SIGILS

OF THE

OLD GOD

J. P. MOORE

SIGILS

OF THE

OLD GOD

J. P. MOORE

DRAGON MOON PRESS

Sigils of the Old God

ISBN 13 978-1-897492-88-8

Printed on acid free paper

www.dragonmoonpress.com

ONE

THE OLD WIZARD opened his arms above a cut deck of fortuneteller's cards, perhaps trying to draw the world's attention to the stern face of the hierophant. The man on the creased card sat atop a throne between two pillars, raising one hand. Jacob could imagine the hierophant's silk robes flowing with the sharp movement.

"Dr. Thomas Rutledge!"

Sam's accent banged on the back of his tongue. The accent had Slavic notes, but was a rougher song than Russian. He looked at Jacob through thick gray eyebrows. Crust and lice nits littered his wild beard, which found order in just two braids bound at their ends by chipped wooden loops.

There was the lord on the card, and there was Sam sitting on a crate in the November chill before a sputtering orange fire of hatcheted lobster pots. The surf sounded behind Jacob and echoed from the cliff face just behind Sam. The effect only stoked Jacob's headache.

Two women stood behind Sam, their shadows falling back into the mouth of his cave. They were short and thick, mountain women with large hands and dark hair. Their eyes sat slightly too far apart. Red blotches blossomed on their cheeks, the residue of a childhood fever. They moved in jerky fits, uncomfortable with their own joints. They must have fed on gruel and pork fat, and a healthy dose of folklore in a deep Eastern European fog. Behind them, two stocky men cut fish. Hoarse cries of desperately starving children bounced from deep within the cavern. The whole group of them looked like a shipwreck. A Gypsy nation had set them adrift out of fear that they would cause too much trouble, and the sea disgorged them onto this shelf of stone, into the stink of rotten fish and gull droppings. They were just more flotsam and jetsam washing up the beach from the wharf.

"This card typically refers to someone who gives advice," Sam said. "Someone who answers questions. Rutledge is a professor at the college for women."

"Here in Jamesport," Jacob said.

"Yes. A man who can answer questions that most have not yet considered. He is a man who has seen dark rites in Africa and South America."

Icy mist drifted from low clouds this morning, breaking now and then into spurts of bone-chilling rain. Jacob lifted his Stetson and ran his hand through his wet hair. Blond strands fell back in front of his eyes, beading at their tips with drops of water. Jacob could not help but smile. This job was close to his apartment just up the hill from the wharf, close to the warm quilt that lay in a heap on his bed.

Sam was not done. The whole affair wanted to be a ritual, and Sam would not dismiss Jacob just yet. Jacob sighed. Why these cards and this script? Or, when Papaya called him, why bird bones cast across her floor to name the victim? Surely, Jacob thought, there was a better way for the Old God to communicate with him.

"Rutledge is a guide," Sam said. "He is a most important man. But he, like the others, has tread where he should not. So, you must do what you do."

Sam leaned back on his crate to stretch his back. The crate creaked, threatening to explode into splinters beneath him. The fire described new shadows over his bulk as he shifted. One black tooth, scars across a broken nose, the beard of a crazed prophet—still, his eyes were keen. He gripped the smooth plank of driftwood on his lap, the plank upon which the cards lay, perhaps thinking that the wood would keep him from falling. The wizard smiled and laughed. His fetid breath through the rot of his gums made Jacob's stomach turn. It was a horrible smell, as if Sam had plowed the stinking, bubbling muck of the bottom of the bay into his gullet with his open jaw.

Jacob blinked and turned his head to the surf, imagining fresher air blowing from the sea. He could see *M'Lass* beached not far away, between Sam's cave and the wharf. The college—it would be a simple walk back to the wharf, up the street to town and turning west to Millionaire's Row. But first, before any of it, he would pass *M'Lass*. The steel-hulled fishing schooner had slid silently onto Jamesport's sand one October midnight in 1890, a full year after its celebrated launch and subsequent disappearance off Providence. Salvagers left her. Conventional wisdom insisted that she was haunted. She was little more than a witness to Jacob's comings and goings across the beach, and a catch for the wind, twisting it into eddies that wailed like ghosts through her railings.

He knew that wailing. He heard it in his dreams. He heard it as he washed his face in the basin atop his dresser, staring in the mirror at those boy's eyes, wondering how that boy had come to resemble one of the crazed ex-Confederates whom he and Ida had pretended to evade in the Chihuahuan Desert so many years ago. He heard the wailing as he stared through the warped panes of his apartment window, huddling under the quilt that his mother had made, the last thing he had of her. Those shreds and tatters. He would stare as he shivered beneath them, watching rain and sleet fall to Jamesport, waiting for the crow.

Sam once said that he owned Jacob.

"I woke in my cave," Sam said. "I saw it on the wall, in the rock. You belong to me."

These jobs for Sam always started the same way.

The crow would appear at Jacob's window and tap on the glass. It would hop down to his bed and drop a flaking mussel shell to the quilt. The shell was like a long-dead sorcerer's fingernail. It signaled Sam. A scrap of brown milkweed, curling like a tuft of witch hair, meant that Papaya was calling him to the swamp. That was rare, but always paid more.

The shell. Sam. Jacob would descend the dark stairs from his one-room hovel, past the doors of opium addicts and murderers and into the street. Portuguese crones wandered the early morning, seeking scraps of food in the milky fluid that ran in the gutter beneath a thin layer of ice. It flowed from the top of the hill, where the Eriksson hotel and the Jewish cemetery sat opposite one another on the edge of a better part of town. His street took several maze-like turns there, ultimately joining Oceanview. Fine carriages jingled and jostled on that avenue, carving deep ruts as they headed to and from the estates of the wintering New York elite. The wind slammed against their marble castles. It wailed of ancient calamity, of skeletal settlers perishing in the cold and native shamen conjuring sickness from bonfires that cast wagon wheel shadows from stone circles.

The wind had touched it all. Its frozen rain had made the ropes stiff and slippery around the necks of witches. Zealot priests had stared sternly at the ice on those ropes, perhaps as sternly as Jacob regarded the frost that sketched devilish geometry on his window.

"Well?" Sam asked. "What are you waiting for?"

Jacob shook his head, sending drops in all directions like a dog. He nodded and turned, replacing his hat before dropping carefully down the slick stones onto the thin beach. He followed his own footprints back to the wharf, past *M'Lass*. He wondered, as he always did, if it had all been his imagination. What if he turned and saw nothing? No cave. No fire or Sam. But the wind through *M'Lass* scolded him.

Of course Sam was there.

And, of course, Dr. Thomas Rutledge had to die.

Jacob had two handlers. There was the sorcerer Sam, sitting below the cliff with his fortuneteller's cards. There was also Papaya, the witch of the salt marshes north of Jamesport who had escaped slavery just before the Civil War. She divined Jacob's victims by throwing chicken bones onto the floor and singing words and half words of an ancient language that could not escape her thick Gulf accent. The crisscrossing patterns of the bones spoke to her.

Papaya and Sam named Jacob's victims and, he guessed, arranged his payment through unseen strands of the rest of the Old God's web. The murder would make it to the newspaper within a day or two but was rarely a front page headline. Often, it looked like an accident or, in the case of vagrants, the inevitable. Payment was always waiting for Jacob at Chang's import shop in town, often by the evening after the murder.

Victims often had stumbled upon an artifact or a document. Jacob would have to recover these for Sam or Papaya. Other times, the victim was a non-person rambling insanities in Portuguese to rats with rot-caked fur in the dark end of one of Jamesport's alleys. Jacob would still take something. In the bottom drawer of the wardrobe in his apartment, beneath the holster that had belonged to his father, a sack held these souvenirs. Many coat buttons. A couple of rings. Other trinkets. Jacob's latest prize was a pair of glasses from a prominent lawyer who had climbed too far into his own family tree, uncovering an ancestor's papers from the witch trials centuries before. The lawyer had learned of dark meetings by standing stones. He had uncovered prayers that breathed evil into the breezes that rippled the black water of the salt marshes. Sam wanted the crumbling letters that described these rites, letters that the lawyer had found beneath the floorboards of a dark home beside a florist's shop. The florist claimed that none of his flowers would bloom in the shadow of those brooding gables.

Jacob's first shot grazed the lawyer's brow, chipping the left lens of his glasses.

They all had offended the Old God. That was what Sam called him. Papaya named him "Papa Bacalou." Whatever he was, he kept the world at arm's length. Jacob was an agent in this, and perhaps he was alone. He had never met others. The drunken vagrants, though—he wondered if they had once been like him. Maybe they had served the Old God. Maybe they had seen too much and outlived their usefulness.

The door of his apartment building was open to the street, rocking and creaking in the wind. A pungent smell—not death, but something close that the immigrant family in the apartment near the stairs might have claimed was cookery—bulged through the doorway with a weak heat. It was human heat and, Jacob decided, a human smell that fell to the icy sidewalk. A cold wind from the sea made short work of it, carrying it up the hill to the cemetery. There, Jacob guessed, it died. He climbed the stairs to his own door on the second floor.

His apartment was a single room. A bed sat against the wall. The quilt his mother had made was half on the bed, half on the floor. Near the door, a pan of water sat atop its stand, below a mirror. His armoire stood beside this, leaning with the uneven floor. That was all.

Jacob opened the armoire's door, then its lowest drawer. His father's belt and holster were there. His father had been a sheriff, but the holster's badge was missing, leaving the ghost of a star in the leather. Jacob took the holster and strapped it around his waist, underneath his denim coat. The revolver was fully loaded. Loops on the greasy leather belt hugged six extra rounds.

The crazed ex-Confederate, too young to have actually fought in the war, stared back at him from the mirror. He straightened his Stetson and wiped leftover sleep from the corners of his blue eyes.

Patting his pockets, he felt a lump of cheese he had bought the day before. The cheese was hard and waxier than the paper in which the old vendor had presented it. He devoured the cheese and felt ready. He needed nothing else. There was nothing left to do.

Still, he decided that a trip west down Oceanview to the end of Millionaire's Row should wait until dark. He would use the afternoon to learn what he could about his victim. Not that it mattered. He did so more out of curiosity than anything else, but there were few places left for him to go. He had exhausted the Jamesport library, even the special collection that dissolved into mold under the watchful eye of a pale, purple-lipped crone who seemed more ghost among the basement stacks than a living librarian. The drunks in the bars of the wharf—they had taught Jacob much. The sea had many mysteries, and they knew of several. One of those drunks was obsessed with *M'Lass* and seemed convinced that, in another state of consciousness before his introduction to opium, he had even been a mate aboard the ship. He spoke of its beaching like he were on the deck, even though the schooner had already and mysteriously been abandoned when it slid onto the beach. In the end, the drunks were no better than the vagrants whom Jacob had killed. They rambled and spat, losing themselves in nonsense rants against the moon, the endless dark waters, or the shapeless things that lived at such depths that no vessel could reach them.

He could still count on the Historian.

The Historian squatted in the abandoned fish market across the avenue from the wharf. Jacob did not want to learn his name, feeling it probable that Sam or Papaya would eventually identify him as a victim. The Historian seemed harmless, though. His insanity kept him occupied. He spoke as three people, each with a different voice. But he knew everything. His voices told stories from before the millionaires from New York City, before the Portuguese and, it seemed, before the original settlers ejected from Massachusetts Bay in the 17th century. The Historian had encyclopedic knowledge of the region's oddities—the strange runic glyph on the bay side of the cliff, the mysterious ruined tower in the center of Jamesport, the skeleton in medieval armor that clammers had lifted from the muck of the salt marshes, and much more.

It was a short walk from Jacob's apartment, back toward the abandoned market by the wharf.

Jacob stepped over scraps of the market's fallen roof, around the icy puddles of mud and decades of fish rot. Occasionally, Jacob would see a vagrant in the market, a drunk or opium addict dying in the corner or rambling over wet tinder, trying to start a fire. Not today. Only cats and rats scampered as Jacob made his way to the heavy door of the icebox on the rear wall.

This was the Historian's cell. A prison, perhaps. Or a monkish hermitage. The Historian sat atop a mound of fish skeletons, each perfectly cleaned of meat by vermin.

"Tell me about Dr. Thomas Rutledge," Jacob said. "Tell me about the college."

The Historian hissed and leaned into a shaft of light. Jacob rarely saw that face, and shuddered whenever he did. The Historian had been burned, once. His skin was stretched and splotched. He had no eyes, only empty sockets. He had no nose, no hair. He was a mouth wearing burlap sacks. His arms and legs twisted in strange directions, like one of Ida's tortured dolls. The limbs had all fallen off and young Ida had sewn them back on herself, though in the completely wrong positions.

Ida, yellow curls over blue eyes, sunburn and freckles— Jacob's younger sister had been a tomboy, down to the trousers and shirt she wore as she rambled with Jacob through the desert. She tortured scorpions, and bore the pink scars of those deeds on her thin forearms beneath thin blonde down. But she had a doll that she prized.

The voice of the youngster, the highest and youngest of the Historian's three voices, spoke first. It was impossible to discern as either male or female.

"Eliza Stephens helped the orphans. And the women."

"She founded the women's college," Jacob said.

"Yes," the youngster replied, though the gruff old sailor—a second voice—interrupted. "She died after the war. Her husband had passed. You must know about him. The iron king of New Jersey. And her son was a drunk."

Jacob nodded.

"Whitebirch is the oldest mansion in Jamesport," the sailor continued. "It's at end of the point. She left the entire estate to the college. Eliza Stephens College for Women. Delicate women, though they are a strange lot. They become the whores and wives of the millionaires in New York. The women are secretive. They protect each other. But if one steps out of line, they destroy her."

"He doesn't care about this," the third voice said. It was a whispering, hoarse rasp in the Historian's throat. "Get to the point."

"He cares," the sailor shot. "And he needs to know about the rock."

"Yes!" the youngster said. "Executioner's Rock!"

"I know about the rock," Jacob said.

"Warlocks!" the sailor shouted. "The priests forced warlocks to walk from that rock. Like a plank on a ship. Just beyond the mansion, at the very tip of the cliff. That's the Executioner's Rock."

"I know," Jacob replied. Executioner's Rock was second only to the Mystery Tower in the square in Jamesport folklore. "Tell me about Rutledge."

"Rutledge," the hoarse whisper said. "His collection has grown so large that he has taken all of Whitebirch to himself. Scholars from Boston used to visit. But no more. He lets no one see it."

"The women live in the Larchmont estate," the youngster added. "The college owns that mansion, too. No one goes to Whitebirch anymore."

"Enoch Larchmont threw himself from the rock!" the sailor yelled. "Decades ago, during the Panic!"

"Tell me about Rutledge's collection," Jacob said, sighing.

"What will you give us?" the youngster asked. "We're hungry."

There was a quiet moment, during which the Historian sat very still, huffing. Clouds of breath billowed from his throat.

"I have six bullets in my revolver," Jacob replied. "And six more on my belt. I can give one to you. It would only take one to silence all three of you."

The Historian groaned and recoiled out of the light. The youngster spoke first.

"Why do you always threaten us, Jacob?"

"The collection," the hoarse voice said. "It is full of strange things. Idols and implements. Remains. The professor studies these things. Things from dark places, from jungles. He started off innocent enough. But something went to his head in those places. We know nothing more."

"Is it enough to let us live?" the youngster asked.

"It's all that you know?"

"Yes."

Jacob retreated from the icebox.

"Forgive us," the hoarse voice said.

"Or shove it up your ass!" the sailor shouted.

Midnight found Jacob on the sidewalk of Oceanview, walking to the end of Millionaire's Row. The avenue was still, though each mansion had a window or two that still burned with a warm but nervous and furtive light. Some mansions had their own generators, which clattered in the otherwise quiet night. All but the two mansions of the college—they were completely dark.

He had passed the marble wonders, stopping only to admire the Forsythe Castle. Robert Chandler Forsythe had channeled all of Ivanhoe and King Arthur, all of the history of the Crusades, into a massive fortress. Where the others were careful and delicate expressions of French-inspired gentility, or tried to evoke the American spirit of a rustic who had simply gotten very lucky, Forsythe's home was a bold and undeniable statement of lordship. If there was a king of Jamesport, it was he. Forsythe had amassed a fortune in oil that the others only expanded through their industries of steel and railroads. And he was a benevolent if unreachable and unassailable king. His fortune had brought schools and churches to the squalor of the Portuguese neighborhoods of Jamesport. It had repaired and modernized the ancient sewer throughout the city. He, a devout Catholic, was listed as the chief benefactor of the city's historic synagogue, and the Jewish cemetery. The sight of that fortress, a skyline in and of itself, still occupied Jacob's thoughts as he reached the modest Larchmont estate. Beyond, Whitebirch was lost in the mist, if not the shadow cast by the Forsythe castle.

The rock, Eliza Stephens, Enoch Larchmont—the Historian's hoarse voice was right. Jacob had little interest in that history. Still, he felt the power of the place tingling across the back of his neck. He knew that feeling. It arose when he scanned the tree line on the edge of the salt marshes by the railroad. Sometimes, looking past Sam into the cave, he noted it. Definitely near *M'Lass*.

It may have been the chance of atmosphere. Now, the air was very cold. The rain had stopped and a thin fog crystallized into tiny slivers of ice right in front of him. They danced and shattered in his breath. The midnight moon, waxing this week, was a yellow smudge at the top of the sky. He suspected, though, that it was more. Here at the point and in those other places, powers leeched through the ground from a deep, hidden source. The history of suicide and sacrifice may be important for coaxing all of that from the ground, as if suffering and lament were a magnet for magic.

To be in bed beneath his quilt, Jacob thought.

He left the avenue for the lawn of the Larchmont estate, cutting across those grounds to the wall. He climbed, dropped, and sat with his back against the cold stone. Looking across the yard, he could barely see the edges of Whitebirch. This furthest mansion on the cliff was a hectic arrangement of the best of New England's old homes. The architect had intended the aggregation to be grand and beautiful, but the overall effect was almost nauseating for being so jumbled and dizzy. Crammed gables and ornamentation pointed in odd directions. In the dark and fog, however, Jacob could see little more than the bulk of the thing. From this angle, he had no sense of the best way to take it.

Jacob looked to his left and right, up and down the wall. He could hear the surf slamming against the cliff. It felt like a dangerous place, not because of the anger and evil clinging with breaking nails to Executioner's Rock on the other side of the mansion, but because the grounds dropped into a sheer cliff on three sides. This was the very end of Jamesport, where two rocky points choked the ocean into a bay of so much salt, so much poison seeping from the salt marshes that no settlement could survive on those lower shores. A single storm, a stiff breeze, even a bad thought would blow both of these mansions clear off the cliff, right into that stagnant, stinking bay. They were not the marble monstrosities that surrounded the Forsythe castle. Isolation rather than opulence seemed to have been the point of both Whitebirch and the Larchmont estate.

Two gaslights burned not far to his right. That, Jacob thought, was the main gate. He narrowed his gaze and could see light reflecting in ice on the big flat stones of a walkway. That led to a door. He could see dim light there, as well. A shadow broke the light. Someone was inside and awake, roaming.

Jacob moved quickly across the slippery grass. He avoided the light as he reached the walk, but it did not matter if Rutledge saw him now. Jacob was focused, in an unwavering state that he knew only in these moments. It felt somewhat like a dream.

He stepped onto the porch and approached the door. A man sang inside. Opera. A cracking, wavering soprano. Jacob reached for the doorknob. In the greater mansions, the newer ones like Forsythe's, butlers and guards, porticos and atriums, gate after gate—there was no easy entry. Whitebirch had been the first, and so the first to be outdone.

The door was unlocked. Jacob paused, suddenly concerned. He pushed the door, which whined as it arced inward.

The singing stopped.

A man stood in the foyer. Stairs, red curtains, and rich wood paneling all rose into darkness around him. He carried a tarnished metal tray with a pot of steaming water, a teacup, and a small oil lamp. He wore a tattered scarlet robe that trailed long loose threads behind him. Gray hair fell in matted strands from beneath a soiled sleeping cap. Legs and arms were stick thin, swimming in the robe.

"Dr. Rutledge," Jacob said, lifting his revolver.

The man smiled, a motion that seemed so foreign to that face that the wrinkled cheeks looked like they would crack. His black eyes were wide, but not with fear. Excitement. He took two breaths, started to talk, but swallowed. He shivered, closed his eyes for a moment to calm himself, and spoke. Serene, quiet, measured.

"I have been waiting for you," Rutledge said. "It has been a long, long wait."

Jacob squinted and lowered his revolver. He knew he was making a mistake as he did it.

The smile wavered on Rutledge's thin lips before recovering. With a sudden and powerful jerk, he launched the tray. Jacob stepped to the side, flinching as boiling water splashed across his wrist. The lamp shattered against the wall.

"Catch me!" Rutledge shouted, disappearing into the dark.

TWO

HEAT BLOSSOMED ALL around him as the lamp ignited the curtains. The dry fabric burned quickly and drifted in glowing, feathery straps to the carpet, which began to smolder. The flames rose high into the atrium on either side of the door, catching a valance that ran across the top of the doorway. It became a fiery symbol framing the entrance. Woodwork near the ceiling caught as well. The whole house groaned, an old man awakened by great pain.

A crack—there was a muzzle flash in the corner of Jacob's vision. The shot missed, thwacking into the wall. Jacob dove and spun, craning his neck to see into the hallway. The firelight revealed a passage that ran into the belly of the house, with an open door into an adjoining chamber along the way. Cases of dark curios stood between roughly carved statues, some of such strange contortions that Jacob could not tell if they were animals, monsters, or men. He had no time to investigate. He darted into the hall and peered through the doorway, then entered with deliberate steps, leading with his drawn revolver.

Dim light from the outside, from the gas lamps by the front walk, fell through a window of ancient panes. The world through that glass was twisted and hazy. There was a garden of thin, sick trees, and a view back to the outside of the atrium. The fire had broken through the roof like a waterfall of orange and yellow.

Jacob was in a small dining room of silk wallpaper and rich mahogany appointments. The table was a heavy, beastly thing that was much too large for the room, and might have hailed from a castle in old Europe. The chairs were gone. Scratches and grime marred the surface from the careful arrangement and rearrangement of countless small figurines. Many of these faced one another, like a child's toy soldiers. A whole brigade was of stone, carved in a consistent and detailed style. These were strange forms, with mouths in their stomachs, eyes on stalks or in their palms, three or even four arms. Some stood upon eight or nine legs, poised for attack and balance. Other figures were wood, and reminded Jacob of warriors in reliefs at Chang's import shop. Indian or Chinese. Still others were crude forms of men, carved from bits of tusk or woven from dry brown reeds. All of the shadows of these figurines flickered in the light, some enlarged to giant proportions against the wall, overlapping in frantic dance, fighting, and rape. It was any of these at any moment, any glance.

The center of the table drew his attention at last. There, a mound revealed itself in the light as an arrangement of stone skulls. Children, Jacob thought and swallowed hard. Exaggerated ridges above the eyes and along their scalps confused him. Horns, crags, shapeless accretions of mud had hardened into glistening, glassy rock. These were monsters, or deformed apes plucked from the dark heart of the jungle. The sockets swallowed the light and regarded the legion of figurines with uncaring emptiness.

Movement to his left—a form flew from a shadow, through another doorway. Jacob leveled his revolver and pulled the trigger. The report scattered beneath a devastating crash from the atrium. Jacob steadied himself. He reached for his belt, feeling for extra bullets. Five shots left in the gun, six in his belt. He would have to remain calm.

He peered into the next room. It looked, at first glance, like a library. Rolled manuscripts and open tomes covered low counters. But he saw ranges along the wall. Pots and pans marched in line, hanging from hooks. It was a kitchen, but Rutledge's collection had spread to every surface.

Jacob dove through the doorway and smacked his shoulder against one of the counters. Three shots from Rutledge whistled overhead, flying into the dining room. The third struck the mound of skulls with a hollow sound, but with enough force to send the bony dome of one skull into a cloud of grit that shimmered like gold dust.

Two lines of electric bulbs lined the back wall, throwing a dim orange light. Their wires met in the center of the wall and dove into a stairwell. Rutledge flew down those stairs. Jacob shot twice, striking a heavy pan that rang like a cathedral bell.

The fire's roar sounded through the walls as it flowed between the studs and pried apart the joists. The hallway behind the dining room was now ablaze. The shadows of the figurines, of the skulls, were frenzy.

Jacob rushed to the stairs, which were slippery with black mud. He paused to catch his footing and looked back as the fire engulfed the dining room, wrapping its fingers about the frame of the kitchen doorway.

The bulbs reached down a short tunnel at the bottom of the stairs. Smooth brick walls made a gentle bend not more than ten yards ahead. A narrow pair of rails ran down the center of the floor. The black mud, the rails. Coal, Jacob realized.

He took slow steps. There were wide puddles, and Jacob wondered if the water had seeped through the cliff from the surf far below. Wet coal grit echoed beneath his boots, but a comforting quiet nonetheless filled the tunnel. He felt safe beneath the bricks, sure that they would protect him if the house collapsed.

The lights flickered and went dark.

Jacob heard a voice. Rutledge. It sounded like the professor was right in his ear.

"We are all fallen angels of the Old God."

Jacob whirled, swinging his arms but hitting nothing. A boot struck him in the gut and the air leapt from his lungs. He slammed into the wall, dropping his revolver to the floor. He fell after it, reeling from the attack, his brain sending bright spirals into his vision.

Rutledge spoke again.

"I have seen it. The answers are so crushing, so disappointing."

The hoarse voice bounced throughout the tunnel. Jacob could not fix the source. He had lost his bearings altogether.

"But liberating," Rutledge continued. "Do you wonder how you came to be here, looking for me?"

Jacob blinked and shook his head to clear his eyes. He felt the floor for his revolver and landed upon the warm grip. He pulled it close.

"You deserve to know the answers," Rutledge said. His tone was calm, though there was something at its edge. Measured, but forced, the cadence threatened to break into howling laughter or an insane, raw-throated scream.

A sudden shuffling sounded to his right. Jacob fired and glimpsed the hallway in the flash. Rutledge fled around the bend. Jacob stood, dizzy at first but gaining balance, and vaulted down the tunnel. He turned, nearly slamming into a wheeled bin that had toppled from the tracks, spilling coal. Straight ahead, the tunnel turned upwards, perhaps to the street.

But Rutledge, Jacob knew, had taken another route.

Electric light leaked through a rough hole in the wall. A pickaxe and sledgehammer leaned against a pile of broken bricks. Jacob ducked through the hole into a tight space of sharp lines between shelves of rock. He crawled, following the light, the sour smell of sweat, and the sound of breathing that he guessed was Rutledge, but which sounded with each second more and more like the sighing of the cliff itself. The cyst opened, spreading into a natural cavern so large that Jacob could not even see to its far side. The air of the place was stale and musty, with a hint of the sea. Large electric bulbs dangled from poles that ran in a long line, down the sloping, gravelly floor and toward the left-hand wall.

He saw skulls, like the skulls on the table in the dining room. These lay with other bones, a sprawling sculpture of slaughter. Where he saw figures, most seemed human with two legs, two arms. But some had other limbs. Still other odd shapes— curves in the spine, spikes from the femurs, extra joints in the fingers. Fans like the sails on the back of a fish spread from some shoulder blades. Wings.

The house hissed far behind and above. The narrow end of the cavern was bright with fire. It was a smiling maw, the rock formations like teeth. Smoke billowed through. Whitebirch was falling and there was no going back.

Jacob clenched his jaw.

Fear sparkled in his gut as he gazed at the bones. Some of them bore deep cuts and scratches. In some areas, thin stalagmites rose from the bones to catch milky drips that fell from the darkness above, from the invisible ceiling.

"Fossils," he whispered.

He stepped onto the pile, following the string of light bulbs. A taut twang shot through the bones, like the cracking of ice on a winter lake. Beneath this sound, he imagined the hollow, wet cracks of the ancient bodies splitting and the screams of these creatures. The devil's cherubs, these malformed, scrawny things hovering on giant insect wings, snagged in a net and slain, discarded here. All around him, now—cries and screeches had buried themselves in the smooth rock and in the pockets of air between the bones. Each step released them.

Panic flared. He opened the cylinder of his revolver. Two bullets. He walked and, his hands shaking, reloaded the gun. He dropped bullets into the pile. They fell through the gaps and cracks, gone forever. Four in the cylinder, now. That was all.

What beast, he wondered, had lived in this place and taken these creatures into its gullet? Now slithered off to the sea or sky, space itself, or deeper into the cliff.

A much smaller creature answered this thought, buzzing about his head. It was brown and black, an insect, its body so plump that it dipped with each beat of its wide wings. Then, several more were circling about him, knocking into him with audible thuds. One landed on his arm. It was long, like a grasshopper or a praying mantis. Serrated pincers grew like tusks from the sides of its head, below two eyes faceted in plates of crustacean armor. The eyes turned independently, both finally gazing at Jacob's face through pinholes in the chitin. Two barbed quills slid from beneath its wings then, and began exploring the sleeve behind its body. One of the quills shot longer, doubling its length as it plunged through the thick denim and pricked Jacob's arm.

He brushed the thing to the bones, then smashed it with his foot. Yellow slime burst from its abdomen.

Now there were more of them, on his shoulder and chest, reaching with their long front legs toward his neck, probing with their needles, articulating their jaws, scraping these mandibles to make a cricket's music. The trill sounded like frantic hunger.

Jacob took wider steps. The panic jumped up his spine and hit the bottom of his brain, the animal part that had made the creatures in Rutledge's figurine army do such grotesque and horrible things to one another. The edges of his vision blurred as he ran, his boots beating fossils. The air was thick with the insects, now. He swatted at them, feeling their leathery plumpness against his palm.

He could see the edge of the cavern. The smell and sound of the surf was all about him. His breath was dry in his throat. He did not care about Rutledge, about the job. Any second, he knew, bony fingers would grip his ankles and pull him down into their clacking depth, where the devil's mantids would devour his flesh, his brittle white bones left to become stone for a curious but equally unlucky explorer eons away.

He fell into a round tunnel, a natural pipe. The insects launched from him and gathered several steps behind him, as if the air of the sea was noxious to them. Jacob huffed and stood, holding still for a moment with his breath clouding in the electric light. His heart beat hard. He braced himself against the feeling that the tunnel was spinning.

"Answers," he heard.

Rutledge. That voice rattled through the tunnel, rising and falling with the waves of the ocean against the cliff.

"The beasts of the jungle, the savages dancing around bonfires, between standing stones. Sacrifice and murder for the Old God! Everywhere!"

Jacob moved slowly forward, reaching a boulder-strewn cavern that opened onto the gray mist of midnight. Thomas Rutledge stood in the mouth of the cave. He was just a silhouette.

Jacob pointed the gun. His hands were still shaking. His breath was hard to control. Staring down the barrel, he braced his wrist with his left hand.

Rutledge raised a finger.

"Kill me," the professor said. "It does not matter. There is no stopping what comes!"

Rutledge crouched. Jacob shot, almost out of a twitch. Two bullets went over the professor's head. Rutledge was going to jump. Without thinking, Jacob holstered his revolver and rushed the professor, grabbing him by the threadbare lapels of his robe. The professor smiled, fat gray whiskers cracking through the crust of dried drool about his lips.

"I have told you all that I can," Rutledge whispered. It barely rose above the crash of the surf far below.

Rutledge placed a quick kick to Jacob's shin, then a knee to his groin. Jacob, wincing in pain but trying to hold, lurched just enough for Rutledge to break free. The professor fell back. Jacob craned over the ledge, watching Rutledge fall into the dark. The sound of the surf swallowed the old man.

That was certainly the end of Thomas Rutledge. The collection, the mansion. Rutledge had said something about answers, but they were now gone. Rutledge could not have survived, but Jacob had not seen the death. He had not heard the last, raspy breath of a life misspent on questions that no human should pursue. He had not seen the last twitch of fingers that had traced glyphs and sigils of an incomprehensibly dark magic. Sam would consider the mission a failure for the lack of proof.

But there was something in Jacob's right hand. Two ends of a broken cord fell from his clenched fist. He opened his fingers.

A flat rectangle of carved wood bore the relief of a small winged beast. It was heavy, and ran the full length of his hand. The beast was a bat-like thing, but the ancient artist had captured a humanity in its gaze. Perhaps it was the shape of those large round eyes, or something of the artist invested into the grain of that wood. Rutledge must have been wearing it around his neck. Jacob sighed as he looked at the relief. He carefully wrapped the cord about the slip of wood and placed the thing in his pocket.

Jacob mulled over his choices. He had never failed a mission, and was not sure what would happen. Would it be better to drop with Rutledge? No, he thought. But he had no intention of heading back to the cavern of slaughter.

He looked down again. He saw nothing but the sheer cliff face. There was a black shadow above him, a long point of rock. Between here and there, he saw enough crevices to make the climb. They were spaced in nearly perfect arrangement. And, beyond the crevices, beyond the shadow, he could see the orange glow of fire. He realized, then.

Executioner's Rock.

The air was calm as he climbed, but the surf reacted to his presence. It jumped, roaring and howling like wolves after prey that climbed a tree. The last leg of the climb was a reach. A sharp rock edge dug into his fingers. But he rose, his entire weight upon their splitting tips.

Before him, five low standing stones ran in a row like the toes of a dead giant, half-buried at the end of the cliff. The air was heavy and still. He looked past the stones to the swirling flames that had been Whitebirch. He could hear shouts, and then a roar as the mansion collapsed in bright yellow sparks and billowing smoke. It had been the oldest mansion in Jamesport, and it had seen perhaps a handful of deaths at the rock. Not the warlocks of centuries before, or the sacrifices of whatever beings had raised the stones before that, but Rutledge. And Enoch Larchmont.

In the morning, curious folk would pick through the smoky ash and find the remnants of the strange collection of idols and figurines, of the life that had been Rutledge's. But no answers.

Jacob's thoughts returned to his failure. He tried to reassure himself that Rutledge must be dead, but he wondered if he should even try to collect payment at the import shop. He wondered if he should appear before Sam at all. The trinket in his pocket could pass as proof. Perhaps it would be all right.

Something caught his eye on one of the stones. There was movement there against the background of fire.

It was a black bird, a crow.

Jacob stopped and looked at the thing. He sighed. A light breeze brushed its feathers.

It held an object in its beak.

A mussel shell.

Jamesport was awake. Not its inhabitants—its empty streets and dark windows oozed a fidgety energy. The last possible leaves clung to the trees and shivered, sensing that the events on the cliff rather than the coming winter would somehow lead to their fall. Creaky signs swung in their hooks, though there was no breeze. Flames in the gaslights flickered and twisted in trance-like dances of abandon. The midnight fog was gone. The moon was dim and frail but wide, appearing much too close.

Jacob walked with his hands in the pockets of his denim coat. His left hand was a fist, clenching Rutledge's idol. He looked at the sidewalk in front of him as he walked, counting the bootscrapes, cracks in stoops, empty flowerpots. When he looked ahead or to his sides, he felt vulnerable.

He was thinking about escape. An inelegant, potentially unfinished mission—it was bound to happen. There was no way that Rutledge would have survived the fall, and Jacob could present the idol as proof. To Sam, this would be like any other mission. But Jacob had seen far stranger things than a man surviving a fall into the sea from a great height. And Sam might have seen it all. Sorcerers and witches with their animals, the crows delivering mussels and scraps of silk weed—who knew what those animals saw, and how they might have reported that sight to their masters? There was a fair chance, Jacob thought, that Sam had summoned him for punishment. Escape from the whole enterprise would be the only thing to save him. Jacob smiled as he considered this, comparing himself to men in mundane work who grow tired of their jobs. He imagined them, accountants or lawyers, killing their bosses and fleeing. He stopped walking.

To escape, he would have to kill Sam and Papaya. Or would there be others to channel the will of the Old God? Perhaps that force would break its silence, break the barriers that forced it to communicate through witches and sorcerers, and strike at Jacob itself.

He lifted his gaze from the sidewalk. To his right, the nation's oldest synagogue faced an enormous gothic church across the park. They were like two old men staring at one another over a chessboard. Between these two gray faces, right below the heaviness in the air that marked the spot at which their gazes met, the ancient Mystery Tower stood. It was short in comparison to the two behemoths, no more than two stories opening to the sky in a ruined or unfinished edge, with eight tall arched openings at its base. Those entrances were quite close to one another, so that the whole thing stood upon eight narrow columns of stone that seemed inadequate to hold the weight of its upper half. There, layer after layer of flat stones piled into a cylinder, joined with a mortar that had withstood countless nor'easters, and perhaps more. A local scholar, a colleague of Rutledge's at the women's college, once gathered students and peers in the park to show that the tower was just a mill, erected by Scottish settlers well within a timeframe that most folks would consider normal. Case closed, he thought. Yet, more fanciful tales persisted. Vikings, of course. Monks from Ireland. Egyptians or Phoenicians. Or others. The vagrants who typically inhabited the streets at this time of night generally stayed away from the thing. Jamesport had whispered a different secret to them.

Jacob looked at the tower, then at the church and synagogue on either side. He wondered how the tower had gotten here, and how he had come to witness it. As the days had passed and the number of victims climbed, he had wondered more and more about how childhood ramblings in West Texas had led to this place, this time. He remembered climbing a cliff face to ruins cut into the very rock. He remembered Ida falling. He remembered crouching in a corner of that dead, abandoned place, sobbing. After that, nothing.

He lowered his gaze again and continued past the park, finding himself at the top of his own street after several minutes. The Eriksson hotel was as quiet as the rest of the city, though there was light in two of its windows. Across the street, the old Jewish cemetery occupied an odd, asymmetrical plot where two side streets joined Oceanview. The decorative iron work of the fence was lost beneath countless coats of black paint. A dozen or more small stones marched along the top of the tombstone just inside the bars.

He thought of continuing down Oceanview to the import shop, seeing Chang and acting like everything had gone off as planned. He could try to collect his payment. But he knew that Sam would not take well to the dishonesty, and there was no guarantee that the payment would be there. Perhaps Chang received messages from crows, prompting him to count out the bills from hidden safes in his storeroom. What would happen, Jacob wondered, if he tried to cheat the Old God? It was not worth the risk. Jacob had plenty of money stashed beneath the floor in his room, and in caches around the city. It was best, he thought, to face the thing. He thought again of shooting Sam.

Jacob turned and went down his street, toward the wharf. He reached the bottom of the hill without any sense of having made the trip. He imagined tumbling down the hill with that foul fluid in the gutter, catching himself before falling through the grate into the sewer.

The bar on the corner showed the only signs of life at this hour. Jacob heard a fiddle and laughing. He could smell the smoke of cigarettes and pipes. He wondered if it was real, or a haunting. Perhaps his attention would startle the ghosts into disappearing, snuffing away into the high clouds by the moon.

It was real. One drunk stumbled into the street, looked at Jacob with surprise, and vomited on the sidewalk. A ghost, Jacob thought, would do something more interesting than that.

The tide was to the middle of the beach. Jacob could not see the posted chart in the dark, so he did not know if the tide was coming in or going out. No matter, for he had enough beach to hike to Sam's cave and hoped that he would not be there long. Jacob was frightened as he walked by *M'Lass*, thinking that it could read his thoughts about Sam and might unleash an attack. He kept the ship in the corner of his sight.

He could see Sam's fire, the orange flames silhouetting the old wizard's bulk. Jacob pinched the idol in his pocket, wondering once again if Sam were a figment, a construct of imagination justifying an urge to kill. The idol offered no answer. But seeing Sam, seeing the fire, was something. Sam already had the plank on his lap. Jacob could see the deck of cards.

This was strange, he thought. The crow never came at night, and never anywhere but to his sill. But here was Sam, seemingly about to give him another job. Jacob remembered the images on some of those cards—men pierced by swords, a fool crucified upside down. Perhaps Jacob was to draw his own punishment.

Sam was alone. The cave was silent. It would be easy to shoot him.

Above, the wealthy in their castles made sense of the fire. Many of the windows were lit, particularly at the Forsythe estate. Powerful men gathered there, sharing nervous talk over brandy. No doubt, there would be petitions and proposals in the morning, complaints that the fire brigade was too slow, too noisy, or both. The college might hold a memorial for Rutledge, an awkward affair in the morning from which teachers and students would wander, wondering if the destruction of the mansion and the disappearance of the professor really should mean anything at all to them.

"Typically, your work is more..." Sam looked above Jacob, perhaps looking for a word in the dark part of the moon. "Elegant."

"Rutledge is dead."

"That is true. I know it. You can rest easy."

Jacob's right arm relaxed. He did not realize until then that his palm was resting on the revolver.

"I—"

Sam waved it away.

"There is new information. The situation has changed. There is a need for your services. Immediately."

"What's going on?"

"Do not worry. The Old God understands chaos. Rutledge used it against you. You will not be paid, as a warning to take more care, to be more decisive. But that is the extent of your punishment."

Sam leaned back and stared at the cards. Finally, he pointed at them.

"Cut them!" he snapped.

Jacob was confused and curious. He reached forward and felt along the edges of the deck. As always, one card caught his fingers on both sides. He lifted. He had taken most of the deck, leaving just several cards behind. Sam took the top one, biting his bottom lip as he looked at it. He scanned it from corner to corner, his dark eyes devouring it. He let a long sigh through his nostrils and turned the card to Jacob.

Jacob had seen this card. It was much like the figure from the day before. It was a woman, though, sitting between the pillars. She held a rolled scroll in her lap. Her blue robes fell to a crescent moon, which had landed at her feet. She looked from that card, meeting Jacob's gaze with calm, resigned to dying at Jacob's hand.

Sam once drew this card and named the wife of one of the railroad barons. She had dabbled in fortunetelling and séances, like so many bored wives of the cliff mansions had. Suffrage or the occult. But she took it further, gathering twelve like herself and leading them to a rock landing on the shore of the bay, beneath weathered marks on the cliff that some said were Viking runes. Rites, sacrifices—there were rumors of blood and screams among the rude, dumb folk who lived on the edge of the salt marsh. They spoke of an odd smell, a skunked rot that bubbled from the dark water any morning after these women danced naked in the moonlight. None could say where she had learned such rituals. Even the Historian knew nothing.

Jacob found her in her bath, her skin pale white and loose. She looked ancient. He shot her in the head. The bullet passed through her skull, smacked into the porcelain and shattered the tub. Her corpse fell to the floor with a splash of blood and steaming water. That was a decisive, indisputable death.

Before he pulled the trigger, she whispered to him.

"I am a witch," she said. "You cannot kill me."

Her body, the water falling to the floor—it reminded him of a mackerel falling from a net at the wharf.

Jacob knew one other witch. Just one.

"You know who this is," Sam said.

Jacob nodded. This was not Sam's normal ritual.

"Papaya," Jacob said.

"You must go now," Sam snapped.

THREE

A COLD WIND FROM the north brought the stink of the salt marshes over Jamesport. Jacob walked to that edge of the city and stood before a small chapel near the rail yard. Paint peeled from the church's clapboard walls. Its roof and steeple pointed in somewhat different directions, giving the impression that it could not bear the weight of the universe that it had long described to its parishioners. Its cornerstone began "16," but the decade and year had weathered away. Tombstones crammed every space around it. Each leaned to different angles. Many, particularly in the oldest corner, bore the death's head, the winged skull carved in stone. These were like a flock of beasts, like the fossilized creatures of the cave beneath Whitebirch.

It was still early, just past six in the morning. The sky was clear. Red splashed across the eastern horizon, signaling that a storm was coming. A crowd of a dozen gathered before the door, which was closed. Each shifted from foot to foot, straightening formal garments that were stiff and old. There were no children and no women among them. They were odd folk, bearing the features—a sloped forehead above a prominent brow, a withdrawn chin—of the swamp dwellers. At first Jacob wondered if this were a mass, but it was not Sunday. The sects that had risen among the rude peasantry of the rural parts had all taken different tacks on observance, so perhaps this chapel had fallen into the hands of a more radical minister. Jacob saw the old caretaker leaning against one of the tombstones. He held a shovel in his hands and poked at the ground. It was to be a funeral.

Jacob continued past them all, taking a complicated path among the stones to a ramp on the far side of the property. The slope of packed gravel ran down to the foot of the marsh, into the stinking black water. The marsh had grown over the old road, and had cut at the high ground of the chapel. When Jacob reached the bottom of the ramp, he looked left along the ridge. The chapel hung several yards over the edge. A haphazard construction of rotting planks and sheets of wood strained to keep the building from sliding into the muck. Along the sheer face of the hill, he saw the heads of caskets poking through the mud. Each sat at a different height, so that the line of them looked like sour notes of a dirge running along a staff.

He turned to the marsh. A path on drier ground led along the left bank of the flooded road. The land there was muddy, but traversable. The right bank, however, dissolved into clumps of grass and mud that spread, impassable but by canoe or other boat, to the ocean. Jacob could follow the path north to Papaya's shack, contending with just a few swift and cold streams. He would pass other ruins, other forgotten places. There was the shell of a schoolhouse. The worm-eaten frame barely supported its steeple, which still held a bell though the clapper was gone and the metal was green and chalky with a thick patina. It stood in a depression that the swamp had once and suddenly flooded. Closer to Papaya's shack, a whole settlement sat silent on a wooded hill rising on the eastern side of the submerged road. Square, spartan dwellings surrounded a well that could never have yielded fresh water. A revivalist colony had built the settlement decades before the Civil War, but disappeared. They had left no clues of their demise, but plenty of evidence of their lives—place settings on tables, unmade beds, open books. A child's doll, decapitated, its porcelain fingers broken, lay beside a fallen chair. It was all still there.

Jacob had not slept at all, but had gone straight to the swamp from Sam's cave. He had thought about stopping to see the Historian, but decided against it. It was not better to know more in this case. Papaya had not called him nearly as often as Sam, but she always treated him well. She always fed him, cared for any wounds. Indeed, on one job that Jacob had underestimated, a vagrant in a Portuguese slum had slashed his gut with a jagged knife. A single shot ended the man, but the wound was deep. By the time Jacob reached Papaya's shack, the gash was swollen with such fever that he could barely rise above a stoop. Papaya set him in her own bed, dressed his wound, and fed him a fiery gumbo that ultimately rejuvenated him. In his memory, Jacob held flashes of her puttering about the place, preparing his salves and meals, and singing spirituals and psalms in her thick voice. Such a voice from so thin and frail a woman.

He was now unsure. Those memories sent his stomach spinning. He had to stop walking. A cold wind rustled the swamp grasses. He watched as they bent toward him, looking like they fell beneath the rampage of an invisible beast rushing at him from the sea. Thin trees on strange, small hills bent against this rushing onslaught. The rising sun offered some warmth, but not enough.

Strange feelings, he thought.

His stomach calmed and he knew that he had to push northward to Papaya's shack. Still, he hesitated, as he had the night before in Rutledge's atrium. He should have killed the man right there. There would have been no fire or mysterious cavern. He should have dropped him right on the rug. But Jacob had paused.

And the fear—ancient bones, even if they were of an extinct devilish race from the far past. Why had they frightened him? It was not the bones or the strange insects, he knew. But there was something in the air. Not quite a smell or a feeling, it was something that set his heart beating faster and brought terrifying images to his mind. He was feeling it now in the marsh, as he had felt it walking past *M'Lass* earlier. He wondered if he would soon be a babbling vagrant, sought by his successor for knowing too much. Jacob would be wishing, waiting for the bullet to the head. He would leave his apartment and sleep in the mud of the abandoned fish market to the sound of the Historian's voices yelling at each another.

Jacob shook his head, lifted his feet one after the other, and pushed forward, past the schoolhouse. His path wound long around its flooded yard, and the settlement of the lost revivalists peered down on him from its hilltop perch across the road. Passing these landmarks, he found himself surrounded by the swamp. The ridge of the path marched north like a spine. To his west, swamp reached all the way to the northeast corner of the bay. The road and rails to far Boston were imperceptible in a greenish morning haze. The swamp spread east to the ocean as well, a field of waving rough grasses broken here and there by hills.

Soon, as the sun reached higher into morning and the stiff breezes settled into a persistent wind that pushed against his progress, he began to hear Papaya's song.

The ground rose. Jacob climbed this knoll, gripping smooth trunks of young trees. Far to the north, dark clouds marched along the horizon. He thought he saw the flash of lightning— such a rare thing for this season. Agitation buzzed through the air, much like the agitation in Jamesport the night before. He noticed the calls of birds and frogs. They were chaotic, without rhythm. The coming storm set the hairs on his arms standing.

Beneath the energy, beneath the calls and cries, he could hear her singing. Her voice was a calming thing in the chaos. He always heard her voice when he approached her home.

The shack was close to the bottom of the hill. It was gray, warped boards gathered into a box that stood atop stilts. The thing had no business standing, looking like an explosion had blown it apart, followed by each stubborn piece snapping back into place. There were gaps, missing chunks, lines that were completely off level.

He brought his hands to his hips, resting his right palm on the grip of his revolver. He felt along his belt—no bullets there. Whipping the gun from the holster, he flipped the cylinder open. Two shots left. He had not stopped to retrieve ammunition. He hoped two shots would be enough. Papaya always seemed harmless enough, but she was powerful. If an old professor could do what Rutledge had done, there was no telling what Papaya might do.

Other sounds intruded. A train from far back in Jamesport howled. A plop in the water at the foot of the knoll—a frog or other little beast jumped away from him. A screech dropped from above, where a carrion-hunting bird, high and unseen, circled.

Jacob returned his revolver to its holster and hopped between clumps of dry ground toward Papaya's shack. He tried to move quietly, but he had no doubt that she knew he was coming. She was a witch. She had ways.

Papaya stepped onto the porch, shaking a blanket into the wind. She avoided looking at him, though her wry and sarcastic half-mouthed smile joked with him. Jacob waved. She turned her back to him and laughed. She was tall, gaunt and skeletal. Old loose skin, black as lacquer, hung from her arms. She wore a long, dirty robe and a kerchief over her hair. A turquoise rosary draped around her neck. Her laugh and her song filled the swamp. They got down into the muck and made it bubble. They launched into the air and blasted the clouds.

"Jacob!" she called. "Come up, now."

She beckoned him up the ladder. He climbed, smiling and self-conscious. He was unsure of what he should do. One bullet now, and it would be over. But he had to get inside. The peasants of the swamp could be watching.

There was a mud brick hearth. Flames lashed at a pot that bubbled with stew. Papaya took a bowl and spoon from the table. Both were of the same shining yellow wood, and both were comically large.

There was her bed, where she had nursed him back to health. And the table. She had served him the spicy, slimy swamp gumbo every time, from the same pot. It was actually quite disgusting, despite what it had done for him once. It was sweeter for the motherly pride with which she presented it. Jacob looked at the bare spot on the floor. She would cast her bird bones, there, reading the death of this or that person.

"I don't think I called you," she said, staring into the stew.

"You didn't," Jacob replied.

She squinted. Concern knit her long face into wrinkles. She was starting to understand. He would have to act quickly.

"So, why are you here?" she asked.

Jacob sighed through his nose. She looked at his eyes and squinted. Her pupils went wide with realization. She stepped back.

"Don't do it," she said. She held the spoon before her, perhaps hoping that its glistening back would shield her.

Jacob swallowed hard and turned from her gaze. He could not look at her.

"I—"

"It's Sam!" she said. "He wants to take power from me. Don't do it!"

Jacob looked at his hands, at the floor. A bad move. She could strike him. She could take one of the heavy skillets and level him. She did not, but stood shivering, grasping at things to say.

"I fed you," she said. "I took care of you. I was loyal to you."

He pulled his gun from his holster and weighed the weapon in his palm. Nausea gripped his stomach. Jacob closed his eyes and gnashed his teeth. What was he doing? Why and for whom?

Papaya knelt before him, her hands clasped together in prayerful pleading. She rocked back and forth, nearly singing.

"No. No, please."

Jacob continued to stare at the revolver. Perhaps she was not so powerful, just a messenger.

She went silent. He lifted his eyes and found hers, wide and piercing as she pried into his skull. He felt her moving through his head, parting his tissues as one would part fronds of growth in a jungle. She peered into this dark corner and that, saw his memories of youth in the desert and the deaths of everyone around him. She went through each of his jobs, the wound that he had suffered and which she had nursed. Jacob saw these things as she did.

Then, Rutledge. Sam. This moment.

She broke the stare. Jacob fell back into the chair at the table, the bowl of gumbo before him like nothing was happening.

"I have seen everything," she said to the floor. She turned her eyes to Jacob. They were tired and wet, tears welling in the lower lids. "They will wake the Elders. They will use you. You must be stopped."

Papaya moved more quickly than he thought possible. She grabbed an iron skillet from a hook and spun. Jacob loosened, letting himself fall beneath the swing. The skillet knocked the hat from his head, but missed his skull.

Jacob rolled from the table, ending flat on his back with the gun pointed between his raised knees.

"It will not come to pass!" Papaya yelled. She barreled down on him, raising the skillet high to bring it smashing upon his face. He pulled the trigger, the shot sending the skillet away sparking, spinning, and singing.

Papaya stood dumfounded, staring at her hands for one moment before violence erupted on her face again. She lunged.

He shot again, and she dropped.

"Papaya!"

The voice came from outside. Jacob turned to the doorway and saw a form in the light, a young woman. Though her eyes were bloodshot and dark, there was something soft in their character, in their shape. She was nonetheless striking, her cheekbones high and wide so that the rest of her face tapered to a point at her chin. Mud caked her wild blonde hair. Her skin was gray and her lips blue. She wore the rags of a dress that may once have been glorious. It was a white summery thing with lace.

The woman gasped, bringing her hands to her mouth. Her fingernails were as deep blue as her lips.

The gray woman darted out, jumping from the porch and landing with a messy splash. She stumbled forward, and began to run. Jacob's heart beat faster, and he went after her. He launched and landed near her, gripping a scrap of her dress. It tore away, brittle and dry. She made no noise as she went. Indeed, her limbs and legs cut through the water and mud like they were nothing. Jacob, though, made great and noisy splashes as he struggled to pursue her. She was fast, and the distance between them grew. He stopped once, lined up a shot and squeezed the trigger. The revolver made a soft click, its chamber empty.

The peasants of the swamp were now darting through the grass, dark shapes in a rising swamp haze. Their calls mixed with the screeching of birds and the wide-throated belching of frogs. The woman ran deeper into their world, though was certainly separate from it. She was thin and quick, while the swamp folk were more like Sam's thick, rough women.

They reached a ledge of dry ground. Jacob rose into the wind. The water of the swamp felt like it was freezing into his skin. His feet went numb, but he was now gaining on her. He chased her for some time, dodging low and scraggy brush that whipped at his denim coat. Breezes mounted the ledge from the swamp, and his wet clothes went stiff with ice. Pain began to thud in his head. Mist swirled in tendrils between him and the woman. The ledge became firmer and wider. They moved among trees. Thin vines tangled around his feet.

A hill rose suddenly before them. It was a lonely pyramid, an unexplainable feature in the landscape. Young trees and low brush wove a tangled barrier over its craggy surface. It was not an easy climb. He lost sight of her, the fear of a second failure spiking. She would tell the swamp dwellers, the angry subjects of Papaya's swamp kingdom.

He climbed, feeling terror grow in his gut, terror like that which had gripped him in the cavern of the bones beneath Whitebirch. Stones jutted in unnatural angles. Moss and dirt filled rectangular spaces—graves or doorways. A hum, a vibration deep in the hill, set Jacob's molars shivering against one another. The brush thinned as he went, and the trees were gnarled and twisted as they leaned toward stars so distant that Jacob would not have seen them in the night, let alone in the thickening morning haze about the hilltop. The trees reached for something, reached perhaps to lift their roots and separate themselves from this strange place.

The brush eventually gave way altogether. There was an arrangement of standing stones at the top of the hill. The Historian had once spoken of such monuments, like this and the one at the head of Executioner's Rock. The child's voice said that even the natives had avoided these places. Jacob found that he could not see straight to any of the stones. They appeared unfocused, or in double image. When he was able to fix one in the center of his gaze and force it to be still, it shot a pain into the back of his skull that was so intense, so searing that he had to stand with his eyelids clenched shut for what seemed like minutes as nauseating patterns spiraled out of hell to fill his dark field of vision.

The gray woman was gone. The swamp dwellers were silent. They, unlike him, knew to stay away from this unholy place.

Jacob holstered his empty gun and turned. He walked at first, then began to run through the brush and whipping branches. He was thankful to crash into the cold water. He had lost his bearings, and spent several seconds fixing his position. It was almost noon before he reached Papaya's shack, and before his heart calmed. Though the swamp dwellers were still near—he could sense them—they left him alone. He had killed the witch and climbed the summit. No doubt, they thought him to be quite dangerous.

Jacob stood below Papaya's porch, whispering to her, to the absence of the song in the air.

"I'm sorry."

He climbed the rungs and found her body where he had left it. She was splayed in a haphazard form, beside a fallen chair. Her blood had begun to clot on the floorboards. He felt that, even in death, she might have taken a more studied pose. But she was like any of the others. Now, she was nothing more than a heap. She had cast bones on the floor. She had sat there and slept there as she nursed him back to health. She had died there.

He looked at her wrinkled cheeks, her long face. No breath. He was not sure why he had expected her to seem asleep.

Jacob found his hat and placed it back on his head. He

approached Papaya and tugged at her turquoise rosary. It did not yield, so he slipped the thing over her head. He stood, carrying the necklace to her basin. The water turned pink with the blood that had soaked into the thong.

He took this single thing, but not as proof for Sam. The wizard would know that she was dead. He would see it in Jacob's mind, like Papaya had seen into his mind. He took it for himself.

FOUR

"SACRIFICE!"

It was the sailor's voice. The Historian recoiled with disdain. Or fear.

"Sacrifice! The Old God was always here, and these beasts were killed for him. The Elders sacrificed them. They used his power, but he got even in the end."

"How long ago?" Jacob asked.

"Before man," the child answered. "Before the great lizards."

"Before the new gods," whispered the quiet one.

"The cavern," Jacob said.

"Those creatures, those angels. They were sacrificed."

Jacob looked at the ground by his foot and sighed. The Historian knew everything, and could just tell him. Like getting missions from Sam, conversations with the Historian had to be rituals. They had to be difficult.

"Papaya said that someone is trying to bring the Elders back," he said.

The Historian was silent for a moment. A loud sigh fell from his throat.

"If that's true," the sailor said. "We're all in trouble."

Jacob frowned and closed his eyes. He felt the cool breeze from the street, from the collapsed front wall of the abandoned market, against his back. He opened his eyes. Two insects—

small, like gnats—twirled in a shaft of daylight that reached through a hole in the ceiling. Rainwater, for the rain had started again, dripped through that hole as well, thwacking against the refuse on the floor. There was no sound louder than the Historian's raspy, uneven breathing.

"Why did I have to kill Papaya?" he asked.

The Historian shrugged. Gestures were uncommon, perhaps requiring all three voices to agree.

"You should ask Sam," the child said.

Jacob blinked.

"Papaya said that Sam was trying to steal her power."

"Ask him," the child said.

"What's going to happen?" Jacob asked.

"We can't tell you the future," the child replied. "We don't see that. You know that."

"Don't tell him," the sailor spat.

"I must," the quiet one insisted.

And then the sailor: "We can't!"

"Jacob," the quiet one whispered. The Historian leaned forward. Jacob could smell his breath. Musty, dead. "You are in danger."

"Be careful," the child said.

The waves lapped against the hull of *M'Lass*, as if the beached ship had just landed at the edge of the tide and the sea were pushing it the final few inches into place. Beyond the soft breaking waves, the sea was a mystery of mist and thunder. The storm of the day before had retreated, the wind shifted so that fog from that front flew back to shore. Now there was thunder far to the west. Thunder in November.

The rain had passed, at least. Tiny drops of mist still gathered on Jacob's shoulders and the brim of his hat. When he looked down, a stream of water poured onto his boots.

Jamesport's nervous energy seemed to be rising. Paper boys were hawking the morning headline with gusto. "Fire At Whitebirch A Mystery." News had always come to Jamesport. Panics in New York and politics in Boston. And, decades before, there had been the war. Jacob's deeds often failed to make headlines. The newspaper readership had become jaded on the festivals and doings of the wealthy, who had their own channels of news to keep up with one another. Jamesport therefore rarely generated its own headlines. This morning, the second morning after the fire, the city was still excited. Folks on the street did not seem to know how to react, having only read of such things taking place in distant cities.

Jacob bought the paper. He was concerned about one line.

"The chief of police reports that the circumstances surrounding the fire at Whitebirch, and the disappearance of Dr. Thomas Rutledge, are mysterious and suspicious."

He had left the newspaper on his bed, and felt nervous to the point of nausea as he stepped on the sidewalk, on his way to see Sam. Dry, clean clothes—he usually relished small pleasures like these, for they were short-lived. Now, however, his mind spun on the conversation with the Historian and a plan to rid himself of Sam.

There were questions, to be sure. Chief among them: who was the gray woman of the swamp? But none of the answers mattered any more. For Jacob, this morning was about escape. There was a nearly-botched job at Whitebirch, then the order to kill Papaya. Both jobs had attracted undue attention. Perhaps Jacob was losing his touch. Perhaps he was close to being sent from the Old God's ranks. He had no idea what was on the other side.

Escape had always been a fantasy, even when he had not realized it. It had been a fantasy all his life, back to his days in the desert with his sister. Escape had been forced on him, by disaster and plague, and the unexplainable but undeniable urge to take the trance-like journey northeast to Jamesport. Over many years in Jamesport, escape was a glowing ember at the edge of his dark thoughts as he took one victim after another, amassed a small fortune, and did the bidding of forces that he never questioned. Mysteries piled atop one another, and he vowed to deal with them all one day down the road. Now, the pile was so high as to be unapproachable and unscalable. Best to leave it all behind.

Escape, however, would require one more action. One more bullet.

Jacob stepped onto the stone near Sam's cave. He thrust his hands into his pockets. In the right pocket, Papaya's cold rosary wove itself like a thin garden snake through his fingers. In the left pocket, he still carried Rutledge's idol. The wood was so smooth and cold, so worn, that it did not feel like wood at all, but rather like a river stone tossed by the water for generations.

Sam's cave came into view through the mist. Jacob stopped and his heart jumped. He wondered if he had made a wrong turn, or walked too far. There was nothing outside of the cave—no chair or crate, no fire. Sam and his weird entourage were nowhere in sight. The cave itself seemed unreal behind the whispering, twirling haze.

Just looking into the cave, Jacob felt colder. It might not have been the darkness, or the breeze from the sea. There was a silence in that yawning maw that was icy and dead. He looked about. The stones were littered with scraps of stuff washed up from the sea—twigs, dead fish ensnared in knotted twine, lacy sheets of dried seaweed. Jacob stood in the same spot he had always stood. How many times had he watched a card turn? Dozens.

The mountain women, odd men, crying children from deep in the cave, the fire that seemed never to be warm enough—now there was nothing at all.

He stared into the mouth of the cave. The word itself, he thought. Mouth, swallowing, belching ancient air from the depths of history, the depths of the Earth. He waited for Sam to wander from the dark. There was only a low, far-off groaning of air through the pipes of the planet.

A tortured squawking interrupted the thought. Jacob squinted and put his hand on his revolver. Just inside the cave, a metal cage held one live crow and several corpses of others, their torsos marred with bloody gashes. The live one had pecked them to death. Jacob knew these birds. They were the messenger crows that had brought him shells. Indeed, beside them, mussel shells filled a pan. Were there that many victims, or that many assassins? It was proof that Jacob had not imagined Sam.

Jacob kicked the gravel at his feet. He exhaled and watched his steam rise to the far, dark roof. Darkness obscured everything ahead of him, as well. There was a smell, not just the sea but also a touch of sulfur and must. Fungus and swamp. That, he imagined, was the heart of the world—musty, slimy, hot and decaying. He looked about once more. His eyes settled on a dim green light that did not waver as he squinted. It revealed the edges of stone formations near it. He groped toward this light, keeping his eyes fixed on its center. The gravel gave way to bare rock, which began to rise. There were puddles emitting the heavy, nauseating stench of the deep sea. The tide must have brought water here.

Jacob stopped and took another breath. The air was getting colder, much colder. It was heavy in his lungs, stretching them tight. He felt like he was losing his breath, much like he felt in the cave of slaughter beneath Rutledge's mansion. He forced one more deep breath, which helped somewhat to dispel his anxiety.

The green glow was right in front of him. He could now see a path diving to his left into the rock. It became a wide way, smooth and round like the tunnel beneath Executioner's Rock. The walls of this tunnel glowed green and misty, with no warmth. A thin layer of slimy fungus emitted the phosphorescence. Jacob worried that the mist would set his heart alight and shine through his ribs if he were to breathe it.

Squinting, he saw several sets of dark footsteps leading down. One segment of the tunnel far below was dark. Struggle and confusion had smeared the glow from the rock.

Jacob loosened the revolver and felt for the bullets on his belt. He swallowed the air once more and shuddered at an itch in the center of his chest, almost driving him to cough. He wheezed it out and began to descend. The way was treacherous and slippery. He tried to take it slow, but his feet slid. He moved them rapidly forward to catch his footing, but this only made the slide worse. As he reached for the walls at the edges of his fingers, he found no hold. The fungus slime dragged and piled on his fingertips, leaving deep, dark gashes in the wall. Not even halfway down, he fell to his rump and slid several yards before coming to a stop. Looking back, he saw his clumsy footfalls. The light had dimmed wherever he had touched.

He was breathing hard, the sound of it echoing in the tunnel. He tried to silence it. He heard his heart, and the howl of the wind far above. His chest burned, and so he spat the air violently from his lungs, only to gulp it back. He did this several more times until, finally, his heart began to slow and his chest relaxed. He swallowed hard, hoping the boulder in his throat would fall upon his heart, upon his twisting stomach.

Jacob crept the rest of the way, reaching the edge of the dark span of the tunnel. Beyond, the phosphorescence continued for a short stretch and turned to the right. There were several heaps on the ground there.

The wind rose and fell through the cave above, from the beach.

Jacob stood, feeling the cold slime plastering his pants to his legs. It covered his hands and filled his cuffs.

The heaps on the ground—four men, two women, two very young children. They were all dead. Ghastly wounds broke their chests and spilled their bowels. One child's head lay smashed, looking like a piece of fruit. The arms of the woman beside him twisted in strange ways. The corpses seemed much like stone, with glowing fungus advancing over them at an almost visible rate. They were in a haphazard arrangement, having huddled for safety in this corner only to be slaughtered all at once. Jacob recognized the wizard's wild eyebrows and beard. The center of Sam's face was smashed inward so that his profile was a sickening line.

Jacob shivered and looked to the left. The hallway continued perhaps a dozen yards before joining a larger space. He listened to his heart, the surf, and something else. He pulled his revolver from the holster, relaxed and tightened his hand on the grip.

A mechanical noise, machinery in motion, fell to him. Next, he heard a spinning moan that rose to a high-pitched whine.

"Wooee."

The mechanical clanks, followed by the whine came again and again from above, and came closer. A form entered the green light at the top of the ramp. The thing was large and boxy, but a kind of man, its feet clomping on the stone. Between each step, it moaned. The creature moved slowly, and did not seem to see Jacob.

Jacob considered his options. It was still several yards away. He could dive to the left, but it would notice him. He might lose it in the tunnel, but he had no idea how fast or aware the beast might be, or how far the tunnel went.

The form was still indistinct, a silhouette in the phosphorescence of the cave. Its long arms ended in different tools—a ball on the left, while the right broke into a sinister claw of long, skeletal fingers.

Another choice—open fire.

He gripped his right wrist with his left hand, leveled the revolver, and squeezed the trigger.

The bullet smacked square in its chest, making sparks there. The beast stopped and went silent but for a soft click and hum. Jacob fired twice more, and again sparks flew from the thing, from its head and left shoulder.

The creature stood still, whirring and clicking for a moment before moving forward, faster down the ramp. Jacob fired again. Sparks everywhere, but nothing deterred the thing. Jacob turned, slipping in the slime as he went, falling to his hands. The beast was now at the corpses. Jacob sent one more shot into its legs, but it had no effect. It was upon him, reaching with its claws. Each finger was a razor. It caught Jacob's heel and sliced through the leather. The other hand came. A canon ball smashed the ground, sending slime and grit all about. Jacob twisted, pulled the trigger three more times, but emptied the cylinder after only the first. The claw came again, slicing Jacob's forearm. The revolver jumped from his hands.

Scrambling with his heels, he found traction as the beast raised its iron ball. Jacob squirmed and was up, running. The empty holster slapped against his thigh. His arm sang with pain. He took solid, heavy steps so as not to slip. The thing behind him whistled and began to move again.

The tunnel ended in a natural cavern. Stone formations reached up and down in the fungus light. Jacob bobbed and weaved among these, the beast remaining close behind. Jacob's feet splashed now in water. Whirring, whining, stomping—it was right behind him, swinging its ball into the stone, smashing it to grit and gravel.

Jacob could see the far wall in front of him, an unbroken field of phosphorescence. He looked left and right for a break or tunnel. There was nothing. Jacob was tiring. The sprint had drained him. Now, the cold water rising to his ankles fought his progress. It would only be seconds before he reached the wall. Jacob glanced over his right shoulder. The beast was reaching for him. He could hear the splashes of its steps. Jacob veered left, hoping to earn a second or two. The thing made the turn with him. His legs were now burning with the strain, his chest heaving. It would not be long at all.

The water shot up around him, filling his mouth and nose, wrapping around his head. The floor had given way or he had stepped into a hole. He had no sense of the beast, of anything but panic and drowning. He vaulted forward, hitting stone every way he turned, cutting his hands and fingers as he flailed. The beast would smell his blood in the water. He saw nothing but white light pulsing at the edges of his vision. His chest was ready to explode and his mind was about to shut down.

At last, his fingers found a shelf. Gripping it with both hands, he pulled with the last of his strength, perhaps only to smash his head into more stone. But he broke the surface with a gasp. Gulping air and water, he pulled himself to the edge of the pool.

He was in another cavern. The fungus light was strong and there was no beast in sight. An icy breeze touched upon his bare head. His hat was gone.

Before him, hewn steps rose to a landing flanked by a pair of ancient columns.

Jacob climbed the stairs on his hands and knees, for fear of slipping. He looked back, seeing the pool from which he had risen. It was a dark break in the green glow, which covered every stone surface here as it had in Sam's lower cave. He saw the trail of his own crawling as smudges in the stone's aura. Before him, the short flight of steps led to a landing with just enough space to stand before two columns. Jacob could just make out their ornate caps below a bare frieze. The columns and the doorway between them were tall enough for Jacob to pass through, but he imagined anyone taller having to stoop.

He felt the weight of the world above him, and worried about air. Fear started as an itch in his lungs as he breathed the must and funk of the fungus, and grew from there. The weight above him, the stone and the history, could be his tomb. He would die here, to be found in a far-off time by a being who would wonder how Jacob had come to be here, what role he had played.

His heart quickened as he remembered the insects in the cave of slaughter. He stood still, holding his breath, listening. He did not hear their wings, or the trill of their jagged tusks. He stepped, listening for the pop of soft insect bodies. Nothing, just the squelch of his boot sinking into the fungus.

The small entryway opened into a large cavern. The light of the fungus revealed a broad space of finished stone. The walls curved on either side to describe a circle, but the chamber was so large that the far side was indistinct. He could see a ceiling, but could not tell how high it reached. The sound of his steps in the fungus echoed far and high. Looking down, he saw the blocks of the floor, their irregular shapes a primer in an unnatural geometry that made him nauseous. After seconds, those lines began to undulate like a stormy sea. He closed his eyes tight and shook his head. He could walk just a minute or less across the endless cavern before having to steady himself once more.

As he moved, unsure of where he headed, the walls and ceiling peeled away. It was just the floor and darkness. Forms and figures pressed on these like pressing on a taut sheet. A hand here, or a long face there. There were sounds, as well. He was not sure if any of this was real, or if the lines on the floor were doing something to coax these things from his imagination. Nevertheless, the sights and sounds brought a primal, animal fear from the base of his brain. These were the noises that the gibbering fools in the alleys mimicked and the sights that they chattered about as they wandered through the shadows. But it was more than that. All about him, strange creatures rose from the muck, taking all sorts of insect shapes. Some had eyes on stalks. Others had mouths in the centers of chitinous chests. They gathered in formations, arrayed against one another in the ghost light of the fungus. They were, Jacob realized, the armies of figurines on Rutledge's table. He imagined these creatures, legions of them, burrowing into his skin and chewing through his tendons and fibers, snapping them like piano strings to curl back in sharp, stiff spirals. They would leave him an empty sack, a husk.

The sounds became louder, feeding these images and his fear. The floor went wilder, its waves higher, tossing Jacob into the dark air. His point of view flew up and down, high into the sky to see twisted and stretched souls pouring like a waterfall from Jamesport's cliff into a whirlpool of black sludge in the center of the bay. And, his sight sank to the depths of that bay, where clouds of black silt, the decomposed slime of millions of dead, roiled in currents of icy water. It all spun. He felt his stomach lurching to vomit, but it seemed ridiculous and futile to do so, like his body were already flinging apart in bloody, fleshy shreds at the pressure of this world's spinning. His lungs exploded with the acrid air that expanded within him.

It stopped so suddenly and with such a definitive silence that he wondered if he had died. His skin cooled and his racing mind cleared. It was a beautiful escape, so deep that even the sound of his breathing went far off from him, dissipating into nothing in the darkness.

Jacob shivered, bathed in sweat, and opened his eyes. His vision was blurry at first, but cleared as he blinked. The confusing, undulating floor had calmed, but still punished his direct look with nausea. His lifted his gaze, finding the foot of an altar directly in front of him and, upon its flat and undecorated surface, a large bundle. The fungus had only crept up its base, but the green light revealed folds of cloth wrapped about a small creature of human proportions, a chimp or a child. Jacob squinted and leaned forward, peering into the shadows of the beast's empty sockets and reaching to touch the dry teeth of its death smile.

"A mummy," he said to himself, and the whispered word sped down through the folds of cloth, shooting throughout the lines of the floor. The sound came back to him, his own whispered voice but with a deeper-throated character.

"Forsythe," he heard.

"What?" he whispered. Then, louder: "What?"

His words echoed up the chamber, running the edges, spiraling up and driving back down to him as an exclamation to replace his question. It was coming from, or through, the mummy.

"What!" the corpse said. "Forsythe!"

"I don't..."

"The king on the cliff has cast his vision down, down into my depths."

Jacob swallowed hard at the nervousness that jumped from his stomach. Sam and Papaya were dead, but this was a task. This was the voice of the Old God. The corpse, its dry lips stretched over jutting, twisted teeth, continued to whisper.

"He has seen what he should not."

"Forsythe," Jacob said. "Robert Forsythe."

The name went into the stone itself, running veins of gold

and silver through the granite and shale to find the sea, the surface, the sky and the stars.

"Kill him," the voice said. "Do my bidding and you will be free."

He heard water and smelled the sea. He had been walking for a long time. The cavern had pinched into a tunnel that ran straight and level. As he walked, the sound grew louder and louder, lulling him into a trance. For hours, it seemed, he took one step after another in the rhythm of the waves, of the sea that he heard echoing through the fungus glow around him.

He saw the hole before falling into it. It was an absence of light from which rose a pillowy burst of sea air that held him aloft for a second before losing him. Jacob fell forward, smacking his chin. He spun and bounced into sharp stone as he tumbled down a dark slide. It left him in shallow, icy water. He lay still, gnashing his teeth against the pain that exploded throughout his body.

Jacob opened his eyes to dim light. He could see an opening not more than twenty yards away. The light rippled on the surface of the water, reflecting through the mouth of the tunnel. He could not see the hole through which he had fallen from above. Beside him, ancient steps led from the water to a rough landing, but there was no way into the stone. Scraps of bracken and billows of foam floated on the surface of the water. The smell was rotten. This was Jamesport Bay. He had started in Sam's cave, just beyond the wharf, and had traveled clear through the cliff to the other side.

He tested his arms and legs, craned his neck—bruised and pained, to be sure, but nothing was broken. The slice on his arm was tender and swollen, but blood had crusted into the cut and his shirt, and had somehow held in the fall and the water.

Jacob sloshed down the tunnel, his steps echoing like waterfalls. He could not imagine the mechanical beast following him to this place, and so did not take care to go quietly. He reached the mouth and breathed the poisoned air deep into his lungs. It made him dizzy and sent nausea to the top of his throat, but it was air. Gray, flat clouds high in the sky—these were indistinct through an oily haze, but it was no ceiling of stone, no cave. Howling from the swamp set his nerves alight, but it was not the automaton.

Metal clanged above, probably a chain against a flagpole on the grounds of one of the estates. Jacob crouched low beside the cliff, waiting. He saw nothing.

A small beach of muddy sand spread from the foot of the cliff to his right. Boulders had been arranged purposefully on the beach into a circle surrounding a stone block much like the mummy's altar in the underground cavern. Jacob had seen pictures of this beach and read history, explanations, and conjectures much like those that learned men had advanced about the Mystery Tower in town. Researchers spoke of this place as a dark corner of the world, a place in which the local tribes had killed their own to appease a spirit in the bay. Here, the witch he had killed in her tub had danced in dark ritual.

Jacob knew of another mystery on this beach. Vikings had carved runes on the cliff wall, right above the boulders. These men had layered the letters over one another into a puzzle, into a bloom of lines and corners that reminded him of frost on his window.

He touched his tender jaw and clenched his teeth.

Forsythe.

He closed his eyes and felt for his revolver, remembering immediately that it was gone.

Forsythe, then freedom.

FIVE

THE FULL MOON drew brilliant outlines on scraps of speeding clouds. The ocean was violent against the cliff. The air on the ground, however, was still. Jacob stood behind Forsythe Castle, staring at the rear facade. There was a complicated arrangement of steps leading to a locked and certainly guarded back entrance. Trees might have provided cover if he were to travel to either side, presenting the possibility of entrance through the kitchens. He would run the risk of alerting the servants.

No, he thought. He had no revolver. This had to be exact. He had to get very close, very quickly. There was no margin for the sloppiness of his last two missions. Though failure and death were beginning to rank equal to the escape he would earn through a successful mission, he was somewhat thrilled at the prospect of killing Forsythe with his bare hands.

A burst of intuition lit the way for him. He saw nothing at first. But after blinking, he noticed a path winding through the ice-glazed fronds of a giant willow. The path then went along a line of oaks, to a trellis. Climbing this, he could reach a ledge leading close to a second floor porch so wide and tall as to be the most obvious feature of the rear facade.

Jacob moved, clenching his fists against the cold. He parted the branches of the willow. Tiny icicles showered him as he stepped into the cavern below the canopy. The behemoth trunk was a twisted beast in the silent ice cavern of its fronds.

A whispering breath touched upon the back of his neck, and he whirled about to face only the darkness. Ghosts, he thought. Jacob saw stones in concentric rings around the great tree, and wondered if they were graves. There were many stones in mysterious arrangements in the swamps and on the cliff, and even in Jamesport itself. Some were thought to be graves, while others may just have been ceremonial or other markers. As he walked the outermost ring around the willow's trunk, he imagined cold stone skulls turning and peering through empty sockets from below. Dry straps of tongues licked fossilized teeth.

A breeze rustled the willow fronds, only lightly at first and then with more fervor, until the entire tree was shaking and the noise was a din that filled the night. The ice shattered into crystals of frost that floated in the air, seeking one another, seeking a surface upon which to draw their fragile lace. Fear pushed Jacob to move faster and faster through this place. He was now sure that the stones were graves, and thought he heard their broken fingernails scratching at the ground below him. This was a burial ground for witches, or worse. They were waking, throwing the darkness from them like a heavy quilt, throwing it out upon Jacob.

Either panic or the forces decomposing in the dirt made a confusion of the willow's cavern. All lines bent with those rings of headstones, so that any travel across the space curved, bringing Jacob closer and closer to the massive trunk at the center. He was forgetting Forsythe, forgetting escape from Jamesport. The trunk's great veins spiraled with his movement. The tree spun, its fronds growing around him and wrapping under him to close the cavern completely.

Another breeze, and the rustling was a whispering voice of breathy syllables piled atop one another. They sorted as they traveled the shivering twigs, settling into a sentence that repeated again and again.

"Free us to be free."

It sounded with each circuit, dying in volume as Jacob careened closer and closer to the trunk. He slammed into the wood, hugging it with his arms and legs to stop the movement and rising vertigo.

The air spoke once more, wet and windy against his ear.

"Free us to be free."

Jacob fell to ground, looking up to the trunk. The bark shifted and crawled like centipedes to form a circle, inside of which two triangles touched point to point in the shape of an hourglass.

He looked left and right, but saw nothing,

"Destroy the sigil," the voice said. "Destroy the charm. Free us to be free."

Jacob stood, backing away, tripping over the low headstones as he went. The hourglass symbol glowed an eerie yellow that faded as he went. The frozen willow fronds gripped his shoulders, pulling him. They caressed his face and neck, his arms and legs. He went limp, taking no steps but moving through the ice wall as the fronds passed him from one to another.

He fell gently onto the lawn, the cold jolting him back to wakefulness. The whispers of witches, however, still smoldered in the back of his head.

Jacob placed one foot, then the other, gently down to the floor of the porch. The loggia was large, closed on all sides but the columned opening to the back lawn. Sound bounced from wall to wall, amplified against the stone. His steps were quiet, but the rising wind across the columns played the house like a giant instrument, eliciting a wailing groan that rose and fell.

There were three doors clustered directly in front of him, in the center of the loggia's inner wall. Separate from them on either side, pairs of smaller doors also led into the house. A large pediment capped the central three doors, from which a relief of angels stared with open mouths, bellowing silently at the sea.

The pair of doors to the left was open an inch. Jacob smiled as he moved across the loggia, passing a chaise and a small table set with a chessboard in mid-match. The bellowing angels watched him go the whole way.

Jacob hooked his fingers on the edge of the door, cringing at the weak whine from the hinges. The sound thankfully died halfway through the arc.

He was in. He had taken Forsythe Castle. All was silent, and there was sufficient light creeping through the rooms from a central gallery. He was in a girl's bedroom with pink wallpaper shot through with silver swirls. Plaster angels in each corner of the ceiling looked from deep shadows, observing the center of the room's red carpet with little interest. A Greek goddess, however, regarded Jacob sternly from a mantle.

A girl, no more than twelve, was in the bed. Long black hair twisted with her nightgown and sheets into a picture of restless, almost violent sleep. She breathed loudly through her nose, her breath clouding in the cool air above her. She was perhaps a bit too old for the childish flourishes of her furniture, which was dainty and white, unsophisticated in its play at French royalty— oversized dollhouse furniture rather than real appointments.

As the goddess of the mantle watched him, Jacob watched the girl. Her face remained in shadow. She did not start or twitch as he, the nightmare that everyone had told her did not and could never actually exist, moved across the carpet, out of the cold spilling through her open door.

The private chambers in such homes were typically

connected. He had not studied this house. He had not studied the den of one of his victims in years, trusting his intuition to carry him through. It would only be several rooms, perhaps several maze-like corridors connecting them, before he was standing over Robert Chandler Forsythe, contemplating a million ways to stop that man's breathing as quickly and as silently as possible. Through the private chambers he would go undetected by servants and guards alike, all of whom would have dumbly expected evil to enter the same way as visitors or deliveries. Only the angels, gods and goddesses, Tudor royals, and whatever other nonsensical faces, would see him through their blank marble eyes. Some were already aghast, sculpted to witness his invasion.

The large door leading deeper into the center of the house was closed. Jacob guessed that it led to the gallery. A smaller side door was open. This led into a dark closet which opened into a bathroom. Beyond, another bedroom, another closet, and so on. The doors connecting these spaces were all open, a clear path through the residence quarters of Forsythe Castle. Jacob clenched and opened his fists, and moved on.

The wife's bed was unmade but empty. A host of pastoral maidens, togas practically flowing from their ample bodies, from the mural and onto the floor, regarded the bed with wide eyes. Some hushed their voices with frail, bent hands. None seemed interested in Jacob's passage through their field of vision, into her closet and the master bathroom. The possibility of intimacy in an adjoining room seemed enough to monopolize their attention.

Two doors led from the master bathroom, one only opened a crack. A plush rocking horse stood spooked, a comically panicked look in its glass eyes. Beyond, another angel peered from a ceiling corner, its arms spread to present a dark wicker and uncomfortable nursing chair. The angel looked away from this chair, away from the door to the unseen source of light, high-pitched snoring. There was a baby sleeping in that room.

The next door led into Forsythe's closet. Beyond, the wife was in her husband's bed. There were no angels or maidens guarding her restless slumber, through which she had twisted her legs in heavy, dark quilts and nearly maneuvered herself out of her nightgown. Her blonde hair was a nest-like tangle over her face. Rather, deer and other forest creatures, animals that a man like Forsythe might hunt and kill were he a proper English lord rather than an American corporate baron, pranced freely across the walls. A single face peered through a prominent gathering of foliage directly across the room and stared right at Jacob, smiling with a sinister grin. It was reminiscent of the Green Man of ancient European lore, dark and stern but with peering, bright blue eyes.

Jacob stood in the threshold of that room for one moment, tracing the foliage pattern of plaster on the door jamb with his fingers. Swirls and swoops, vines and leaves. The trail ended with that green face of the wilderness spirit, its wry smile perhaps signaling that the whole mission had been a farce or a riddle. There was Forsythe's wife, his room, but no Forsythe.

A weak light fell into the room and against the mural's left cheek. The room turned a corner at that far wall, heading out of view to the right. There was noise around that corner—shuffling, breathing, light humming of a song. Jacob crossed a short span of hardwood floor to a dark green carpet. He clenched his fists again, his heart now beating more quickly and a smile spreading across his face at the possible imminence of the act. He glanced once at the eyes of the spirit on the wall and stopped.

The humming continued, growing just a bit louder.

The woman in the bed had not moved. Behind him, the baby still slept, as did the little girl in the room off of the loggia.

Jacob had passed no sign of witchcraft, no hint of insanity in the home. There was nothing like Rutledge's collection. The cavern of the willow was peculiar in the back of the estate, but one did not travel far in Jamesport without stumbling over such things. It had been here before Forsythe, and perhaps had no connection to him. And, it was a song drifting from the right, not incoherent babbling. Most of Jacob's victims approached or had crossed the edge of sanity. Forsythe was not the type.

Jacob relaxed his fists and traveled to the far edge of the room. He stood directly in front of the mural, staring down the green face's quiet, knowing stare, and turned right. A short hallway ended in a tall door, most likely leading to the gallery. Mid way down on the right, a small room opened from the hall.

Forsythe was there. The shadow of his movement wandered all over the walls of the hallway.

Just a few steps, and Jacob was behind him. Forsythe was leaning against a table, his back to the door. He moved stacks of money into piles. Jacob could not help but smile. What else would the barons of Jamesport do in the middle of the night in their mansions but arrange and rearrange their money? He was the perfect caricature of wealth, if not for his striped pajamas and wild, though thinning hair. Short, stocky, barefoot, a wife in his bed but lured from sleep by piles of cash.

Forsythe went suddenly still. His breathing and humming ceased.

"Robert Chandler Forsythe," Jacob said quietly.

Forsythe turned and backed into the table, knocking one of the stacks which spilled in a slide of fluttering paper to the floor. His face was pudgy and ruddy, and bloomed with recognition.

"Jacob!" he said. "Why..."

Jacob's heart leapt. There was no collection of oddities, no insanities. But Forsythe knew him. None ever knew him. This was not a mistaken target after all.

"Jacob, sit!" Forsythe beckoned to a rickety wooden chair that would have looked more at home in the Portuguese slums than here. A table, one chair, and a small fireplace with a decorative but not opulent marble mantle. Upon the mantle, however, a glass jar held something indeterminable through the scratches of a rough inscription.

Jacob stepped forward.

"You want your pay. The world goes to hell and you just want to get paid. I understand! I have it all here. I under—"

Jacob took two steps, gripping Forsythe's neck and squeezing the baron's voice box with his thumbs. He crushed the man's throat shut, ending his voice. The wound on Jacob's arm reopened under the pressure of his deed.

Someone had scratched the jar with a very fine point. The symbol, two triangles meeting point to point within a circle, was traced again and again so that the strokes were thick, though hasty and sloppy. Lines and swirls surrounded the sigil, all the way around the back of the jar. The jar itself looked to be of a gallon size. Its lid was heavy and solid black marble, polished beyond sheen to a point at which it swallowed rather than reflected the weak ambience of an electric light on the table.

Jacob turned from the mantle back to the bedroom. There was no sound, no movement in the shadows. He turned back to the jar on the mantle, lifted the lid and peered in, immediately struck by a musty and rotten stench. Inside, a small black and leathery husk, fist-sized and roped with ripped and dried vessels, sat in bits of its fibrous matter. He did not know what it was.

He placed the lid on the table behind him, thinking only the words of the willow, that here was a sigil and its charm. The promise of freedom demanded that he destroy both.

But quietly. He considered his options, which narrowed to carrying the heavy thing out with him.

Jacob heard stone sliding on wood, the lid across the table. He spun to see the wife, her soft beauty lost in restless sleep and deep lines of horror and anger. She held the marble lid high, and came upon Jacob with every intent to smash his skull.

Jacob sidestepped, extending his leg to trip her. He cupped her mouth to stifle her scream and, with his other hand, pushed her forehead hard into the mantle. She went limp and slid to the floor, leaving a thick trail of blood down the side of the fireplace.

Jacob threw the jar down upon her head, which made a hollow cracking sound before the jar struck the marble, exploding into shards. The leather bundle rolled to Jacob's feet. It stopped there, but seemed for a moment to live, its leathery surface going smooth and wet, its chambers contracting in succession. It was a heart, and for that few seconds it beat.

He crushed it beneath the sole of his boot, expecting it to gush blood. As soon as he touched it, however, it went dry and brittle again.

Jacob dashed through the bedroom, passing breathless, hysterical crying from the nursery and bounding across the daughter's carpet to the loggia before, he hoped, the servants had any notion that anything worth their investigation had happened.

This would be a crime for the headlines.

The wind was rising, bringing a bank of ocean fog to hide the moon and make broad blurry spheres of each of the gas lamps in the rear of the Forsythe property. The air within the willow cavern, however, was still and dry. It was also cold—so cold that it prickled into frost on the walls of his lungs. The light beneath the willow fronds was oddly different from the outside, as well. Bright blue light from a full moon of another time and place fell through gaps in the leaves and sliced across the rings of stones. The stones within this light sparkled, studded with diamonds or tiny globes of ice. The trunk was dark, with no sign of the sigil that Jacob had destroyed. The witches, and all feeling of them, were gone. Jacob's chest heaved, and the fronds waved with the wind outside. That and the rising clamor from Forsythe Castle were the only sounds.

"It is done," he said.

Voices shot from the house. Jacob had no reason to be concerned. The willow was near the edge of the property. From here, it was just steps to a rough trail that ran in defilade along the cliff and into Jamesport. Still, he was afraid. First, there had been a voice in the subterranean temple, then voices below the canopy of this willow. The latter seemed to have gone silent. Jacob had just committed the murder of the century, and knew that he had to leave Jamesport.

They had promised him he could. "Free us to be free," they had said. Jacob wondered if that had been the last that he would hear from them. Free, they were on to greater things, and he should now just leave. Or, the forces behind the unraveling of the Old God's network had caught up with these voices as well, and would now track him down. Either way, he felt uncomfortable leaving without an acknowledgement of his deed, a confirmation that he had, after two sloppy missions, finished this one.

"You needn't be afraid, Jacob."

Jacob turned. Forsythe's daughter stood framed in parted willow fronds, the mansion's light reflecting off of the willow's ice in a brilliant corona around her. She stepped into the space, letting the fronds and the light close behind her. Her hair and gown were disheveled, and her eyes nearly closed.

"I must escape," Jacob said. "I have to go."

Saying it, he realized he had nowhere to go. His life had known West Texas and here.

"You can't," the girl said. "Not until we free you, and it's almost time."

"I killed Forsythe. I broke the jar. What else?"

She smiled. Dark eyes, stiff black hair, sleeping gown–she looked innocent and demonic all at the same time.

"You've done well, and you're almost done. There is one more victim."

Jacob sighed, his breath signaling a sharp rise in the wind that sent the fronds alight with frenzy. They moved in the same direction, toward the mansion. As the wind went from rush to roar, they shivered and spun, sending icicles in all directions.

"Kill the Historian."

SIX

JACOB'S DOOR WAS open just an inch. He stared at it for a moment, trying to remember the last time that he had been in his apartment. That was to gather bullets the day before last, before heading off to Sam's cave. He was sure he had closed the door. In fact, he remembered the ritual—closing the door, locking it, looking all around the edges at familiar marks, dents in the wood of the jamb. He found nothing new now, so no one had pried the door. Next, Jacob looked at the door knob. Nothing there but the reflection of the dim gaslight on the wall behind him. The knob turned easily. The bolt above it was simply unlocked. There were no scratches about the keyhole.

He pushed. The door slid open a bit further before stopping against something soft and heavy. He looked through the opening and saw his mirror, which reflected the wall above his bed across the room. Dust floated in shafts of orange light that fell through the window panes. The sun was rising over the eastern sandy point of Jamesport.

Jacob reached for his holster, forgetting again that he had lost his revolver. The pain in his forearm, bandaged with a strip of cloth from his shirt, reminded him. The scene came back to him at once—cowering beneath the mechanical beast in the cave, beneath the suffocating weight of stone in the glow of the fungus. His heart jumped at the thought that the thing had tracked him, indeed had beaten him to his apartment. Jacob went as still as he could, waiting to hear the whine and moan, the mechanical clicks. He heard nothing but a horse on the street below.

He could see another small slice of the room through the gap between the hinges. He studied this, rising and kneeling, leaning to get as much of a survey as he could. The door had stopped against his mattress, which was off the bed and spilling its stuffing from a cut down its center, head to foot. The wardrobe just beside the door had thrown its contents straight out, the drawers extended so far that they tilted to the floor. Jacob saw bullets, the souvenirs of his jobs, his clothes all about, with some of it reaching clear across to the window. The mattress stuffing sat atop this mess, so the wardrobe had been the first target.

The intruder had pulled the bed from the wall. Jacob could not see behind it, to the floorboards in the corner. There, a compartment in the floor hid much of his earnings.

Jacob slammed against the door, pushing the mattress just enough to allow him to squeeze into the room. The door creaked, the sound running into the stairwell, up to the roof and into the sky. The world knew that he had arrived. He felt the weight of a gaze fall upon him.

Something crunched beneath his feet as he reached the table below his mirror. The lawyer's turtle shell eyeglasses. He checked his pockets. Rutledge's idol and Papaya's rosary were still there. They had stayed with him through his journey in the belly of the cliff and his mission to kill Forsythe.

The window was open. The curtains were blowing straight with stiff gusts of wind, like two ghostly arms reaching into the room, rising and falling. The floor below the window was wet with rain from a burst that had lasted just minutes, but which had filled the gutters.

Jacob raced to the corner behind the bed, nearly slipping in the puddle. The floorboards were misplaced, and the compartment below empty. Thousands of dollars were gone, though his mind immediately began running through his inventory of caches throughout the city. He had hidden two hundred or so in each. Another two thousand around the city, but so much more had been stolen from his apartment. He felt dizzy and braced himself against the bedpost. Cool air fell over the side of his face. The curtain reached up and brushed his cheek.

There was mattress stuffing in the compartment. Several bullets, as well. A corner of his mother's quilt fell into the space from its heap on the floor. There was a button from the waistcoat of a shopkeeper who had delved into a hobbyist's history of the ruined stone tower, and had stumbled upon shocking secrets. Sam had arranged a handsome payment for that man's death, and his sketches. The button had come from the wardrobe.

The intruder had gone straight for the compartment, had stolen the money, and then ransacked the rest of Jacob's apartment, starting with the wardrobe.

Jacob looked down. He looked past his hands, which were brown with the stain of the cave fungus and still felt the soft warmth of Forsythe's neck. He saw but could not consider fresh blood spreading through the bandage on his arm. It did not hurt at the moment. His torn shirt, his pants, his coat and boots—all were damp and filthy. His mind, though, locked upon a single question.

What else had the intruder wanted?

Jacob gathered cleaner clothes from the floor. He cleaned his wound in the basin below the mirror and washed his face with the pink water. Washing his face and licking his lips, he tasted salt, behind which rang the metallic tang of his own blood. He had no second pistol, but he had a second Stetson. It sat beside him on the floor overturned. He took it, brushed it off, and fit it to his head, feeling suddenly more human and refreshed. He turned to survey the room once more and frowned.

Not only had the intruder known about Jacob's money, he had known exactly where to find it.

Jacob wanted to sit, to sleep, to fade away. Now was not the time. There was much more to be done, money to collect. He had counted on this money to take him from Jamesport, but none of that would matter until the Historian was dead. Now, however, Jacob was also a target. Certainly, many had reason to despise him, but his safeguard had always been in his stealth. No one knew him. Those dead, his victims—they had either forsaken all of the living, or had exercised such insane tendencies as to be shunned by friends and peers. Who mourned the rambling drunk in the alley? Who mourned a man like Thomas Rutledge? And, more to the point, who among the thin ranks of mourners had the inclination and skills to track Jacob, overcome his stealth, and rob him? Forsythe was a different kind of victim.

Did the Old God have a rival? Jacob imagined a legion of assassins working for another arcane presence, another ill-tempered thing that wanted nothing more than to be left alone, its secrets protected.

Kill the Historian. Jacob's taskmaster brain silenced the other distracting thoughts. Go to the abandoned fish market and kill the Historian. Collect the money hidden throughout the city, including two hundred dollars in a hollow in one of the market's walls, just steps from the Historian's perch. After that, escape. Additional tasks surfaced. Jacob might also need medical attention, and the types of physicians who exercised the necessary discretion came at a price. He would need a new revolver, and they were not cheap. Chang's import shop was the safest place to purchase one, though the proprietor's role in all of this was uncertain.

Each of these, he realized—the Historian, the doctor, Chang—represented a potential threat. Each was a clue back to him. Forsythe could have bought the world ten times over. Certainly, his death would not go unnoticed or uninvestigated.

Jacob heard shuffling. Shuffling and breathing just outside his door. He waited for the mechanical moan, the clicks. Would the thing have walked the streets to reach him? Perhaps it had tunnels to reach any place in the world.

He heard nothing but the shuffling and breathing, though the shuffling sounded like several. They were close to the door. He rushed to the window, nearly slipping once again.

He climbed over the sill and slid down against the rough edge of the window ledge. He gripped the wet stone with the tips of his fingers. The wound on his arm seared, seeming to rip longer. His right hand released and he swung for just seconds, looking down to the sidewalk. The street was empty but for a wandering vagrant. She was a crone of the alleys, an old woman who had probably lost her husband to a whaling accident, or the war, or to Jacob's revolver. She shuffled, mumbling, in a ratty coat that looked like burlap, and with a thin dirty kerchief over her head.

She was below Jacob when he let his fingers slip, just as he heard movement in his apartment.

It was only one story, perhaps just ten feet, but Jacob hit her square. She was fragile. Her cry was harsh and loud, running from deep in her gut and warbling the loose skin around her neck. She lay on the wet sidewalk. Jacob, unscathed, rose and stepped one step from her, but turned. She reached to him, dragged her body toward him.

Jacob glanced up to his window. There was a shadow. He squinted, turned from the crone and ran down the hill to the abandoned market.

Exhausted and breathless, with a nauseous dizziness rising in his gut and sharp pains in his shins, Jacob rounded the corner across from the wharf and ducked through the closest gap between the crumbling wooden planks of the market's wall. He stopped for one moment to collect himself. No one had followed him. The wide, empty marketplace spread before him. Water cascaded from several holes in the roof. The scene was otherwise still. The ocean breeze did not blow through the buckling columns or rusting joists. The rotten stink of the sea had instead settled into a palpable, heavy sourness that gripped Jacob's coat and wove itself into the denim. It filled his nostrils and lungs, forcing the air out of him and making a much greater labor of his heavy breathing. His nausea spiked. He leaned against a metal support, welcoming its coolness against the back of his neck.

The Historian's cell was not more than two dozen long strides across this end of the market. Jacob went, crouching low and looking to either side. He spun to land against the freezer door with his back. After a moment surveying the quiet market and the early morning street beyond, the beginnings of the wharf's day with its ringing bells and shouts, Jacob pivoted into the Historian's cell. No one had seen him. He was sure of it.

The beast was already aware, already awake. The Historian leaned into the light, revealing his rough marbled face, and scowled. A low whine escaped with his breath. The sailor's voice was the first to speak.

"I smell fear on you, Jacob. More than usual."

There was little to be gained from hiding it. Whatever senses this beast possessed, whatever prescience it had, it could at least see straight through the assassin before it. Jacob lowered his gaze to the edge of the Historian's perch, where years if not longer had made a gray muck of refuse that melded with the floor.

"I am sent to kill you," Jacob said, stepping forward.

"Why?" the child asked. Then, the sailor: "We knew this day would come. Some of us may have denied it, but I was right all along. I knew it when you stepped into the market—today, but also the first time years ago. I could feel it in the hairs on my neck!"

Jacob was halfway across the chipped tiles of the freezer's floor, but stopped. Ending the Historian would indeed end the story as he knew it. Sam and Papaya were gone. Forsythe had bankrolled the network. The Historian had been the closest to a guide that Jacob had. After the Historian, there would be only Jacob. There were others on the edges—Chang, for instance, who laundered Forsythe's money. And there were friendly doctors, an occasional lackey who provided transport or left a crucial door unlocked. But of the central figures of Jacob's life in Jamesport, the Historian was the last.

"He hesitates," the harsh whisperer said. "He questions whether the escape they have offered is true, or if it is a false promise to lead him to one more murder after another."

"You are the last," Jacob said.

The child laughed, nearly giggled.

"We aren't the last," he said. "Jacob thinks we're the last, but he doesn't get it. He doesn't really know that he's hunted, does he?"

"He must," the sailor said. "How could he miss it? They pillaged his apartment. They sent the automaton."

Jacob took another step forward, a small step. He flexed his fists.

"You see, Jacob," the whispering voice said. "They will use you, but they hunt you. They will not let you escape."

"What are you—?"

He saw the explosion before hearing or feeling anything. The rear wall to the side of the Historian bulged, the tiles separating and shattering. A jet of flame shot through the hole, pushing the Historian from his perch and blossoming before Jacob in an image of hell. Jacob was lifted from his feet, flying back out of the cell to land in water and roll, stopping in a folded heap against a steel support.

He rose to his knees, gripping his head and squinting as a second explosion expanded slowly, a ball of fire from the Historian's cell. Jacob watched the door swing, pop from its hinges, and sail across the floor. The ocean stink, the dust and crusted seaweed, the dried scraps of fish flesh, the trash—it all rolled into a wave that spread from that explosion and shook the supports, broke the columns.

Jacob gasped as it came to him. It hit him in the gut, twisting him around the support and throwing him face-first through the wall. He landed in the street upon planks and splinters. He exhaled in a long whine, turned over onto his back and stared into the bright gray of the sky.

The sound pounced upon him. It was thunder and dynamite, the screaming of wrenching metal. It quickly rose to become a muffled, high-pitched buzz in his ears that suddenly ceased, leaving nothing behind it. The sound felt like a liquid filling his skull.

Jacob rose to his elbows, which immediately gave way.

Figures gathered around him. Onlookers. Good Samaritans. But he was wrong.

There were three of them. They wore gray half-capes with high collars, hats almost like sailors' caps. Young women.

One spat on him and spoke. Her voice was so distant that he could not hear it.

Another held his shoulders.

The third bent over him, drawing a cold shadow to cover him. He shivered, prompting a tighter grip on his shoulders. This third woman reached for his mouth with a cloth. A sweet and pungent smell filled his nostrils, setting them afire as his vision dimmed from the edges, leaving just a small dot of consciousness at the center that lasted a moment before blinking away to blackness.

Ida sat on a boulder in the middle of the cut. She had drawn her knees to her chest and perched atop the stone like a vulture.

"Let's climb to the ruin," she said.

Soon after, she was already in the cave. Jacob was several yards, the toughest yards, below the rough steps that led into the cliff dwelling.

They had seen the place a thousand times. They now ignored the warnings about entering it.

Jacob blinked as a drop of sweat fell from his hairline, down the bridge of his nose and hung for one suicidal second at the tip before falling to the canyon floor. He looked down, expecting to see it fall. The floor was far below.

He sighed.

"This isn't real," he thought.

"Come on!"

Ida was beckoning, yelling, but it sounded like she was under water.

"This isn't real," Jacob said again, aloud.

"It happened," came a voice. "See it again."

Jacob reached, feeling for a handhold. The sun was at the top of the sky, shining right into his eyes. He saw nothing but Ida's sun-wrecked silhouette in his failing vision.

Pain exploded in his head. He shut his eyes so tight that he saw spiraling patterns, a million suns. The pain spiked, then receded into a dull throb that he feared would be with him the rest of the day.

"Not real," he said through clenched teeth.

The pain rummaged through his brain, shifting from the rear of his skull to the front, moving from side to side.

"Nothing yet," said the voice. An old woman. Almost grandmotherly, but insistent and curt.

Ida reached through the brilliant sunlight, taking Jacob's hand and pulling. Jacob was dizzy, thankful for the bracing grip of his sister. The two stepped into the shade of the cave. There, Ida crouched, peering through an ancient window into an empty chamber. A doorway beyond led to stairs that climbed the rear of the cave to a long gallery on the level above.

"Why do you think they lived up here?" she asked.

"A flood," Jacob said. "Or thieves."

The voice came from him, but he did not will it. It was in him, sounding from him, but he did not think those words. He kept thinking to himself, "Not real." He was a child, perhaps twelve or not even. Ida was just nine, curls falling over her eyes and the scars of scorpion stings covering her forearms. Ida, who had died.

At this place.

Yes, Jacob realized. Ida would die here.

"I'm remembering this," he thought.

"Go along," the voice said. "Do it. We must see. There are answers."

Ida scrambled along the wall, beneath the gallery. The wall opened, there. A black tunnel led into the cliff. The sound, the air of it—it was evil and dark. The breath of the underground carried whispers of horrors and disease. Jacob could understand none of it. It was the gibberish of stone and dust, but it got between his teeth and clotted in his throat. He needed water.

Ida was standing in the entrance to the tunnel. Jacob's heart shot into his throat—he knew what was going to happen. He could hear the skittering in the world below, the rustling. It was playing before him again, and he wanted to stop it.

"You cannot stop it," the voice said. "Do what you did."

Jacob looked to the ground beside him, to a shattered pot and the untouched bare footprint of a denizen of this place, a man dead for eons. He stared at these for long seconds, thinking that he saw fingerprints in the clay of the pot. He waited.

The rustling grew to a roar, and a black cloud burst from the mouth of the cave. Ida stumbled back to the edge of the cliff.

"Bats," Jacob said.

They kept coming, hordes of them in a column, a river of black and gray, of disease and the rotten stench of the center of the Earth.

Ida spun her arms to balance but fell back.

"This is it," the voice said.

Jacob rushed to the edge of the cliff. Ida was still falling. Dust clouded around her as she struck the ground. Her neck was twisted, her body broken.

The bats clouded over the canyon, a roof over this simple scene, this single death.

Jacob blinked hard. He wanted this to end.

"See it through," the voice said.

Something in the cave. A furtive, desperate growl that rose and fell in a threatening, primal melody. It filled him, set each of his fibers ringing like guitar strings. That shivering, that ringing—it never stopped. Its tone spoke to him, drove him from Texas after the plague had taken his mother. It sent him to Jamesport, to Sam for the first fateful errand.

"Do you enter the cave?" the voice asked.

"No."

"This one knows nothing. This is a waste of your time. Send him below to me."

Jacob opened his eyes. The world beyond him was a blur of light and soft colors, blues and pinks. A few brilliant streaks of gold twisted through like cloudy swirls of paint in water. He blinked several times, and each time the scene shivered with a touch more detail before fading again into fog.

He was in the center of a large room. His head was lolling. He could sense that movement now. A marble floor. A ceiling deep into his vision, far above and dark. A forest all around him. White shot through it—a white chair rail. The forest was a mural. Gold cherubs hovered in the blue sky that, as it went higher, faded into night and stars. It was all painted with exquisite detail in the brief moments that he could see it, when he blinked.

The three women in gray sat before him in identical chairs of heavy wood with ornate knots like swollen knuckles. The chairs formed an arc in the center of this large room. Several younger girls in white stood in front of a closed set of double doors, the only exit. High windows let moonlight fall to the veined brown marble floor.

The woman in the center was blonde and young, with high and prominent cheek bones and cold gray eyes that pierced Jacob. Her mouth was wide, and her jaw a severe line dipping into a sharp point. She spoke.

"Mother has been through him," she said. "He has nothing. He knows nothing."

She gestured to her right, to her identical twin. The two laughed, pleased by the result. The one to their left was different, with soft features and brown eyes beneath black hair. She was quiet, but furrowed her brow in concern or annoyance as the two blondes laughed. Her face was somewhat flat, and her eyes small and disconcertingly far apart. Her skin was as smooth as porcelain, and just as white.

Jacob's stomach growled. He was famished, and his mouth was as dry as it had been that day in the desert.

The blonde in the center snapped her fingers.

"Water!" she shouted. Her voice was clear and sharp.

One of the younger girls—white cloak and skirt, curls—rushed in with a tin cup. She pressed it to Jacob's lips and tilted warm, sweet water into his mouth. His throat would not open at first, but finally parted to let the water through. It felt like nothing, but shot through him, his limbs and head, bringing clarity to his vision almost at once.

"Ida," Jacob moaned.

"What does he say?" the brunette asked.

The blonde on the left leaned forward to answer. Her twin in the center clicked her tongue and donned a threatening scowl that silenced her sister. The brunette sank deeper into her chair.

"It doesn't matter," the leader said. "His sister. Dead, now. It doesn't matter."

Jacob tried to stand. Straps held him to the chair at his wrists and ankles.

"Where—?" he began to ask.

"Where are you?" the leader interrupted. "This is the Eliza Stephens College for Women. We are the last."

"I—"

"You are Jacob of West Texas, assassin for the Old God. You have much blood on your hands. You belong to Mother, now."

"You have for some time," the twin said, giggling.

The leader smiled, tossing a half-hearted "Hush!" to her sister.

Jacob pulled again at his restraints, then looked across the three women assembled before him. The twins regarded him with boredom and disinterest. The brunette had compassion in her eyes. She moved to the edge of her chair and leaned forward, holding a goblet with both hands in front of her knees. The cup was gold and covered in jewels, and was like Jacob's imagining of the Holy Grail. When her gaze met Jacob's, she turned her eyes down, looking past the goblet to the floor.

The two blondes suddenly snickered. The leader waved to the young girls in white, who immediately went into motion, each taking a position on either side of the double doors. They opened those doors.

Jacob saw an opulently appointed sitting room beyond. There were plush chairs, tall vases, thick curtains. But he heard something—clicking, whirring.

The beast of the cave stepped into view, its metal feet pounding on the marble floor.

Jacob fought his restraints, but they held. The blondes were laughing now, looking back and forth between him and the beast as if watching boxers approach one another. This was sport.

"You have not been properly introduced," the leader said. "This is Tinker, the first of Professor Rutledge's experiments."

Tinker entered the room, ducking through the doorway. As he approached the three women, he slowed and stood tall in the light. Metal plates covered his entire body. Some of it—the round joints at his shoulders, elbows and knees—looked like medieval armor. Some of the metal, however, was boxy like ductwork. The pieces were irregular, so that rivets ran in strange, crooked lines that crossed one another with unsettling asymmetry.

Tinker's arms bore the same implements that Jacob had seen in the cave. There was the claw of blades, their points almost scratching against the floor. The metal ball on the other arm was shiny, but covered in dents. These locked into his arms above the wrists, leading Jacob to think that the beast might wield other tools.

A loose metal plate, held by rusting rivets, clapped against Tinker's torso. Jacob imagined devilish machinery, an unholy mix of organs and gears, behind that plate. Tinker chugged and whirred, then reached a pause, a moment during which the mechanisms behind the panel wound back or reset with a low groan that sped to a whine. The beast's whole frame relaxed, only to tense and shudder as his clockwork snapped into motion, building to the next whining release.

Tinker's head was a simple metal can. His creator had cut a hole for the face and set a curved plate of thick glass to contain the viscous, clear fluid that almost filled the can.

Within, the face of a child looked dumbly, unblinking to the world. A boy. His eyelids were open to different heights. His eyes pointed in different directions. There were cuts on one freckled cheek. These were open wounds that might once have been ghastly, bleeding gashes. They were now dead and white. Fine red hair flowed and waved like a low flame above his ears, just below the level of the fluid. The boy's mouth wrapped around a leather tube that reached through the glass. The moan was not just mechanical. It sounded through that tube as a voice, as well.

A caged thing. Jacob had seen his anger in the cave. Now, he saw Tinker's grotesque imprisonment. This was a dead child, made to be alive.

He wondered. What had Rutledge done?

The goblet-bearer leaned forward.

"Now?" she asked.

"Yes," the leader said.

The young woman stood and, bowing, brought the cup to Jacob's lips. It was red wine, deep and purple.

"Drink," she said.

"Take him to Mother," the blonde in the center said. "Do not delay. The moon is still full enough tonight, but it wanes. There is not much time for Mother to convert him."

Jacob took a long sip. It was smooth and full, but it burned in the back of his throat.

The goblet-bearer whispered. Jacob thought he heard: "I am sorry."

Heat rose in his gut. He belched and tasted the wine, but also bitterness. The edges of his vision went hazy, and his head fell back against the chair. He saw, in the dark of the domed ceiling, ribs of ornate plaster scrollwork cutting through the mural of the night sky. Far, infinite stars shone through thin clouds, even through the overpowering light of the full moon.

Then, he saw nothing.

SEVEN

TINKER WAS CARRYING him, one arm beneath Jacob's neck and one beneath his knees. Jacob was still groggy and somewhat nauseous from whatever the sympathetic witch had served him from the jeweled goblet. Sharp pain sang from his joints and the tips of his fingers tingled. Jacob wondered if this was happening at all, or if it was a journey to a new corner of his unconscious. Would the witches wander through his brain again? He felt no presence.

Jacob tried to survey his surroundings but was constrained. He turned his gaze down his body and saw a thick rope winding around him. Beneath the rope, a sack of white linen like sailcloth ran up to his neck, where the rope ended in a noose that cinched the sack shut. He squinted, and saw scribblings and sweeping symbols painted in rough strokes on the cloth.

The world around him, or what he could see of it, was empty. Clumps of glowing, moonlit snow. Stiff, still grass. Tinker's clockwork steps and moaning barely rose above the wind. Jacob knew that he was on the cliff. If he peered through the space between Tinker's arm and boxy torso, He could see the Larchmont estate a few dozen yards behind them. Tinker's dark footsteps, perfectly spaced, led back to that place.

A dim orange light reflected from the glass covering Tinker's face. Jacob turned his head and saw a small structure in front of them, its walls glowing with light and warmth. The structure was a simple box, a wooden frame with blank white walls that shook in the wind. A wide, pointed roof seemed much too large, perhaps plucked from a different structure. Jacob realized that it was a Japanese tea house just as they passed over the threshold. Tinker stopped before taking a series of steps to turn in the tight space. He moved toward a stone stairway that descended through a framed hole in the center of the floor.

As they went, Jacob's senses twisted. Several times, he felt like he was falling down the stairs, but Tinker held him. Bile rose and mixed with fear in the back of his throat. It was vertigo, fueled by sulfurous vapors in shots of shrieking wind from the darkness at the bottom of the stairs, beyond the short reach of the moonlight. In between those gusts, a low drone set the stones buzzing. Jacob knew the sound. It was the wings of insects, the same that he had seen below Whitebirch.

The insects were in the air, now, alighting upon the sailcloth, exploring it with their needles and testing its thickness with their jaws. They landed, did this, and immediately lifted again. Soon, they were surrounding Jacob and Tinker, clouding the faint phosphorescence rising from the stone but perhaps guiding the pair through a maze of ancient tunnels.

He thought he heard Mother speaking, far away at first but suddenly close, in his ear.

"The mantids will not attach to this one," she said. "He is not a suitable host. We were wrong about him, but I must investigate. He will still be useful for a time."

The world spun as Tinker stood him against the stone wall. Tinker was gone after that. All movement and sound ceased. His existence went as still and silent as stone. He could move only his eyes. Everything else was unresponsive to his wishes. After some time, he heard chirping and squeaking. Tall forms approached in erratic trails as they weaved among each other. They came closer, and Jacob's vision sharpened. They were ant-like, though walked on two legs. These insects moved claw-like hands rapidly against their mouths, gathering foul-smelling slime from beneath their mandibles into gluey balls that they slapped onto his body. This ichor hardened quickly, encasing him. They covered his face. He could see nothing through the shell. He could do nothing but breathe and moan through a tube that was jammed into the softness behind his tongue. They pushed the flying insects down that pipe, and he felt the mantids' tiny limbs and needles scraping against the roof of his mouth, pushing and resisting. His captors forced the beasts until they had nowhere to go but to burrow through the back of his throat.

He wanted to scream, but he could not find the breath.

History. Jacob now had hints of times long past, times that stretched back through incomprehensible spans to an Earth unknown, and to horrible upheavals that he could not imagine but which he felt in his blood. The carrion mantids, twitching in between his muscles and growing fat on his fluids and tissue, excreted this awareness into him.

He could see the larger creatures moving outside of his shell as smudges of black and brown against a green light. They jammed more of the insects into his throat, but he did not feel them any longer. His body was riddled with them, now. Perhaps he was more of their flesh than his own. But he still had his thoughts, and still had sanity in them.

Sometimes, though, he felt Mother in his mind.

"Show me what happened next."

Ida was dead. She was a split thing, her limbs pinned beneath her torso in unnatural angles, the ropes of her gut stretching across the flat bed of sandstone upon which she had landed. The flies had already been sitting on that rock, alighting to avoid the impact only to later land on the bloodied, already baking edges of Ida's wounds.

A shaman found them. He wandered in a peyote haze and did not even believe that Ida was real. He then accused Jacob of killing Ida, and waved a long black feather whenever his old wet eyes found Jacob in the chaos of hallucinations. But something in Jacob's grief won over the shaman. Jacob looked at the man, at his shining red skin and the coal black of his eyebrows, at the reflection of the sun over the canyon on his bald head, and said only, "Help me."

Jacob would not speak again until meeting Sam fifteen years later.

The shaman led Jacob to his shack and offered food. Jacob stayed through the night, returning to Ida the next morning. By then, her bones were white and dry. What was left of her blood and flesh had gone black in the sun. Vultures, vermin and insects had taken what they could of her, leaving only fibrous sinew on those bones.

"She is in the sky and the rock," the shaman said. "This is a holy place."

Jacob felt the bats in the tunnel above and the spirits who walked among those ruins. And one other thing—the growling beast of the darkness. He could feel the rumbling in his belly as the thing sat in the cliffside, staring at him through the rock.

They placed her remains on a rickety cart and covered her with a sun-stiffened, ripped cloth. A burro with pink scars of scorpion bites along its neck, scars like the ones Ida had shown like trophies, limped as it pulled the cart. The animal nodded its head with every step, nodding in answer to the question that ran incessantly in Jacob's head. "Is this real?"

Their mother had already died. The pink froth that had bloomed out of her mouth had made an oily stain on the wood floor. Jacob's father could not wash it away, no matter how hard he tried.

He was next.

The sickness, whatever it was, took the whole town. All but Jacob.

He saw the shaman once more. As Jacob left the town, as he lost his thoughts in the steps of the horse that bore him northeast, he passed the shaman. The old man averted his gaze and waved his black feather.

"Demon," the shaman said. "You are a demon."

"He was right," Mother said.

There was no telling how long he existed in this way, encased in that chitin, controlling his breath between fits of fear that set his muscles twitching. Each time, countless times, the mantids burrowing through his body calmed him. They released a toxin that deadened his muscles. Forgiving calm washed over him, filling him with peace until even the fear went hiding in dark corners of his being. This calm would last for a long moment before the fear rose again, shooting through the shaman's words with a sound like that of Ida slapping against the ground. It shot through his father's hacking cough and the priest's droning, nasal eulogy at the head of one of the mass graves. But between the moments of fear, Jacob's mind did the closest thing it could to sleep and he remembered things that he had forgotten. The shaman lay in one corner of his shack mumbling incomprehensible things through his hallucinogenic dreams. One thing, though, had followed Jacob for years.

"You are no longer yours."

The words had been there, under the surface, all along. As Jacob remembered them now, his mind turned to the gaping mouth of the cave in the West Texas ruins. He climbed up from the stained rock and found Ida's last footprints in the sand. He stood in the cave mouth, the wind of those words at his back. They pushed him into the cave, down a ramp so quickly that he struggled to stay on his feet. He halted in a silent space, feeling the darkness around him like he felt the chitin that the strange creatures had slapped in glistening handfuls onto his body. The darkness constricted his lungs in the same way, pushing him into short and shallow breaths.

But he felt another presence. He heard that growling and breathing. Jacob felt warmth across his back. A searing pain ran from his head to his tailbone, opening him to allow something to step into him, don him like a suit. Another need. It stayed locked within him. Heeding its wishes, he headed to Jamesport. He was an urchin, a thief. He eventually found Sam. And thus, he was here.

Wherever here was.

He was not his own.

Part of him did not want to trust these memories. Were they even his, or did the mantids feed them to him?

There was no telling how long he was like this. But it ended.

The casing around him peeled away in soft, waxy chunks. Perhaps he could have broken through all along.

He looked at his hands in the dim green light. They did not look different in any way.

The strange creatures were around him. They were similar to the mantids in some ways—triangular heads, thin limbs, chitin armor, though mottled with yellow spots and cloudy shapes. Their mandibles clacked as they ingested the plaques of waxy debris that had fallen about him.

Jacob did not trust any of this, either. He was not sure what he was seeing or who was seeing it. He could feel bulges beneath his skin. He sensed not just the pain of his own fiber, skin and bone, but the pain of the creatures within him as they tried to hold fast to his body. He remembered what Mother had said, that he was not a suitable host. He felt their desperation as he had been desperate to leave his own imprisonment. They were not there willingly, but were under a command.

But they did their work. When they wanted him to move forward, he did. It was not an entirely unconscious choice. His limbs sensed their signals and he could decipher them, like he was willing it. There was another brain within him, and he had a choice. But the more he refused to obey, a tingling sensation deep in his core grew and grew until it was burning, threatening to boil his brain in his skull and split his skin at his sides. As soon as he heeded those impulses, as soon as he stepped forward, calm filled him. And so, they taught him to follow their wishes and he craved that calm. He needed it.

Walking was difficult at first. Another sense plagued his balance, almost like having another pair of eyes staring into a different angle. The larger creatures seemed to be expecting this. They held him with their cold, thin fingers—twigs wrapped around his biceps. They guided him, steering him so that he would not trip.

He saw something in their faceted eyes. Malice and mischief, contempt. He had seen it in the eyes of the blonde twins. These were the women of the college. Transformed. Corrupted.

This was a wide natural cavern, a formation of glassy, globular stone with a low ceiling. The green light reminded him of the fungal light he had seen in the chambers below Sam's cave. But the stone here was clean.

They guided him to the brightest point. Leathery webs held the nexus of the light, a stinking and pulsing mass of fungus suspended between the floor and the ceiling. It had no distinct shape, but was solid, its slime held in place by dark, tight fibers that were like a net of veins. In each space between these veins, a milky pale eye with a flat black iris, a fish's eye, stared into the cool wet air.

This was Mother. She was the nucleus, the queen of whatever plane this was.

"You are not yours," she said.

One of the creatures tapped his shoulders. He turned. Two of its many hands presented a gun belt, a holster, and a revolver. His revolver, which he had lost in Sam's cave. He took it, and felt relief as he wrapped his fingers around the grip. He squeezed hard, hoping to feel pain but finding none. When he relaxed his fingers, however, he felt warm blood rushing into his palm and knuckles. Instant strength and power filled him, and he thought of shooting Mother's brain and everything else around him. The mere thought of this, however, lit the burning within him.

"You will go to the import shop," Mother said. Her voice came from that mass, but also echoed through his body, fed directly into his flesh through the carrion mantids. "You will find the man named Chang. He is the last. You will do everything that I bid you to do, and you will be free."

Jacob looked into one of Mother's eyes, wondering if those eyes were actually dead, or if they saw him. He wondered if he was seeing or hearing any of this, or if it was fed to his senses. Perhaps he was still locked away in the chitin, or dead, his corpse pinned beneath debris from the explosion in the marketplace.

He tried to raise the revolver. He imagined pushing the burning back into his feet, which seemed to succeed for a moment before the punishment rose in geysers. He tried to fight it, but the pain grew and grew, pushing his eyes forward in their sockets. He screamed, doubling over. His body shot back to standing. The pain lingered for several more seconds to make a point, followed by the cool calm. He sighed into it, wanting it more and more.

"You will go to the import shop," she repeated. "You will find the man named Chang. You will do everything that I bid you to do."

She paused.

"And then I'll be free?" he asked.

"It will become increasingly difficult to resist."

Jacob walked Oceanview, beneath the shadow of the Eriksson Hotel and past the old Jewish cemetery. He went further in the cold twilight, passing the park of the stone tower, the church and the synagogue. The moon was an oval, diminishing into its last quarter in a clear, cold sky. The moon had been full when he last saw it. He had been entombed for several days.

Jacob shook his head and returned his gaze to the sidewalk. At first, he walked with blinders, like one of the horses on the street. It seemed to be the best way to avoid angering the mantids squirming under his skin. Evening travelers avoided him, silencing their conversations as he walked by them. He wore his coat, and it had been cleaned. He therefore did not appear disfigured or in any way that would have frightened them. He was able to keep a normal gait, despite the pain that his skin sounded at any stretch. It was something else that alarmed them, and he wondered what it might be. He realized that, as he clenched his jaw and stared at a moving space just a yard in front of his feet, the intensity of his stare—not his, to be sure, but borne from the purpose of creatures within him—must register with a deep, forgotten fear in the pedestrians around him.

It did not matter to Jacob. They did not seem any more alive than they ever had. Potential victims, that was all they had ever been. Less, now—rotting meat on skeletons thrown down the sidewalk. Their ugly asymmetrical faces bore boils and pimples that gleamed in the dying daylight, and their shrieking voices cracked and broke in their throats. It was all so clear, and lit a headache that started to flare in the back of his skull. He tried to close his eyes to calm it, but that only invited vertigo from patterns of light which gave him the sensation of falling into an abyss, into the center of the globe.

He walked without thinking of where he went or how to get there. This reminded him of strange tales of men and women who simply climbed atop horses and left their homes, never returning, only to be discovered miles away, living whole new lives. Something pushed them, something over which they had no control. He took step after step, feeling the same way. But this was not what he wanted. This was not the escape that he had sought, and which the witches had dishonestly promised.

Jacob stopped, standing still for several seconds. The urge to move forward grew in his gut and up through his spine. It increased until it was a ramrod of hot steel through his trunk, and its flames singed the bottom of his brain. He closed his eyes tight and ground his teeth even more firmly. The pain increased, its hum rising in volume in his head until it drowned out the surprise and concern of walkers-by, who nevertheless continued to walk by.

One short step, more of a shuffle, calmed the fires a small bit. It was a second of respite before they jumped back. A small shuffle forward, and slightly to the side—the torture returned afterwards, but this step slightly off track but forward had given the same short relief.

Jacob experimented for several more minutes. Though he could not stand the pain at its sharpest, its various levels remained predictable. He was able to build tolerance to the milder punishments. If he walked forward, he felt a numbing peace. This actually buffered him against any punishment that might come from an errant step, and gave him room to steel himself against the results of taking even several more steps from the course. In fact, the first hints of punishment were warmth, which was actually welcome in the cold of this December evening. That did not last long. As the pain grew, exceeding his tolerance, he could correct and enjoy the reward, then begin his deviation all over again.

Jacob was able to pull himself a full block to the side of Chang's shop, but this depended upon moving diagonally across an empty lot. It also increased the time of his trip. The walk to Chang's might have been no more than a twenty minute stroll, but Jacob had stretched this into more than two hours of small steps, stops, corrections, and deviations. He had not anticipated a second smoldering, punishing heat deep in his gut. This steadily increased as time passed. The mission was under a time limit, as well. This did not bode well for his efforts at avoiding the deed. Not only had he reached a point at which his only choice was to walk an ever narrowing circle around Chang's Import Shop, anything short of a beeline straight to the door would simply take too long.

He closed his eyes and stood still, feeling the mantids shiver and this newly discovered punishment of delay climbing up to his throat. It was like heartburn now, but it would soon become intolerable. His eyes still closed, he took a single step back, away from the shop. The other pain climbed his spine, beginning as a pleasant warmth that exploded into an inferno.

Jacob wondered how he must look, performing the moves of a choreographed dance over the landscape of Jamesport with his eyes closed. It was now too late and too cold for many to be about, but the few passers-by must have been affected by his behavior. He did not notice.

One more step back, and the pain flared, both in the back of his neck and in his throat. He would not be able to experiment much longer. Time was running out.

Chang might be able to help him.

Jacob opened his eyes to swirling light framing the import shop's entrance on the corner of Oceanview and Bristol. One road went to the mansions, the other to the public beaches. Jamesport's commerce spread over the intersection—the import shop, the butcher, the grocer. His legs went a bit soft in his dizziness, and he wavered. Several steps forward quelled the pain and steadied his nerves. By the center of the intersection, calm and peace were pumping through his veins.

The bells atop Chang's door jangled as Jacob pushed. Chang, standing behind the counter, looked up from his books. Chang's face was young and smooth, but his hands and neck bore deep wrinkles. Thin strands of black hair crossed his bald head. The man's energy was boundless, and his speech forced through his accent with such verve that it became a rattling jumble in his mouth. The mechanisms of his tongue and teeth could not keep up with his thoughts.

"Jacob," he said, lowering his chin so that his eyes looked over the rims of his small glasses. "Where have you been? I have something for you."

It was the look that always accompanied payment, though Jacob could not imagine how he had earned anything over his past three jobs. Perhaps he was here to receive something from Mother.

"What?" Jacob asked.

Chang stepped from behind the counter. He wore a long black robe, looking like one of the Confucian scholars gesturing from the bas reliefs that lined his shelves. The place was littered with such things. Chang insisted that each piece had come from a temple, a ruin, a treasure house of a court official or emperor. All of these things gathered here, in this import shop in Jamesport. Such things were fashionable, now. This shop had once served only as a place for whalers to sell scrimshaw and other crafts for pennies. Now, fine silk panels shot like bars of light split through a prism across the ceiling. Bronze vessels were stacked high. Jade saints and Buddhas sat. Sandalwood burned, sending thin and intensely fragrant curls of smoke into the air. The barons of the castles on the cliff filled their halls with these pieces, picked their teeth and straightened their coats in their reflections in the black lacquer, wondered at taking the exotic maidens who danced in strange, even impossible poses in bright pink and blue paint on large panels and screens.

Chang did a good business. His wares were expensive. He did well for himself. It was not the kind of place in which Jacob should ever have been seen, but he never saw anyone else in the shop.

There was also vast knowledge of the Old God in this place. Chang was a student of these things—things about which Jacob had never thought he would know as much as he now knew. On those shelves, figures of mantid creatures hid in shadows. Hairy beasts roared from mouths in their chests, ruby light twinkling in a dozen eyes arrayed across their bulbous, domed skulls. Soldiers carried weapons of shapes that gave no clue to their proper though clearly lethal wielding. These were like the figures arrayed upon Rutledge's table. These all guarded corners against the frivolity of the commerce that played so loudly in others, with paper lanterns and shining curios.

"Come," Chang said. He slid the bolt shut on the door, and moved toward the rear of shop. Jacob followed, under his own will though clearly doing the bidding of the twitching creatures within him.

Chang stepped through a curtain of wooden beads. It fell closed after he passed, sounding like rain. Jacob noticed that sounds like this, also like the bells above the door, were very harsh in his ears, shooting through and knocking hard on the other side of his skull.

He followed Chang through a short chamber that served as a library, with a collection of manuscripts lining shelves that reached to the high ceiling. Jacob could not read any of the titles. They all appeared in different alphabets, some of which he recognized as Asian or Russian. Other scripts were completely unknown, ornate scrolling lines with dots or angular geometric shapes. But it was not the writing on the spines that always drew his attention. Some books were bound in stone with sharp edges, but deep and soft marbling swirling like mist. Others were leather like a finely appointed chair. Still others seemed to live and breathe, swelling and contracting beneath a cover of skin. It was hard to look at some. They repelled his vision in the way that magnets of opposite poles push against one another. One book seemed not to exist at all under direct sight. He could see it in the peripheries of his vision, but it was merely an empty space when he looked straight at it. He touched its spine and found that it was, indeed, there. The indentation of the writing on the leather was smooth and cold.

They went through another curtain of beads, into the back room. There, wooden crates spilled sawdust and hay onto the floor. Stencils announced provenance in Siam, Ceylon, China. Inside, mostly harmless things—there were tapestries, bowls, and statues like those that lined the shelves in the store. The most impressive was a dancing figure of weathered, green bronze. Jacob recognized the figure. She had two legs, but many arms. The thumbs and forefingers pinched on each hand, with the other fingers splayed carefully. It was a pose crafted over thousands of years to be significant, to channel something. She was eons old but was, by all important measurements, a new god.

Jacob struggled to keep up through a maze of stacked crates, finally arriving at a workbench arrayed with tools that he imagined performed all manner of tasks, from the manipulation of tiny clockwork gears to the rough, jagged cuts of animal sacrifice. Chang brushed them away with his forearm. Jacob winced with the thought that Chang would slice his own arm open, but was sure that it would not be the first time that the table had seen blood.

Chang brought a lead box to the tabletop. It was a large but simple container, old and dented, with the joint of one corner separating. The dim lamp light revealed intricate carvings in the lid—flowing lines embracing into careful, dizzying knots that seemed to tighten right before his eyes. Chang worked the lid carefully. It slid, screeching as he lifted it. He set it carefully aside, but he was not so careful to avoid the thud of its weight on the tabletop. After practicing the motion in the air above the box several times, he reached in and lifted the contents free. It was a book. Faded gold inlay described a carrion mantid on the cover. The book had been subject to torture and fire. Its spine had split, cobweb threads the only things holding it together. He lifted the top half away, cutting the book like a deck of Sam's cards, and set it beside the bottom half, working hard to keep the threads from breaking. Inside, illuminations and black, blocky writing marched in short, tight rows across splotched vellum. It was European, and the writing something like Latin, though it bobbed and weaved if Jacob looked at it too long. He was not sure if this was a characteristic of the book, or of his new sight, assisted or corrupted by the mantids twitching within him. The illuminations showed robed figures in noble clothes, their noses and eyes exaggerated by an artist with similarly corrupted sight, or a simple lack of skill. More decorations, knots like those on the lid, wound through the margins.

"This," Chang said, "is a travelogue of Ireland and Wales attributed to a warlock. It is in some places a bestiary, in others a description of strange rituals among the pagan tribes. The priests say that it is a fake, that the man never left his cell in Britain. Perhaps. But the man claimed a dream sight. And here is one passage."

Chang cleared his throat, looked to muster strength from the ceiling, and turned to the book.

Jacob felt an itching in his right palm. The pain in his gut spiked. This was dragging on, and time was running out. Without thinking, he swept his coat aside and rested his hand upon the grip of his revolver. He shook his head and whispered, "No." Dropping his hand from the grip, however, proved uncomfortable. The pain rising in his chest and neck tumbled down to his palm. Placing his hand upon the grip, wrapping his fingers around to the trigger to draw—this helped. There was no danger, he guessed, in simply doing that.

"'I alone survived the flood,' Tuan said. 'I changed my shape, and so was born many times. I carry those memories, and am the historian of all things for all times. I speak in many voices at once. My suffering has repeated countless times. The world has changed her shape, and so was born many times.'"

Chang closed his eyes, opened them, and leveled his sharp black pupils on Jacob.

"You see," Chang said. "There are answers when you know where to look for them. I think that this is about our friend, the Historian."

With this, he waved his arms over the book in mimicry of a sorcerer casting a spell. Jacob frowned and tightened his grip around the revolver.

"The Historian is dead," Jacob said. "I saw it myself."

Chang paused, looking straight at Jacob, who found it hard to meet the proprietor's gaze.

"Dead," he said. He gestured at the book. "But this says that he does not die."

"The fish market. The explosion."

Chang just gestured at the book again.

"Thousands of years," he said. "Millions of years. Longer."

Chang continued to look at him. Jacob lifted and lowered his eyes like a nervous, submissive dog. He wondered, how could Chang not see it? How could Chang not smell his infection, his mission, in the air? Sweat beaded on Jacob's forehead as each second ticked, and the harsh punishment began to rise in his trunk. He clenched his jaw and closed his eyes, shaking his head to clear it. He imagined opening his eyes to a different scene, to the morning light of his apartment. He imagined the warmth of his mother's quilt.

"But wait," Chang continued. "There are more answers."

He stepped from the workbench, moving quickly.

"You never leave here empty-handed," he added. "Payment, and now answers."

"I have all of the answers I need," Jacob said, under his breath.

Chang reached into a crate, his fingertips raking through sawdust. He moved to another, muttering. He was looking for something. Jacob could not muster any interest through the pain. There was not much time, and he had found no strategy to avert rather than simply delay the end. He forced his fingers to peel from the revolver's grip. His knuckles ached as blood rushed back into them. His palm became red hot. Jacob brought it forward and looked at it. His vision was warping around the edges, and his movements were hard—at least, those movements that were counter to Mother's aims. His palm felt strapped to his revolver by rubber straps, so that any distance from the gun was harder and harder to achieve. It snapped back to the revolver, though, with no effort at all.

Chang was holding something now.

"This," he said.

It all came to Jacob through a haze. There was only one clear notion, one certain answer. The punishment was unbearable, but there was peace to be had. Arriving at that peace meant putting a bullet through Chang's head.

"Are you all right?" Chang asked.

Jacob was hot and nauseous. The world began to spin about the single thing that Chang held. It was a charm of wood on a black leather cord. It was flat, with bat-like ears, and was like the charm he had taken from Rutledge, though its wings were curled about its body rather than furled.

Chang lowered the charm. Concern brought furrows to his brow.

Jacob lifted the revolver. Rewarding cold doused the flame in his chest and throat, beating it back down to his stomach. It still simmered there, threatening. Jacob closed his eyes for a moment as the sweat cooled his brow. For just a moment, he felt near unconsciousness, but it passed.

Chang said nothing, but made whimpering noises as he backed away, stumbling over the crate. He fell to the floor and shielded his face. That would not stop the bullet.

Jacob aimed and flexed his trigger finger forward, then curled it back within the guard. It was not the fire that drove him now, but the promise of peace. A thought rose still to resist. His finger was squeezing, but he ordered his arm a nudge to the right. The shot sparked off the floor at Chang's side. The recoil sent his arm to the ceiling, but it snapped immediately back to train upon Chang, who had rolled and was now scurrying across the floor.

There was no time to resist, now. Jacob had no time to gather his thoughts, or consider any action. His finger squeezed the trigger. The shot thwacked into the back of Chang's head. He flopped to the floor, his feet jerking but soon falling still. Blood spread in front of him from the exit wound.

Jacob made no more decisions. He limped to the rear of the storage room and kicked open the door. His body threw itself into the alley, spilling down a short flight of brick stairs. Rolling through puddles and mud, he struck the opposite wall. The far, cold stars descended to wrap him in their ice, and it was glorious and sleepy. They extinguished the fires burning within him and froze the mantids still and silent. The pain, the fire in his body was now colder than the stone. He was careening through space, basking in blue starlight, leaving guilt and all of Earth behind him as a dot that went smaller and smaller until it disappeared.

EIGHT

JACOB LOOKED AT his hands and blinked. They were not his hands. They were heavy, thick things covered in brown fur. He had jagged claws, yellow and cracked. The hair was thin at the roots, but twisted into matted tufts, even in his palms. He was naked but for the hair that covered his entire body.

His arms were hanging in front of him. Every movement he made hurt deep in his joints, announcing something fundamentally wrong with his construction. He looked up from his hands and body, across an expanse of sand, to the gouge of the canyon in front of him.

He knew this place.

It was the canyon in which Ida had died, the canyon of the cliff dwelling and the cave. Facing it felt like he was looking backwards. To move forward, he had to turn. His knees and hips protested, but he now faced the morning sun, a yellow beast in the sky. He stepped forward and the pain was so intense that he growled and shouted at white wisps of clouds that were so far in the heavens as to nearly join the stars. His feet cracked the dry plates of sand that curled into bowls, waiting for rain that would never come. Water may once have swallowed this whole place. He and Ida used to find shells in this desert, and wondered how they ever could have gotten there. Those memories felt more distant than they ever had, not even his but merely ghosts of things left in the canyon.

Jacob broke the ground with his hands to pull himself along. He headed into the sun at first, toward a shimmering silver mirage of water far to the northeast. Or, perhaps it was actually water. The sun climbed out of view. It was straight above him, then behind him, then gone altogether. Cold seeped from the ground. The desert was a frigid place at night. Coyotes assailed him, but they were like pups clinging to his back and shoulders, chewing at him with teeth that were unable to break his skin. They tried. Their muscles rippled across their skulls as their jaws clenched. He flicked them from his arms. They broke against stone and dead wood, their yelps buried only beneath the sickening wet crunch of their cracking bones.

As he went, he noticed his mouth drying. The dust of his progress rose into his nostrils and caked in the back of his throat. It was unbearable. He could barely breathe through it, but he dared not stop.

The sun broke the horizon and rampaged into the sky once more, beating him with its heat. The mirage receded with each step. It was cruel.

But there was a gift. Jacob sensed it coming from the southwest, so he stopped and sniffed the air. He smelled iron and steam, burning coal. He waited, and saw loose grains of sand vibrating on the ground. The sun was rising and falling quickly, years and eons passing. Tracks laid themselves at his feet. He stood between them. The sun was at the zenith again, its heat pressing straight into his shoulders. It filled his muscles and made dead, shining leather of their fibers. He felt himself becoming a fossil, bones cast in brittle stone.

Rippling in the heat, the train appeared. Something was wrong. It clanked out of rhythm and smoke poured from its cabin. Jacob could smell the sweat and nervousness of the people aboard. The broken behemoth came upon him and slowed its whining wheels, stopping just yards away from him.

Jacob stood, wondering if his presence had made the engineer stop. But it was not so, for two sweaty men in overalls dropped to the desert and peered beneath the engine, ignoring Jacob. Their arms and faces were streaked with black dust. They pointed at this or that piece of broken iron that smacked against others.

This went on for several minutes until passengers disembarked. The conductors pretended that everything was all right, like they were simply standing on a platform somewhere, wielding their hole punches and raising their arms to gather the crowds. Children ran in the sun, pried plaques of dried mud from the desert floor and flung them at one another. The adults spoke to one another, glancing nervously around, waiting for the wide, empty expanse to launch something upon them. They were nervous in the hot sun, in the middle of nowhere. This was an adventure for everyone, even if the adults tried to feign confidence.

Jacob realized that he had a sense for fright. It tingled in the back of his throat, beneath the caked dust. It intensified when he faced it and dulled when he turned away.

Something else.

He could see through them. He could see the blood in their veins, going blue and red as it wound in loops through their bodies. He could smell it. He could smell the metal of their blood in the air, like the smell in the air before a storm. It was distinct from the iron of the train. It was deeper, and was a deep hunger in his gut. It was a sharp tang on the surface of his tongue. It brought drool that fell to the ground and disappeared in the dust.

He could do nothing but feed.

Despite the pain in his joints, and the life and water that had seeped from him until he was just a husk, until he was just a memory of something that had been far greater millions of years before, he launched into them. He broke their bodies and let their blood fall down his throat. He reveled in the metal, in the warmth.

At one moment, in the midst of it, he knew that he was doing wrong. These were innocents.

But it did not matter.

His strength grew. He became something greater again, something that would have far more impact upon the world than any of them. They were slaves like he had been. Now, their blood would fuel him to do enormous things.

Jacob woke, shivering. He had kicked the sheets from his body, and was naked and curled. He had a sense of seeing himself from above, looking like a pale amphibian creature with thin skin, the bones of his spine poking through, vestigial gills flapping, and small gray eyes closed against the light of the morning.

Panic gripped him. He shot upright, sitting, hugging himself for warmth.

It was a small room with a sink, a bed, and a dresser with a mirror. It was empty but for these things. A window looked over a field of fog that swallowed a close stand of trees. These spanned across the left side of the view. They were bare and gray, their limbs like bleached bone, so that the whole stand looked like a column of giant skeletons marching through the mist. The fog was wild and undulating like a stormy sea. It robbed all color and threaded ice through blades of grass rather than let it fall as snow.

To the right, Jacob saw a stone wall that he recognized. Though he could not see far ahead, he knew that the trees and the wall went to a cliff.

This was the Larchmont estate. Standing, he approached the window and looked down. He judged himself to be on the third floor, in one of the dormitory rooms that had once been a servant's room. He wondered if this had actually been a college at all in recent memory, if ever. Or, just a coven.

Jacob closed his eyes, observing glowing geometry fly by his inner mantis sight. He fell back to sitting on the bed and braced the sides of his skull with his palms. He shivered and looked at his hands. They were not the clawed things, the giant paws that he had seen in the desert. But they were dirty. He saw the black bruises, the lumps of the mantids under his skin—black, cracking and oozing like bubonic nodes. He thought back to his dream of striding across the plain, of killing, the taste of iron in his mouth. It all faded and he saw Chang, and his blood. He felt his feet in the soft sawdust as he went to the alley and fell into the slime.

Here, without clothes or gun, he could not imagine that any of it was true. Either the desert, or Chang. The mantids were still and silent. He felt no impulse or command. He wondered if they were dead. Jacob touched one of the dark lumps on his forearm. It had reopened the wound that Tinker had given him. Beneath the pain, he felt the creature squirm. A sickening shudder ran up his arm. The fiery sensation rose and demanded that he stop.

After several seconds, Jacob stood. He pulled the bed sheet around him, hugging it tight at his gut. With every movement, the mantids shifted and twisted. This sparked itching deep in his fibers. He gnashed his teeth against it.

Jacob moved to the dresser, which was empty. He looked at the mirror, which was cracked down the middle and spotted in black and gray behind the glass. He was pale in the reflection, but for what seemed like a red rash around his eyes. Jacob opened his mouth to inspect his throat, to see if it was as red and raw as it felt. He could not angle the light, and saw only darkness where the mantids had clawed to turn down his windpipe, or into the base of his skull.

The door out of the room was open a crack. He hooked it with his foot, pulling it open, sending it creaking to the wall.

Another door opposite the hall was identical to his. Jacob peered out, looking left and right. There were many doors, a dozen perhaps, in this empty hall. To the left, the way turned and Jacob could see light coming up a stairway. To the right, the doors marched in pairs to a dead end. There, a table held a vase with dry, brown flowers that drooped toward their own discarded petals. Above that, the colorless gray light of the outside found life through a circular stained glass window. The design was the seal of the college—the top of a pillar, an eye, all done in yellow, brown, and red. The words around the top edge declared: "Novus ordo seclorum." Along the bottom, "The Eliza Stephens College for Women."

Jacob shuffled, stooped like an old man. There was dust on the floor and cobwebs filled the joints between the ceiling and the walls. The door next to his, toward the stained glass window, was open. He peered in and saw an unmade bed. A brush and powder, along with other effects, sat on the dresser. The window was open, its thin white curtains waving lazily in the cold breeze. The floor below the window was dark with water. The floorboards were warped. The window had been open for a long time, and dust and cobwebs fell from every corner, every shadow, dispelling the impression that the room had been recently and quickly abandoned.

The window here showed that the sun was already burning through the fog and setting the frost gleaming. The mist retreated into thick ribbons that ran across the lawn. Jacob could now see the cliff and the gray sea. He thought that he saw footprints in the frost and wondered if they were his from when he had trudged across this property to reach the wall with Whitebirch, on his way to murder Rutledge.

Everything had changed that night. Or, rather, he had become aware.

Those footprints—he imagined himself moving low and fast across the grass. As he followed the memory of his trip, he saw himself emerging not as a man, but as that beast in the desert he had dreamed. He was not a dry and weak husk in the sun, but a strong thing. Muscles rippled across his wide back and the power of eons of fury drove him forward. He was fat with blood.

He heard wailing. He was not sure if it had just started. It was not like Tinker's whine, but was a ghostly series of wavering notes that seemed fragile, but held their tones for several seconds before drifting into other notes. There was a swaying rhythm to it. Back in the hall, he went to follow the sound, finding himself shuffling with that rhythm toward the window, past more doors, some closed and others open to more dormitory rooms. In that music, Jacob thought he might hear the commotion. Perhaps a fire or other calamity had forced the students from their rooms in the morning, and they left their clothes on the floor and their windows open, the smell of their sleep in their unmade beds, and rushed away.

At the end of the hall, a single door on the left, unmatched by one on the right and shorter by several inches than any of the others, was ajar. It opened out to the hallway, unlike the others. Its hinges were on the opposite side. The music was coming from there.

Jacob stopped. The notes vibrated the air and were somewhat disorienting, but calming all the same. They blended into one another in such a way that made it almost impossible to concentrate upon the melody. It did not help that he did not recognize it.

Inside the door, a tight spiral staircase rose. He could sense the notes falling down the steps like globs of oil.

Jacob climbed the stairs, having to stoop so low that he braced himself with his hands, one on the step in front of him and the other on the wall. There was a moment of darkness halfway up the stairs. It was just him, and the mantids, and the music coming down through this tube. He felt numb, everything in him lulled. He almost wanted to stay there. His joints relaxed and he felt himself falling.

But there would be no escape in that. Just empty time, blissful as it may be, like slipping from consciousness in the alley. But no escape, and it may end at any time with an order from Mother to kill.

He pushed on, climbing into a dim orange light and, ultimately, a space of sharp angles. He was inside one of the house's huge gables.

Across the space, a young woman in a white nightgown rocked and swayed as she sat at an instrument. On one end, a device much like a spinning wheel turned. A rod ran from its center. Cylinders of glass, each smaller than the last, nested within one another down the length of the rod. As the wheel and the rod turned, the glass shone like ice in the weak light of an oil lamp.

She faced away from him. Her shoulder-length black hair bobbed as her foot ran a treadle, causing the wheel and the rod to spin. She touched the glass and, the barest fraction of a second later, a note would sound. She worked the instrument in this way with both hands, moving one hand every now and then into and out of a small trough of water in the front of the device.

There was a bed and a dresser, much like those in the rooms below—small, though Jacob wondered how anyone could have gotten them up the staircase. There were baskets and boxes, bags and crates, all brimming with strange collections. One burlap sack appeared to be full of utensils from the kitchen. The tines of forks were all locked together, bent. Another bulged with cotton stuffing packed so tight that the sack threatened to burst. There were porcelain figurines fit together like an odd puzzle. One box was full of rectangular marble chess pieces, stacked like bricks. On one side, there was a stack of jars. They were full of sand, and had two strange metal connections at the top.

Between all of these things, there were paths—between the stairs and the instrument, with paths leading to the bed and the dresser.

Through the music and the confusion, the pain as he moved and breathed, he knew her. She was one of the witches. She had given him the goblet that began his transformation.

"Who are you?" he asked.

She stopped playing, holding her wet fingers above the glass.

"Isabella," she said.

She continued to pedal. The sound of that mechanism echoed throughout the room, as did the dying wail of her last notes, which turned in the stairwell around and around, gaining life in the spinning before falling into the hall, into the sunlight that spilled through the window. The notes crept into the abandoned beds below, billowing their sheets slightly before settling into the threads.

NINE

JACOB SAT ON the armonica bench.

That was what the instrument was called. It was a glass organ invented by Benjamin Franklin, she said. It used to be in the parlor, but she had brought it to this room, and taught herself to play it.

"The chief complaint," she said. "It is quiet. It cannot hold its own in a symphony."

"I heard it in the hall, in the rooms."

He wondered if the house were somehow able to amplify things that came from above.

Isabella knelt in front of him, wrapping the wounds that wept and throbbed about the mantids.

"These will turn," she said. "You will get a fever of the blood, and you will die."

She had applied a cream to the bandages, a concoction that she had ground herself with a mortar and pestle. This was no smart marble apothecary tool, but a lump of rough black volcanic rock. It seemed more like something that Papaya would have had in her shack. Jacob was amazed that Isabella had all of these things, and wondered what other contingencies she might be prepared to handle. She had food, tools, and now medicine.

The bandages were wet and slick with the muddy cream. The effect was instant, numbing his skin so that he felt he could move almost normally again. It soothed the mantids, as well. The blissful feeling that had washed over him as he fell into the alley after killing Chang now seeped in small doses through his fibers, into his mind. He smiled as the edges of his vision went hazy and the motions of the world slowed.

"The cream will help," she said. "But your body is rejecting them. I am not a good host, either."

Jacob's tongue swelled in his dry mouth. The mantids slept. His wounds were numb and his cheeks tingled. He thought on how beautiful she was—smooth cheeks, a slender neck, black hair falling just below her ears. She did not smile, but he sensed the capability within her. He imagined her reclining next to him, awash in this bliss, this light, moaning and smiling with him as time sped or stopped or whatever it would do. She looked at him, her large eyes wet and warm and lovely. They were chocolate brown, like Papaya's skin and the Chihuahuan Desert dirt in the one rain he had ever witnessed there.

"The mantids control me," he finally said, fishing it from somewhere as a reply to her, though he barely remembered what she had last said. "They made me kill Chang."

"I am also imprisoned. I cannot leave this house."

"I can rescue you when I'm free."

Isabella closed her eyes.

"That would kill me," Isabella said. "Mother keeps me here. I do not know if she intends to bargain with me, or to use me as she uses you."

Jacob was comforted by her confusion. So much mystery—the empty dormitories, the mantids, everything. He felt that she had no answers, either. But he was wrong.

"I am one of the swamp folk. I thought for so long that I had hidden the fact from Mother, but it was stupid to think that she could not see right through me. She knew it all along."

"I don't understand," Jacob said.

He was not speaking to her, or to anyone or anything. At this moment, for the first time since Ida had fallen, he looked beyond the light and sound and into spaces that separated motes of dust. He interrogated the folds and twists that had always surrounded him, had always been invisible, but which he now saw.

Isabella sighed and stood. She began to speak, but her tone was that of a frustrated adult explaining something to a child, something already covered again and again.

"They created us to sacrifice us, to bring the power of the Old God to the surface and send against their enemies across the stars."

"What does this—?"

"They wanted to sleep and dream in the Old God's magic, so they created Mother to do their bidding, to fight their war. She survived them. Now, she seeks to resurrect them."

"And you..."

"And you, Jacob. You see, the Old God was no silent player in this. His servants always worked to end any exploration that might lead Mother to her goal. You would be there, and you would put a stop to it."

Jacob's gaze turned into the back of his head, where he saw all of his victims. Sam's cards announced those first clumsy jobs in the alleys of Jamesport, silencing old drunks. There were many others, witches and sorcerers who had all tinkered with the notion of bringing life to dead things, or who had simply been unlucky to uncover long-hidden and forbidden knowledge. Then Rutledge, Papaya, Forsythe, and Chang.

"Mother infiltrated your ranks," Isabella said. "Sam sent you to kill Papaya, but it was not his order, or the Old God's. It was Mother's. She sent you to kill Forsythe."

She bent forward, gripping Jacob's knees. Jacob looked into her eyes, then beyond. He had been responsible for much of it, and all because he had been promised freedom. Jacob blinked away the guilt.

"Does it matter?" he asked.

Isabella stood again and turned, shaking her head. He imagined her shock at his response, but he had meant it. What did it matter if he killed for the Old God, or for Mother, or for anyone else? None of it was by his own decision, so it was no different to him. The Old God had paid him. Now, Mother kissed him with bliss and emptiness. In many ways, this was easier. The mantids kept him in line. There were no questions, just fire if he made a mistake and blessed ice in his veins if he cooperated.

"You are not wrong," she said. "You, me, everyone on this planet—you see exactly how little it matters. We were created ages ago to spill our blood in sacrifice. We fail at our destiny just being alive."

Jacob stared into the wood grain of the floor, into the threads of her robe, into nothing.

"Yet we fight to live," he said.

She spun back to him.

"The terror," she said. "That is the terror. That is our breeding. That is part of what makes us useful to them. The terror, the fear of death. They offer that to the Old God, or they relish in it themselves. We have arms and legs just to be severed, stomachs just to be cut. We have minds just to be scrambled and panicked. We fear because fear feeds the sacrifice."

"Most people ignore the fear," he said. "They ignore death until it's right on top of them."

His voice was calm, almost slurring. He realized he was just playing devil's advocate. He did not sound like he truly believed it.

"Yes," she agreed, returning close to him. "Love and hope, so that we know loss and sadness. And, when we are brutal to one another, when we fight and torture one another, we are doing just what we are supposed to do. We were designed to perpetuate the sacrifice in their sleep. And we continue, after they have died."

Jacob thought of the figurines in Whitebirch. Terrible monsters, arrayed in ranks and marching upon one another—how many races? How many eons? He wondered. All war, all torture, feeding a gift to the Old God and achieving nothing more. All of that blood, pooling into an offertory cup for the beast in the center of the world. Nothing more.

But it was a purpose. It was an answer.

"I have killed," he said. "Many."

"Yes. You continue to do what you are told."

"What did I free under the willow?"

"You broke the sigil?" she asked sitting back and lifting her hands to her face. "It makes sense."

"What?"

"It makes sense. You broke the sigil. You freed their spirits. The high priestesses. They possessed the Sisters, and have gone below to join Mother. She bid you to free them, and now those spirits have flesh."

"I didn't know," he said.

"You never knew."

"I can disobey. I can do what I want. I can escape."

"You will do what the mantids let you do. "

He wanted to ask if it mattered again. He wanted to let her know that he agreed, that he had always done what someone else had ordered him to do. But it would change nothing to say it, and he was now exhausted. He blinked twice, his eyelids heavier when they rose the second time. Isabella continued to look at him. She seemed to be waiting for him to say something, but he just blinked again, and again, his eyelids heavier each time, until he fell asleep. He had every sense of time passing slowly through the blackness of his slumber.

He was in the desert again, sucking dried blood from the fur between his claws and smelling eons of slaughter on the cold breeze that whipped over the sand and through patches of sharp grass. The blood had not sated him. There was more to be had, more emptiness in his stomach to fill.

He had a sense of feeding far in the past.

When they came, they built temples and homes, cities and walls. They built the perch in the cliff. They built him.

And when they lost the favor of the Old God, he went to kill them. He found ruins, but one slept in the cave. He moved with care down that dark tunnel, and found the warrior priest sprawled upon a stone slab deep under the rock, deep beneath the baking crust. The stone rang with the hammering of the sun, but it was distant, far above. Here, there was just a memory of sun. All was cold.

The Elder was tall and thin, with many arms. It had eyes all over its head. Each was open slightly, blinking in spasms, though seeing nothing of the world in front of it. It saw its dreams of far, alien vistas, of battles waged in other dimensions against creatures perhaps as terrible, or more terrible than it. This one had escape the deluge and the fire, but it knew nothing of the end of its kind. He breathed over the thing, his breath a hot cloud of hunger and thirst that swirled over its body. He smelled its sweat, its sleep, the tang of the blood that seeped like cold syrup to pool in its limbs.

He chewed out the thing's throat, and slurped its blood. And he was full, just that once. As he slept at the Elder's cold feet, the world turned countless times and bats buried him in their waste, yards deep.

Until Jacob and Ida came to the canyon, and he woke.

Now, he stood by the bank of a great brown river. It went, fast and silent, south to a sea that the Old God had pushed from deepest rock to drown the Elders.

"You are not done," Mother said.

Jacob was in her cave, basking in her light. He was dressed again, and armed. The drones were holding him before her.

"You have killed Chang, but you are not done. I have much more for you to do."

Jacob shook his head. Pain answered, dull at first but soon throbbing into a sharpness that threatened to burst his skull from within. All about his body, the mantids shifted and turned, waking him with pain. He had bled through Isabella's bandages, but the blood looked black in Mother's light.

"I thought I would be free," he said. Or, rather, tried, for it made no sound in his bone dry throat.

"You tried to defy me," Mother said. "Now, you must prove your loyalty. Bring me the woman of the swamp."

Jacob saw her in his memory, standing in the doorway of the witch's shack, shocked at the murder.

"The one who saw me kill Papaya."

"Theresa," Mother said. "The one who was dead. Bring her to me."

The mantids were already imprinting the orders upon his thoughts. There was no obeying, for to do so implied that he had a choice. There was, in fact, no decision to make. They gripped upon the fibers and muscles that would make it so, and readied their poisons to correct any mistake he made. They would be more vigilant and more attentive than on the mission to murder Chang.

"She may be animate," Mother said. "She may be a corpse. It does not matter. But she must be whole. If you must silence her, take care that you do not maim her or lose her."

Jacob thought of the swamp dwellers.

"The others?" he asked.

"They do not concern me. Do what you will."

It was calming, indeed a pleasure, to stand in the black marsh water. His feet had gone numb long before, and were perhaps now on the verge of freezing solid. He had followed the path above the sunken road. Reaching the flooded schoolhouse, he stepped into the water, facing the far hill that he had climbed after killing Papaya. His feet might shrivel and go black, and need to be cut from his body.

And what use would he be then?

He reveled in that rebellious thought, a thought that the cold allowed him to have by silencing the mantids. The icy salt marsh extinguished the fire in him. It slowed his breathing and his heart. It sent the mantids into a sort of hibernation.

But Jacob's senses were heightened. Sight, sound and smell—the funk of the bay was stiff in the morning wind that swept from the west. Sulfur and rot, rising into the clouds of the night sky.

He could see past, present, and future, all that would come and had come. He saw a time when the ground here was firm and there was no swamp. Roads ran before temples and torture houses with spires reaching into the stars. He saw calamitous empty times before that, times when volcanoes gorged slow, sliding rivers of viscous molten stuff, and hissing rains of acid pocked the ground. All manner of creatures slaved at this stone. Some were rodents. Others were giants with barbs of burnt chitin for armor, joints clicking as they labored at carving idols that were a terror to behold. The scale of those idols, their impossible lines—they wavered in the heat, or simply tricked his eyes, and he felt nauseous even looking directly at them. Cries of agony shot like lightning from the depths below them. These shouts ran through the mortar as electricity through copper, arcing between the Earth and dead rocks that ignited to become stars.

Jacob was not sure if this was the past or the future.

But one moment, one moment in the entire history of this place, stood out to him. It was the moment that his path crossed Theresa's once again. He could see their paths intersecting in the swamp like roads. He walked forward and she cut him off, and that was another connection in his life with something larger than he, something that he did not understand but which propelled him forward. He could feel the wind on his face as he coursed across the prairie, feet crunching in the glass of the baked sand. His claws, still bloodied, gripped that ground and left specks of that blood in a trail all the way from Texas. It all pushed him forward to the moment at which he would meet Theresa again.

He could not see himself killing her. It was not in the history of this place. But Mother stood ready to change history. Her will seemed as strong as the Old God's, and shot through a vent to the surface, into his limbs and to his palms, where his revolver now rested.

The wind turned and brought the smell of Jamesport, the smell of the milky fluid that ran in the gutter below his apartment. It was full and sickening, roosting in the back of his throat like he had brought it with him. He closed his eyes, feeling again the movement of bounding forward across the plains. The beast in his thoughts smelled the air for blood and snapped at the waning moon.

The swamp folk were watching him. The light of his lantern reflected through their eyes and off the backs of their skulls. They were all around him, inching closer.

A dozen yards in front of him, Theresa sat upon a fallen tree.

The mantids were stirring in the cold, working harder than they ever had to bring his revolver to bear. Jacob stared down the barrel, right at her heart. She did not flinch, but the eyes of the swamp peasants around him glanced more furtively at one another.

"You were with Isabella," she said.

"I was," Jacob replied.

"You learned more."

"I did."

"She descends from the beasts who built the temples of the Old God."

"I don't care about any of those things."

"You descend from them too, but you are different."

The impulse came to pull the trigger. He could not. Rather, he would not. His mind, denying the promise of escape and seeking now to understand what he had just heard, belayed the order. The fire began to rise from below, reminding him that there were two things that could happen to him. If he defied the order, he would burn. If he followed the order, bliss.

But the mantids were slow to respond and weak. The skin encasing them was necrotic and brittle. Jacob's arms began to shake. His aim traveled up and down Theresa's body, then off the mark. Jacob smiled. Theresa reciprocated, and Jacob blinked at the odd scene, a man pointing a gun at a woman yet the two smiling at one another.

The fire rose slowly through his legs, but was nothing like it had been. Jacob remembered the trip to Chang's, and the strategy of straying small degrees off course. The order came to pull the trigger, but he pushed his arm to the side. The bullet sailed past her. She turned her head with it, watching it disappear in the grass.

The pain shot into his joints and stiffened him. His aim landed back to her heart, and his arm steadied. He twisted his body to throw it aside, and had some success, but it returned each time.

Theresa continued to smile. He could hear her voice, though she was not speaking. Rather, he imagined her saying what he was realizing at that moment.

No matter how sharp the order, he still had to choose to follow it. Punishment and reward, the fire and blissful ice— these resulted in a mimicry of automaticity, a masquerade of the likes of Tinker. Jacob could still choose to disobey, if he was willing to suffer the consequences.

Rising fire, death, and oblivion. That was escape. Mother kept promising escape in return for compliance, but it was disobedience alone that would end this.

But there was a failsafe, even if it meant the destruction of his body. The mantids now tried to occupy him completely. They shifted to dig deeper into his roots, into the pathways of commands and blood through his body. This would kill him, but they must have known that. Their will exploded into his brain, unraveling his thoughts and pushing him toward one last act.

They were too weak. Once again, he pushed his arm from any true aim. It ran back again and again, but he used that momentum, driving it far from Theresa each time. He pulled the trigger several times, emptying his revolver, sending errant shots to either side.

Theresa broadened her smile.

Jacob gnashed his teeth against the heat and shut his eyes. Through the rattling, horrid cry rolling up his throat, he saw the prairie bouncing before him. He felt the wind in his matted hair.

The fire boiled his thoughts. It burst through his temples, sending geysers of matter to either side. It went out, leaving numbness and smoke.

The mantids were still.

He slid into the black water, feeling nothing. This was welcome. He opened his hand. The revolver with which he had killed so many lingered around his index finger before falling away, down into the swamp muck, gone forever.

One corner of his mind nagged. It showed him the moon, the stars, a view from the western hills to the coast, where Jamesport was ruined dark spires more ancient than the most ancient of things, and cries of tortured beasts had long ago ceased to beg for mercy.

TEN

JACOB WOKE WITH a headache that shot from his brow straight to the back of his skull. He remembered facing Theresa and falling into the water. He remembered that cold and black surrounding him, surrounding his vision until light exploded from a distant, central point. His last memory was of this woman, of her pale skin and white robes brilliant even through the fiery corona around her.

He thought he was dead, but was instead alone in a cot in an otherwise empty room. The walls were a patchwork of wood scraps. Panels of corrugated metal, no doubt scavenged, lay in a ceiling above him.

Jacob shifted to his side. His headache flared. A door barely covered the exit, light streaming through the gaps.

He stood, bracing himself, but the headache drained from him. Jacob stepped forward and felt pain over his entire body, sharp pain that gathered in knots throughout his muscles. He unbuttoned his shirt and, peering down, saw bandages and dark dried blood. The mantids. They had burst or someone had gone in to get them. Where they had been, there were now pits that had bled into bandages on his arms, legs and torso, gashes that were dry now, or perhaps he had no blood left in his body.

Perhaps he was dead.

His clothes, oddly, were clean. They were not his. Worn dungarees with tattered hems, and a simple white linen shirt which he now buttoned again. There was still mud beneath his fingernails, but he was clean.

His empty gun belt lay coiled on the floor, the holster set carefully in the center so that the faded star was visible. Beside it, his hat—he was not sure when he had last worn it. He took these, donned them both, and moved carefully to the door. The wide brim shaded his eyes. He moved from surface to surface, bracing his unsteady, aching legs. He looked for his coat, but could not see it. He thought immediately of Papaya's rosary and Rutledge's idol.

Jacob's boots stood beside the door, one boot slightly ahead of the other. He stepped into them, pointing his toes and forcing his heel. The boots were dry, and he wondered how long he had been asleep.

He was hungry and thirsty. There was bitter paste all over the inside of his mouth.

He was not only alive, but sentient and thinking. He had no doubt, now, that the mantids were gone. Their toxins and elixirs were gone with them, and he had woken from that spell as he had woken from whatever recuperation their removal had required.

The thirst was becoming unbearable.

He opened the door. The sky was light gray with a few streaks of darker clouds. He could actually see the sun. It was a bright smudge that afforded a small amount of heat on this cold day. It had been November. It had become December. Perhaps that month had passed as well, but it did not feel like it. The death of the year was still present, swelling from shadows and from within clumps of dry, sharp swamp grass. He gathered his arms together over his chest and shivered as he exited.

The room was buried into a hillock, a barrow. Mud and water seeped up through the gravel in his path. Looking about, Jacob saw other hovels like his and, lording above them all, a broken, falling clapboard house of several stories. It was an impossible thing, a structure that looked centuries old at its core, but with rooms and floors added years and years after. Boards crossed its broken windows. The door was gone. White paint peeled from its siding like strips of dried skin on a corpse in the sun. Jacob thought of a fat dead burro in the desert. Ida poked it with a stick until its gasses escaped, filling the dry basin with a flatulent sound and an evil, unforgettable smell.

The house leaned to one side on the unsteady ground, looking like it sank deeper and deeper as he watched. Jacob felt that, if he waited long enough, it would topple over and disappear in the marsh.

Bright daylight lit the top windows. The roof was gone. The bottom floors, however, were dark.

Someone stood in the doorway. She had just appeared there. Theresa, the swamp woman in robes—she was so still and her skin so white that she was like an alabaster statue blocking the way. She beckoned. As Jacob climbed the hill, two stocky men of the swamp joined him at either side. They did not touch him, and took positions in front of the doorway as he entered. She stepped back into the dark entry hall.

Theresa gestured to a chair before a long table. The furniture had once been fine, of dark wood. The cushions had been intricate needlepoint. The table and chairs were now scratched and faded. The cushion gave way as he sat and threatened to fall through. The chair creaked dangerously but held. The numbing cold retreated deep into his core as the warmth of the place penetrated his clothes. The pain of his wounds resurfaced, throbbing.

His coat lay in a heap on one of the chairs.

A mug of water sat beside a plate of cheese. The cheese was fragrant and hard. His hunger spiked. He reached for his coat—it was clean, but still damp in the seams—and pulled it onto his arms. Every motion, everything against his skin caused pain.

Jacob checked the pockets for the idol and rosary. Both were gone.

"Go ahead," she said, her voice high and breathy. "Eat."

He took up a knife. A weapon, he thought. They trusted him with it. The pungent cheese filled his mouth with milky fullness. He bit again and again, fearing that he might choke but his stomach leapt for it. His throat ached, so he gulped cold water. His headache returned briefly, sharply, and receded as his heart pumped it away. All was right for a moment.

The whole time, she stared at him.

Perhaps this was the end. He would spend the rest of his life with them.

She spoke.

"I watched you kill Papaya," she said.

She moved to the chair across from him, and it was like she weighed nothing. The chair did not creak. Her robes settled about her as she lifted thin arms to the table and crossed her fingers. She was like a skeleton. Jacob could see every bone. There was downy peach fuzz on her arms, but it was white like her skin. He looked at her eyes, which were bloodshot like an albino's. Her pupils were black, not deep but a flat, lifeless black. Her lips and her fingernails were purple. She looked dead.

Theresa sat there, her wheezing breath barely lifting her chest.

She was dead. Mother had said it.

He did not answer her. It did not matter, for she continued to speak. She was dead but commanded a legion of peasants. He had no one, and nothing but an empty holster. She could speak, but he could barely mumble through his swollen throat.

"I saw her," she said. "Even though she fought, and even though she saw something of what you would become, she loved you. Better than all of the others. She nursed you back to health. I know who you are."

Jacob wanted to ask, "Who are you?" He could not. He looked at the table, at the dents and scratches. He took up the mug and drank down the water, forcing the liquid into his stomach in gulps that sent pain through his entire chest.

"We took them out," she said. "The mantids. We got all but one." Theresa pointed at her head.

"The one at the bottom of your brain, the one that entered through the back of your throat. It is still there. If we had tried to take that one, you would have died."

She leaned back, eyeing Jacob up and down. He continued to stare at the table, not quite sure what he should think. He could not isolate the last mantid. He could not sense its thoughts or feel it moving. Perhaps it had died, and it would rot, its sacs breaking and sending poison through his body. His life would finally end.

She leaned forward, clasping her bony fingers again.

"This was a home once," she said. She motioned down the hall and to the room around her. "Then a tavern. A way station on the road to Boston. Then a brothel. Now, it is a dead place. A ruin. Yet, it lives and breathes. There is no escape in death."

None of this made sense to him. Jacob felt that there may be answers, but he was missing a key point, an important turn.

"Come," she said. "I have something to show you."

"It is a sigil," Theresa said.

They floated in a canoe on the bay. Jacob squinted at the symbol on the cliff, perhaps a quarter mile to the south. He huddled against a strong wind that whisked the fog from the water's surface and reduced the stench of the bay to short whiffs. One of the swamp men worked constantly at the rear of the canoe, keeping the small craft straight.

The sky was clear, but the sun was harsh and white, cold as it headed toward the horizon. Jacob shivered and brought his coat around him. The gray woman was in the prow, leaning forward from the bench like an Indian chief leading a flotilla of canoes to a raid. Jacob was cramped and uncomfortable in the middle of the canoe, huddled on the wet floor, his wounds singing with pain. Sweat and spray from the wind went to frost on his coat, threatening to encase him in ice. It would be welcome—bliss like the mantids had promised.

Theresa pointed her long gray arm at the symbols on the cliff face. A sigil.

"The things that came to this world," Theresa said. "They invested magic into language—all language. Through this, they built cities under the ocean, carved hollows below the surface, and more. They made this world. We can do little to match their power, but here is a sigil."

"What is it?" Jacob asked. "What does it say?"

"You have a command—a curse or a blessing. You take its letters, and you lay them atop one another. The symbol is as powerful as the command, if handled properly. This one stands over this place, this bay. It is impossible to decipher."

"I don't understand," Jacob said, levelling his gaze at her. She turned, regarding him with frustration, reading his look as obstinate petulance. He persisted, though lowered the brim of his hat, both to avoid her punishing gaze and to further anger her. Theresa did not move, though her expression changed. Her expression went flat as she lost patience with him.

The wind howled, sending water into Jacob's face and causing him to break the stare. The white sun clicked across the sky a few more degrees. The canoe rocked in the chop. The sigil just stayed, the bars of its overlapping runes standing firm. Ghosts of terrible things, images of brutal and unimaginable acts, flitted among the standing stones on the rocky beach beneath the sigil.

"You did not listen to the Historian," Theresa said. "You did not listen to Papaya, to me. You did not hear any of it."

She closed her eyes. A few more seconds passed. Her face was stiff and now she was dead—completely dead. Jacob looked over his shoulder at the swamp peasant. That man listened to none of it, and was preoccupied with the dirt under his thick, cracked fingernails between sessions wrestling with the canoe in the chop. He worked at each fingernail, flicking what he dug into the air.

Jacob thought of twisting his shoulders, leaning, and falling into the bay. That would be it. He could be over the side before the swamp peasant reacted, before Theresa opened her eyes. He lifted one shoulder, preparing to twist, but the pain stopped him. The canoe rocked with him, startling the swamp dweller. Theresa opened her eyes and drew back slightly. She spoke.

"Eons ago, before anything lived on the surface of this world, the Elders came from the stars to worship the Old God. It slumbers, imprisoned in the rock. But its power creates much movement. The Elders went into the ocean and dug into the stone. In those places, they made life. They made their slaves from silt and salt, rock and volcanic glass."

Jacob's heart beat faster as she spoke. His blood warmed him. It leaked into the holes of his wounds and fed the mantid still perched in his brain. He stared at the floor of the canoe, at the black, cloudy water sloshing around his crossed legs.

"The slaves placed stone upon stone to build cities for the Elders. The witch kings slept in those cities, and the slaves worshipped for them, sacrificed one another to the Old God, fought wars in the stars. They made even more horrible creatures waiting to be harvested and sacrificed to the Old God."

She paused.

"How does this matter to me?" he asked.

"The Elders discovered immortality," she said, undeterred. "They took the secrets to their slumber. And now, we fight a war over the fate of the dead."

A cold wind bolted over the bay, slamming into the canoe and turning it. Jacob shivered, plunging his hands into the empty pockets of his coat. He rolled tighter and looked at his boots.

"I had a rosary," he said. "And an idol."

"Done with the history lesson, then?"

Jacob looked at her. She was smiling, her thin lips stretched tight and bloodless.

"My role," he said. "My role and my place in this...I just can't see it."

"How is it," she asked, "that one so steeped in this, one who has killed so many, can be so ignorant? You were a good servant to the Old God. You did what you were told to do. You asked no questions."

"I want out," he said. "I'm done with all of this."

"Where will you go? What will you do?"

He had no answers to either question. Theresa leaned back into the prow and continued.

"We buried the rosary with Papaya. It was hers. She made it with bits of shell and stone that she dug from the swamp mud. The idol belonged to someone else."

"What do I care?" he asked. "If these Elders rise and enslave all of us? What do I care?"

"You have killed. You have turned the wheel, without even knowing the importance of what you did."

"I have to atone?"

She paused and looked past him, nodding to her companion at the back of the canoe. He lifted the oar from his lap and began to row, turning the canoe back toward the inlet.

"I am not saying that," Theresa said. "You want to disappear. You think that this is possible. Back to the desert, or into the swamp. But I have all of your money. From your apartment, from your jars and boxes, buried and hidden in stone walls. You will not get far. This will catch up to you."

Jacob glared at the water of the bay, at the oil slicks that sped by. Everyone had owned him, and had promised or threatened him. Now, Theresa—comply, and perhaps she would return what she had stolen.

"This...story. We can change this?"

Theresa blinked. Jacob realized that it was the first time he had seen her do that.

"Yes," she said.

Theresa remained in the prow. The swamp dweller paddled through a maze of tall grasses bound in clumps of frozen mud. The sky was dark as well, deep purple on the western horizon beginning to arc overhead, to night in the east. There was no moon, and the stars seemed hesitant to shine.

After a short time, fine sleet fell from the impossibly cloudless sky, smacking against the swamp grass with a rushing that drowned even the dips and plops of the swamp peasant's paddle.

But not her voice.

Theresa's voice was clear and loud across the marsh as she spoke of things that made no sense to Jacob. There was the history that went back beyond the Viking tower, beyond the beginning of humanity. She spoke of the Earth as a sacred place, and of the witch kings corrupting it, creating life many times over. Some of these creations were hardy, and lived for eons. Others died quickly. Some were mistakes that lingered, polluting others before dying off or crawling into crags to be forgotten.

The minutes passed. The sky was frozen in twilight. The sleet was suspended, melting against Jacob's face as the canoe carved a visible trail through the floating crystals of ice. Soon, the canoe reached familiar landmarks and Theresa ended her confusing monologue. The abandoned colony, and its mysteries. Papaya's empty shack in the distance, the ghost of her singing lost in the rain.

They reached the flooded schoolhouse.

"There," she said. She pointed straight through the doorway.

The canoe slid into the place, and Jacob felt its power in the back of his head and in his cheeks. It was like the buzzing air before a storm. The single room was not much longer than the canoe. There was little left of the structure. The walls were bare but for blooms of mold that were beginning to glow in the faint starlight. The ceiling had fallen in one corner. A weak tree reached a dry branch through that hole. A rusting pile of twisted metal below this collapse must have been a stove. Along the front wall, a ladder reached through the ceiling, into the cupola.

Theresa leapt from the canoe and dropped into the water. Her robes floated up around her thighs. She moved, barely disturbing the water, and stopped near the stove. She reached into the water and lifted an object that looked for a moment like the monster automaton Tinker's arm—the shaft and the lead ball. Theresa crossed the room and ascended the ladder, her wet robes raining into the swamp flood. Jacob realized that she had retrieved the bell's clapper. Theresa fixed it into the weathered bell and gave the thing a push. Then another, and the clapper smacked against the side and the peal, somewhat soft, sounded over the swamp. She began to descend.

Jacob saw movement in the windows. Shadows crossed in the rising mist. Theresa had reached the water, and stood now facing the canoe.

"I am Theresa Rutledge. Dr. Thomas Rutledge was my father."

The bell rang again, louder and surer. The crust and the patina cracked.

Every window, now, was alive with movement. He looked through, squinted, and saw children. He recoiled, gasped, and nearly shouted as he realized that these were bones, some still with clothes, some with bits of white flesh drooping, waterlogged, from their joints.

"You see," she said. "Death is a matter of design. Some things die. Others just slumber. My father awakened me."

The bell was slowing, its peal weakening as the reach of the clapper lessened. As the sound waned, so too did the interest of those children, those corpses. They began to wander off, back to wherever they slept beneath the black muck of the salt marsh.

"But these children," Theresa said. "These were his first experiments. Failures, but not entirely."

Jacob, wide-eyed, barely able to speak, looked at her. She stared into the water, her arms outstretched in an invitation to embrace. But, as the clapper now just touched the bell, the children were all gone.

"This is why you killed him, and why Mother wants me. I am his first success, a secret art writ in dead flesh. I am the resurrection of the Elders."

All were gone but one—one last child was in the window, its empty sockets and its skeleton smile framed in the flaking wood. It turned quickly, almost playfully, and bounded into the swamp.

The bell was still creaking in its carriage. The clapper now pointed straight. The ringing had fled through the swamp, through the misty rain.

ELEVEN

JACOB'S HEAD CLEARED like after a winter fever, the pressure popping through the cavities in his skull and falling away. He even took a long deep breath, feeling the air fill him where the mantids had left spaces. The feeling tingled throughout his body. He was stronger than the day before, mending. But he was befuddled and frightened. Theresa was a walking corpse, and dead children had risen at the flooded schoolhouse. Mother had a plot to raise the witch kings, and Jacob was somehow in the center of it. He had no energy even for escape, or thoughts of escape, but the mysteries of Jamesport now occupied him. He was empty, sad, and hungry for answers.

Theresa and a party of swamp dwellers led him up a hill. He walked without consciousness, ignoring pain, tripping over roots and rocks in the path. At the summit, he sat within a pile of furs and blankets. Beneath the blankets, in a dark space ruled by his heartbeat, he felt his arms and thighs, his stomach. Where the bandages had been, where the skin had gone black and cracking above the mantids, he felt rough stitches and heat. The swamp peasants had cut away the dead skin, taken the mantids, and stitched him closed.

There was a fire in front of him. Its furious flames shot toward the center of a ring of clouds. These clouds rampaged in the spinning circle, following the standing stones arranged

around the clearing. A chanting voice counted the meter of
this herd, and of Jacob's heart. Every three beats, the fire hissed
and flared in different colors—green, purple, blue. A swamp
woman, shorter and much older than any of her kind, danced.
Her ancient skin sagged from her mouth and eyes, the wrinkles
on her jowls looking like deep, crisscrossing canyons. Wisps of
gray hair at the edge of her turban flowed like scraps of storm
clouds. Her fierce black pupils were hard pearls of onyx in wet,
red eyes. A rosary of bone beads, much like Papaya's rosary,
bounced on her chest as she jumped and spun about a twisted
staff of gray wood that must have rested in the black swamp for
a thousand years.

Jacob turned his head, which protested like he had never
asked it to move in such a way. Indeed, he thought that he heard
creaking in his spine as the vertebrae twisted against one another.
He realized that the witch was the first woman he had seen among
the swamp folk, besides Theresa. There were no children either,
just the seemingly dumb men who followed Theresa, regarding
the world through small eyes with an idiot's calm.

He knew this place, and had been here before. It was the ring
of standing stones at the top of the swamp hill. He knew it not
just from weeks before, from the pursuit after Papaya's death.
He knew it as something else. In a flash, the piles of bracken
and moss fell away. Trees, looking like dead men's hands with
bracelets of thorns, closed into fists and disappeared. Priests and
priestesses appeared about the fire, seemingly jumping out of the
coals. The hill was a giant structure of cut stone, a pyramid, with
hordes of swamp folk dancing with abandon at its foot. Blood
streamed down the steps of the pyramid onto the crowd, as the
priests sacrificed all manner of strange and horrible creatures.
Women, men, and children were a frenzy in the offal and blood
that fell to the ground.

Jacob blinked, and he was back in the ruins of the present. He saw echoes in the land about him, lumps and ridges that, millennia ago, had been the city of a race that lingered now as a clan of peasants in the swamp. Those walls and structures, the very stones of the pyramid, had taken a cloak of moss and vines, or had sunk beneath the black water.

He snapped his head the other way, ignoring the pain that shot sharply from several places where the mantids had been. He saw Theresa.

The dancing witch stopped and stared around the fire. Looking into Jacob's eyes, she forced the corners of her mouth into a deeper scowl than they had already described, and shook her head. Her jowls flapped like the comb of a chicken. She said something that Jacob could not understand, but knew to be unflattering from the harsh, dismissive tone.

Theresa looked at him, "She thinks that you are not worth it."

Jacob squinted at the witch, then Theresa. Who was to say that the witch was wrong? He was nothing, a slave to whomever hired or compelled him. He had contemplated escape again and again, but could not even manage that. He was not worth it.

The witch's eyes were like Isabella's—dark and wide apart. But Isabella's skin was soft and white. She had cared for him, given him succor in the attic to stave off the pain from the mantids. Had he even deserved that?

"He does not think that he is worth it, either," Theresa said. "He thinks that he is a failure. His only failing is that he does not listen."

The witch squinted and muttered something unintelligible to Jacob. It was not just her language that made it so, but a burst of wind that whipped through the stones and eddied about his ears.

"Do you not see it?" Theresa spat, stepping toward the witch. "It comes to destroy him. We have very little time."

The witch stuttered a reply, swallowing it halfway through. Despite the weakness of it, Theresa interrupted her.

"I see it. I am sure that Isabella sees it."

Theresa turned to Jacob. She stared at him for one moment.

"If we had left the mantids," she said. "You would have turned into one of her creatures. Or, you would have died. You are inhospitable to them. Few are like you."

The witch turned her gaze to the ground and shook her head. Jacob looked again to Theresa, who looked through him.

"He knows almost everything," she said. "Whether he realizes it or not. Isabella told him things. I showed him. He resists, but he knows almost everything."

The witch launched forward, vaulting on her staff and landing right in front of Jacob. Her eyes darted over his face, prying. He felt her pressing into his mind, and the mantid woke, resisting. Jacob felt the pressure of both meeting in a sharp, fiery pain in the front of his brain. The witch barked an order, which Theresa translated in an equally sharp tone.

"Tell her!"

Jacob tried to form words. He tried, but managed only a single one.

"Elders," he said.

"What of them?" Theresa asked.

"Elders...dead. Mother tries to resurrect them."

Jacob swallowed hard against the pain in his throat. Just those short words had been exhausting. He wanted to collapse into the blankets and disappear into their warmth. A tomb.

"That is all?" Theresa said.

The witch spat and lifted her arms to the sky.

"She does not think that you are anything special," Theresa said, walking to Jacob's front to separate him from the witch. "She thinks that you are a fraud at best. Or, at worst, an enemy.

You served Mother. And, with the mantid still in your brain, you compromise us."

Theresa moved behind him, and leaned over his shoulder.

"I do not believe her," she whispered, though loudly enough for the witch to hear.

Theresa stared down the crone with a sharp glare that even Jacob could feel in the corner of his eye. The witch huffed and bounced in fury. She shouted things in her language, things that plumed through the hole in the clouds and banged against the hair-thin etching of crescent moon that stood in meek defiance of the growing daylight.

"We will prove it," Theresa said.

She leaned close to Jacob, who braced to smell rot on her breath. Rather, that air from her was cold and floral. Jacob looked into her eyes and saw nothing.

"What are you?" he wanted to ask. But he was unable to move or speak. Without making a sound, with just a twitch of her eyelids, she commanded him to be still and quiet. The mantid released its blissful reward, and calm washed over him. He let this flow and felt the muscles in his face relax. Theresa was right in front of him, so close that he could see fine, soft down on her cheeks. She closed her eyes and was like Ida, sleeping or peacefully dead.

Whirling geometry exploded into his vision from the center and signaled the presence of other minds, of the consciousness of the mantid still in his skull, of the fragmented thoughts of long-dead things, of the buzzing and clicking thoughts of Mother. Indeed, as he thought of Mother he could see her. He saw through the cliff to a glow in its belly, a glow that he knew was her. He realized that he was pinpointing her. From her, he saw beams traveling across the landscape, into the sky.

He shifted, floating into one of those beams. He was thinking and feeling her. Much of it was strange, incomprehensible, too large for him to imagine. He saw her thoughts in glimpses, like the images he saw of the beast running across the desert. It made no sense, and so his brain discarded those things.

Theresa spoke.

"You are there?"

"Yes."

There was no reply. All he heard after was the rush of sounds and images passing through the beam. Mother was shouting, sending all of this through him. Behind him, he sensed another one like her, far away, deep in another mountain. It received, then launched back with its own thoughts. Now, Jacob was bearing the onslaught from two directions.

"You see," Theresa said. "Jacob listens to them, but is not with them. He is like a spy in the night."

The cacophony continued. Back and forth, Mother and her peer traded images and plans, solved and plotted.

"None of it makes any sense, does it? Mother communicates with her kin. Like the cable across the ocean, they send messages to one another. They work together to bring the Elders back to life. But Mother is the furthest along. Do you see her shouting more than the others?"

Jacob did. He imagined himself floating back, looking over Mother. He saw thick lines branching from her as from the center of a spider web. Her messages coursed out in pulses of light and sound. Only several came back to her. Indeed, some of the trails were dark. There were no answers at all. Perhaps those of Mother's kin were dead or silenced, or they had stopped listening. Others answered each of her bursts with a small contribution of their own. But Mother was the loudest and most prolific.

The crone spoke. Short, guttural, insulting.

"How can you disregard him now?" Theresa asked.

Jacob could say nothing. His mind was committed. The more he devoted, the more difficult it was. He felt pain rising in him like the fire of the mantids days before. He was not sure how much longer he could watch and listen.

"He does not have much left," Theresa said. "I must ask now."

Jacob felt Theresa's gaze upon him, again. It fell over him and the landscape about him as a dark cloud. It dimmed Mother's glow.

"Where?" she asked. "Where do the Elders slumber?"

Jacob did not know what to do with the question at first. He felt it bounce through the corners of his mind until it reached the mantid, which seemed to feed the thought into all of the noise, all of the bedlam. Some of the channels lit brighter, or shifted hue. Red burning points appeared on the horizon. Jacob shifted his gaze and found dozens of those points. One was much closer than the others.

It swirled above the black water of Jamesport Bay.

"Come back," Theresa said.

A clap, and it all disappeared. Jacob was back on the hill, though he could see the ghosts of those things—the lines and the red spots. The crone stood far from him, watching him skeptically through narrowed eyes. Theresa was kneeling in front of him, her hands gripping his knees through the blankets.

"Where?" Theresa asked.

Jacob turned his head left and right. He saw the swamp marching in all directions. The edge of gray Jamesport climbed the cliff to marble mansions that gleamed in the first orange rays of the morning sun, which now set the clouds afire as it rose in the eastern horizon. Before the cliff, the round black bay was like a hole in the world.

The red swirl of fire from his vision was there, like a spot after staring at the sun. It faded with each heartbeat.

"There," Jacob said, pointing.

Theresa and the crone squinted. Theresa turned to him.

"The bay," Jacob said.

She dropped, seating herself in the dirt in front of him.

For a moment, there was nothing but the dying sound of his vision. Teresa shook her head and, looking at nothing, spoke.

"First things first. We have someone to rescue."

"Isabella," Jacob thought.

And he was with them, thinking nothing of escape.

TWELVE

THEY GATHERED IN the basement of the dilapidated church at the edge of the swamp the next day. This place was theirs, a place where the edge of Jamesport met the edge of their world, allowing them commerce and connection when necessary. It was also a base from which to launch more secretive missions.

Theresa and Jacob stood with a dozen others around a table. Theresa spoke to the group in a language that was something like a harsh Creole that warbled on the backs of their fat tongues and, at times, reached high into their noses as breathy whistles. A swamp-speak, a language that sounded like the land and the water itself. Croaking and chirps, it rolled into a single sound and stuffed into the spaces of their skulls.

As Theresa finished her instructions, she moved to a thick curtain that was stiff and black with mold. She parted the heavy cloth, revealing a tunnel through the damp dirt, braced with railroad ties. Shaggy roots poked through, hanging in clumps that looked like wigs. Tight rows of rotting wood panels crossed the ceiling in diagonals. Jacob realized that these were the bottoms of caskets from the cemetery above.

The group filed into the tunnel, sloshing through black water that had seeped into puddles beneath their feet. Theresa walked at the front, guiding the expedition with a lantern that reflected fog and mist more than lighting their way. Some of the dozen swamp men carried coils of rope, and Jacob wondered at the plan. The Larchmont estate was abandoned and posed no difficulty to enter. Perhaps the trip through the underground was not so easy. His role in the mission, however, was quite simple. He carried a heavy shotgun and, though he could not speak their language, understood that he was to provide brute force. Many of the swamp men were armed as well, with pistols and short rifles, but Jacob's presence at the rear was, he imagined, like that of a bellowing elephant following a group of clowns into the center ring of a circus. He hefted the shotgun, thankful for feeling much stronger than he had in the days before. There were stiff bandages over his healing wounds, which itched terribly. The pain had all but gone, and he felt vital again.

He was not alone in himself, however. The mantid in his brain had been recovering as well, moving more and learning to act with Jacob on its own, without the network of insects that had riddled his body. He not only sensed its movement, but felt its presence in his senses. There was a metallic smell and taste to everything. There was also glow about the edges of the tunnel, something Jacob attributed at first to mold in the dirt, similar to the effect in the tunnels below the cliff though the glow here was colorless and grainy. He realized that it must be an additional sight, an influence of the mantid trying to see the world through him. The glow penetrated dark spaces outside of Theresa's lantern light. In those spaces, he also had consciousness of his visions at the top of the hill. In one direction, he felt the presence of the Elder's tomb at the bottom of the bay. To its left, he could sense Mother and even see the beams of her communication to her kin across the globe. Jacob blinked hard and shook his head, which cleared these artifacts. His sight into the dark, however, remained.

He tried to gauge their direction as they went, but abandoned the effort after only several turns. The tunnel meandered about roots and rocks, with few straight runs. Soon, however, they came to a broken stone wall that opened into a sewer. They were below the city. Jacob gagged over the terrible smell as they entered the sewer, forcing his breath through his mouth. The stench rose from a frothy stream of water that rushed through a channel cut down the center of the floor. In some bends, this stream had weathered the channel into a wider flow that challenged the party to keep from fouling their boots. Here and there, the tunnel showed other kinds of wear. Stones jutted or had fallen from the wall as roots pressed their way into the sewer. A more calamitous cave-in at one intersection forced the party to crawl through a narrow opening near the floor. The swamp men went through easily, but Jacob became caught. He struggled, watching the lantern bob away ahead. He shouted and his voice bounced through the sewer, echoing against the slick stones. The lantern stopped and one of the swamp men returned, shushing him, grabbing his hands and pulling him free. Jacob's back scraped against a sharp edge, and he was sure that all of his bandages and stitches were cut, for all that it burned. He stifled the scream in his throat, and it rolled there as a harsh growl.

It was more than the pain. He imagined being stuck there, immobile, pinned against the floor within the sewer slime. No one would ever find him. He would shout into the darkness until blood spewed from his throat. His chest would heave against the heavy rock in frantic breaths until his muscles and ribs broke. The darkness, cold and almost palpable, would seep into his joints, his eyes, his mouth and suffocate him until he was silent and dead. And he would be a fossil, like the skulls in the cave of slaughter. Despite all of this, it was a simple thing for the swamp men to pull him free.

Every dozen yards a stream of the foul water fell from a chute above, a twisting slide that no doubt led to the street. A century of falling sewage had also accreted into leathery stalactites. These fell like vines to the floor, and gripped the party like tentacles as they passed through. Peering up, he could see gray light but could not see anything more of the world above. Jacob imagined the water running in the gutter on his own street. It gathered with the rest of the waste on the block, and fell through one of these twisting chutes. Sometimes, Jacob thought he heard voices and laughter from above, or the sounds of horses and carriages. Once, he thought he heard a gun shot. He wondered if these were the sounds of the city, or memories or echoes that bounced through the sewers forever and ever.

Jacob's companions remained silent. Indeed, they moved with such determination that the cascading sewage and the reaching ropes of slime did not deter them. Several now walked far ahead of Theresa and the lamplight. Jacob wondered if they could see in the dark, and if the lantern was for him.

They passed through several intersections, making purposeful turns, traveling short stretches, turning again. Soon, they came to another break in the wall. The expedition paused here, conversed in whispers for one moment, and filed through. Jacob followed them into a natural tunnel of glistening stone. Specks of mica glimmered between thin veins of phosphorescent algae, which colonized just cracks here, but which spread to cover the entire surface further into the cave. The glow of his mantid vision fell away before the green light of the algae. Theresa even extinguished the lantern.

Jacob began to hear the surf. Its rhythm affected their gait as they went, until the line of them marched to the ebb and flow of the waves. The light of the algae vibrated with the rhythm as well, waxing and waning. Jacob became confused as the surf's noise grew louder and louder. The Larchmont estate was on the cliff, but the party was clearly much closer to the surf.

Theresa stopped beneath a rough archway, ushering each of them by until Jacob had passed. They gathered at the edge of a large cavern that echoed with the crashing waves. She spoke to the swamp men, who nodded at each of her instructions. There was a plan, but Jacob could not discern what it was.

As they moved forward, Jacob recognized the place as Sam's cave. He stopped for one moment, confused. Theresa waved him forward, and he tried to convince himself that he was wrong, for the cave would have been a tremendous detour from any path to the Larchmont estate. They wound through stalagmites and arrived at the top of the ramp. This was Sam's cave. There was no doubt. Jacob's footprints were still dark in the algae, but he could not tell if the corpses remained at the bottom. The cage of crows was gone from the entrance. The tide had risen nearly to the mouth of the cave. The moon was still thin, so the mantid's light returned to Jacob's vision as they cleared the cave.

"Where are we going?" Jacob asked.

"*M'Lass*," Theresa said. There was no hint of annoyance or surprise. She was not even looking at him, but rather trying to light the lantern in the wind. Once successful, she held it up between them, pride playing on her face.

"Why?"

"I told you," she replied. "A rescue."

She said nothing more, but strode away from him, her white dress spectral in the lantern light as she bobbed upon the rocks, hopping between puddles and eddies. Jacob frowned and closed his eyes. He listened to the surf and thought of the white froth of the sea spilling over itself, again and again. He imagined a splatter of stars spinning about the crescent moon in the zenith. Seconds passed as he stood, listening. They passed further beyond the point of his last murder, and of Ida's fall. Seconds piled upon the distance from far ancient days of the

Elders and their blood worship of the Old God. He was not sure whether they were here to rescue Isabella or not, and that was disappointing. The volumes of time and distance, however, were too broad and deep. Nothing mattered.

He opened his eyes. The waves appeared first, the mantid glow churning in the corner of his sight as he looked skyward. It was brightest where the water broke against the rocks, but spread across the sea, even faintly to the horizon.

The rocks—the lines of their hard edges appeared in the glow like a sketch happening right in front of him. As he followed those lines, he saw *M'Lass* not far to the east on the south-facing shore. Beyond the schooner, the wharf shot into the glowing sea.

Behind him, the cliff was aglow with a white fire that reminded him of the burning curtains in the parlor of Whitebirch. The cave was a black hole in this bright facade.

The stars disappeared in this light. The breeze died against it. Even the sounds of the surf fell beneath it.

Jacob found it hard to walk. The lines were clear, but the surfaces themselves were not. Jacob took each step on faith that it would land upon something solid. It took several steps for him to become accustomed to the mantid's sight, to seeing the surfaces between the lines. Leaving the rocks was a relief, for the sand appeared oddly more solid.

They soon reached the starboard aft corner of the beached schooner and stood in a tight group at the water's edge. The swamp men dropped the ropes from their shoulders and, all at once, tossed these to the deck. Sharp clangs, each but a striking moment, sounded over the beach as metal hooks caught the rail. The swamp folk climbed and crouched on the deck, securing the ropes. Jacob and Theresa were the last to go. Jacob's feet slipped against the steel hull. His arms ached at the strain but his wounds did not protest too terribly. After pulling Theresa to the deck, the swamp men pulled him, and he was relieved to find the boards of the deck to be easily visible and in fairly good shape. Theresa's lantern created a strange oasis of color in the field of the mantid's sight. It made Jacob think of an artist's unfinished work, mostly sketched but with one small portion painted.

M'Lass had a hull of steel, which was a newer convention. In many ways, however, she was like a far older ship with wooden deck and masts. The masts had long-ago snapped away, leaving shards that described evil points against the night sky. Jacob sat on the deck as the swamp men readied themselves for the next phase of the mission. Jacob had no orders or directions. He lifted the shotgun's strap over his head and set the weapon across his lap.

Closing his eyes, he noticed a sensation that was like water in his ears. It itched or rushed as he moved his head in this and that direction. The sensation bloomed into a sound that inhabited several corners at once. Voices. Whispers. He imagined these as breathy warnings from long-dead sailors. He knew that shipwrights often cannibalized vessels in the construction of new ones. Perhaps the planks of the deck had a history, and brought with them ghosts and curses of other voyages besides the ill-fated maiden outing of *M'Lass*.

Whispers surrounded him now, whispers describing things deep in the cold black sea. Formless beasts enveloped their prey and carried them ever deeper into the crags that split the Earth and brought icy seawater to the Old God's fingertips. At the bottoms of those crags, deeper than any fish or creature that pulled fibrous carrion from drowned bones, bloated corpses of men and far older beings drifted in the dark. Monsters waited in that blackness, their tentacles feeling not for food but for change, for shifts in cosmic energy that might carry them and their brood back to the surface to do Mother's bidding, to sacrifice or be sacrificed.

The voices also railed against dark seas, empty horizons, mirages of mysterious lights that lured sailors and winds that mimicked calls for help from desperate men. Sea wisps—they drew ships from their courses and led them to horror, all for the pure mischief of it.

But *M'Lass* had come back from such a horror. And though her crew had disappeared, she was not empty. She was full of these warnings—not just tales of her voyage, but of all of the voyages that ended in disaster and death. They were in her hold and in the grain of the wood on her decks. Beneath those voices, a nervous buzzing set Jacob's fibers vibrating and made his wounds ache. It was like a million crickets, all chirping a fraction of a step apart from one another, or a nest of bees gathering strength to swarm.

It came from below.

M'Lass had brought something else to Jamesport.

Jacob stood. The swamp men stopped talking and glared at him.

"What are you doing?" Theresa whispered loudly.

He lifted his palm to her, but she followed him as he moved away from the group. He descended the short stairs from the raised aft and picked his way across the deck, gripping what he could against the steep angle at which the schooner had settled. He reached the forecastle. The door was open, the hinges rusted solid. He entered and looked about, not exactly sure what he sought. There was a table, cupboards with empty drawers. Paint peeled from the wall and shreds of rope, once hammocks, draped from hooks in dark alcoves.

There were no answers here, just the emptiness that the first men who boarded the wreck had found. Perhaps they heard the voices, as well. Perhaps that was why they could not leave the wreck soon enough, and why they let it settle into the soft pebbly sand to rot.

Theresa was behind him, pulling at his coat.

"What are you doing?" she demanded. "There is a plan."

Jacob turned to face her, aware of the wild look in his eyes.

"What was on this ship?" he asked.

He could not push the voices from his head. In their nervousness, their furtive insistence, he could sense a horrible presence. He knew that presence, that mind.

"I do not need to tell you," Theresa said.

Jacob stumbled back and leaned against the table, which creaked under his weight. He was certain that there must be form to the voices, and waited to see men appear from the air. There were none, just the ethereal whispers speaking all at once. He closed his eyes and instantly felt the ship rocking. He heard the ropes twanging taut, and the water drumming against the hold.

He could see the faceless sailors, deranged and deformed fisherman who had given up on themselves and their minds to join this voyage. They were the men about whom the crippled old sailors in taverns across from the wharf told stories. These men of *M'Lass* were not the brave heroes of sea tales. No, they were the men who sought and were ready to serve the horrors of the sea. The poison of uncharted nether regions had worked with the salt to twist their joints and ruin their skin. So, when they moved, they were like failed creations, things that the Elders might have discarded rather than sacrifice to the Old God. They threw their limbs in a strange approximation of walking. They grunted at one another. Their eyes pointed in odd tangents from their gaze. Hard tumors studded their faces like barnacles.

These men brought the net to the deck from the bottom of the sea. It unfurled, and there was Mother. One by one, her cloudy, dead eyes came to life. The captain, celebrated in Boston for his antics with women and drink, watched in horror as the beast came alive on the deck of his schooner. He had been swayed and, like so many before him, now regretted it. But the woman who had cast the spell over him, the beauty he could not deny, stood beside him. Beyond beguiling with shocking red hair and porcelain skin, she was one of the Sisters from the college. They had commanded this mission.

They lowered Mother into the hold. The sailors went into the sea mist. Perhaps they were still out there.

Jacob opened his eyes and swept past Theresa, launching back onto the deck and stopping at the edge of an open hatch. Theresa gripped his arm, her dead fingers pressing hard into his muscle.

"There is a plan," Theresa said.

"Who are we here to rescue?"

"There is a plan! We have—"

"Who are we here to rescue?"

She looked at him for several seconds during which even the voices went silent, waiting for her response.

Theresa released her hold.

"Go," she said. "See for yourself."

Jacob looked at the swamp men. They huddled, nervousness clear on their faces. Behind them, through the door to the captain's quarters, he could hear the witch whispering to the captain in the darkness, promising him sovereignty over peoples he could barely imagine. He was a captain of a coastal vessel, a fishing schooner. He wanted so much to be more, but he was not. She promised him vast kingdoms. She promised him her affection. Perhaps she even gave it to him. Jacob heard those lusty wet whispers and shuddered with a chill that shocked his entire body.

This was Mother's ship. She protected it. She enrobed it in terror so that all left it alone.

Isabella was not here.

Jacob lowered himself into the hold, gripping the edge of the hatch and letting his feet dangle in the darkness. He released and landed with a clanging sound upon a grated metal floor.

He could see nothing, but could feel that Mother had been here. He saw flashes of that scene, of the corrupted and deformed sailors tending to her as she, the sole cargo, swayed in the net in the center of the hold. They chanted to wake and feed her. They sacrificed to stir her dormant thoughts. And when she woke, her voice coursing through the metal hull like the peel of a bell, they rejoiced. In her presence, they became more and more deformed, so that even the dashing young captain was no longer recognizable. And the Sister who had led the voyage—chitin grew beneath her skin, pushing at the flesh until it died and flaked away in brittle plaques. And she shed her body like a cocoon, becoming one of the insect servants who would care for Mother in the cliff chamber.

Jacob stepped forward to the center of the hold and stood below the dangling chains from which Mother had swayed with the rocking of the ship.

Mother had been dead and formless, rolling with the currents in the silt at the bottom of the sea for millions of years. Her creators had died beneath the Old God's onslaught. But her life simmered in the center of her mass. She had a singular purpose, a single imperative to corrupt and draw blood, to sacrifice to the Old God in order to aim his favor as a weapon into the stars against a distant enemy.

The voices went silent. The slap of the water against the hull. Jacob's breathing. Nothing more.

Jacob heard the familiar whine and the thumping of heavy footsteps. He froze, looking about.

Tinker.

He could not see the beast. The mantid sight could not penetrate this darkness. Jacob could feel the presence and heard again the whining groan.

The metal monster was upon him. Tinker struck at Jacob's legs. Though still numb, Jacob felt the pain of that strike on his shin and collapsed. Instinct told him to move. He rolled, crashing through debris that went to dust, clogging his nose and throat. He heard the metal ball slam through the floor and strike the hull where he had been. The whole of the ship rang.

Tinker groaned. He was upon Jacob again.

A blinding corona exploded around the beast. Jacob squinted against it. He could see, from the hatch above, the bursts of bulls-eye lanterns. Ropes flew, hooking Tinker's arms. Jacob saw it all in silhouette.

Tinker flailed. Several of the swamp men fell into the hold. More ropes came, and Tinker was soon like a marionette struggling against its master, until he could move no more under the restraints. Swamp men descended those ropes, scrambling like spiders. They landed upon Tinker's shoulders and arms. They covered his head with a burlap sack.

The ropes about Tinker groaned. They had him from every direction. Some swamp men pulled from the deck. Others in the hold wrapped the ropes about the base of a mast for leverage.

Jacob rose and limped toward the automaton. He could hear the creaking of gears, their teeth straining against one another to move. Valves clacked and the whirring had gone to a raspy pant that repeated several times each second. It sounded desperate and frightened.

The swamp men were shouting. Jacob could not understand it. Theresa's voice rose above them.

"His chest! The panel on his chest!"

Crude, tilting bolts secured the panel. One of the swamp men rooted in the refuse at the base of the mast. He retrieved a fishing spear and extended its shaft. Jacob took the thing. Though its head was rusted and loose, it would suffice.

"Remove the electric cell!" Theresa yelled, but Jacob did not completely understand.

He looked to the swamp peasant, who gestured at his own chest as if prying it open. Jacob stood slightly to the side of Tinker and, hooking the panel on the barb of the spear head, yanked several times. The healing wounds in his arm burst into pain at the strain. His vision went cloudy. Strange sounds filled his mind. The mantid in his skull protested at the work with a harsh, buzzing whine. Jacob felt nauseous and faint. He took one deep breath of cold air, pursed his lips, and set the hook once more. With one final, quick pull, he pulled the panel free. It knocked against Tinker's knee as it fell, before clanging like a cymbal onto the floor, followed by the clatter of the broken bolts.

The electric cell was a jar of thick glass filled with sand that glowed. That light, however, wavered. Jacob realized where he had seen such thing. Isabella had a collection of them in the attic of the Larchmont estate.

Jacob jammed the spear head into the space along the cell's side. Tinker shuddered with surprise. The cell popped out with little effort, clanking on the floor before rolling out of view.

Tinker went limp. The swamp men relaxed the ropes, guiding the beast to the floor.

Tinker's arms and legs looked like they had been built from sections of stovepipe. His chest was a dented, scratched barrel. He was a crude, poorly-made thing, patched here and there with uneven strips of metal. His edges were sharp and rough, cut sloppily with tinsnips. He wore the metal ball on one hand. His other arm ended in the blades. He was dangerous, to be sure, but not the terrible monster that Jacob remembered from Sam's cave, from his capture by the Sisters, or even from the melee seconds ago.

Jacob knelt, pulling the burlap sack from Tinker's head. The beast's forehead and nose broke the surface of the fluid in his helmet.

His skin was like gray wax. There, submerged, were the open eyes and black pupils. Jacob wondered what ticked behind those eyes. Was it a brain, shocked to life by the electric cell? Or, was it an apparatus? He wondered if there was really a difference between a machine like this, and the life that the Elders had conjured.

The swamp men were gathering about, now. One carried his shotgun. Jacob yanked the gun from him and turned, leveling it at Tinker's head. He aimed down the barrel. Perhaps Isabella was here, and Tinker had guarded her. This had been a trap, and the swamp men had sprung it.

"Stop!"

It was Theresa. She strode forward and stood right in front of the shotgun's muzzle. She gripped the barrel and pushed it aside.

"This is a rescue," she said.

Jacob blinked and looked at the swamp men. Some nodded, while some merely stared at Tinker, or into the darkness.

"That is my brother," Theresa said.

THIRTEEN

THE SWAMP MEN worked through much of the night at raising Tinker from the hold and lowering him to the beach. Throughout the whole operation, they passed nervous glances to the sky, to the sliver of moon as it slid toward the horizon. The eastern sky went from black to a deep blue as the rising sun reached for Hutchinson's Point at the very end of Jamesport, opposite Executioner's Rock. Tinker was as stiff as a statue as they maneuvered him through the hatch, turning him in different ways and, in their haste, knocking him several times into various structures of the ship. Theresa winced each time.

They would not accept Jacob's help, but rather insisted that he stand guard at the rail with the shotgun, facing the sea. He could see nothing but the glow of his new odd vision, which began to fade as daylight crept closer. He wondered what danger they expected from the ocean, but it was only one of several and not the most important of the questions that consumed him.

Questions about Tinker swirled in a confusing, obscuring miasma like fog over the salt marshes. Tinker as Theresa's brother was, but should not have been, impossible to grasp. Both were dead, the results of Rutledge's demonic experiments like the drowned children in the schoolhouse. But Tinker had caused such destruction, had certainly killed Sam and his family, and had almost killed Jacob. He wondered why Theresa would want to rescue him.

He realized that one might say the same about him. Death and destruction followed him, breathing over the back of his neck as would the beast in his dreams. Papaya, for one. Chang. Forsythe. Rutledge. He had killed her father—perhaps indirectly, but the man might be wandering those dark halls among the devilish curios of his collection now had Jacob not paid him the visit that night. Indeed, quite a bit might have gone differently had Sam not drawn that card. It was the start of all of this.

He knew that was incorrect. Mother was behind most of this.

The swamp men nearly lost Tinker as they dipped him over the rail and lowered him to the beach. He slid a dozen feet, and the yank of that rope pulled the six swamp men up to the rail. A knot of them on the beach were nearly crushed.

Jacob sighed through his nose and peered again into the sea. The first time he had seen the sea, he realized, was here in Jamesport. Jacob had heeded the mysterious call to travel from Texas to Jamesport, moving with an intensity that he now realized matched that of the beast in his dreams. For every obstacle, there had been all too convenient assistance. A silent man with burned and flaking skin had seemed to be waiting to ferry him across the Mississippi just yards from the spot at which he encountered that river. A band of religious zealots in yellow robes paused a ceremony, an exorcism by the looks of the woman writhing on an altar of boughs that they had constructed, to feed him. An old Roma with a deep scar running through an empty eye socket and perforating his left cheek offered him a fire at the feet of the Appalachians. And, Sam. He and the weird women were at the very end of the straight line he had travelled, the line from which he refused to be deterred. Sam, then Papaya, others, and now this.

Was Mother behind all of it? Had she pushed Ida from the cliff, setting all of this in motion?

The line had not stopped in Jamesport. The years here had been like the negotiation with the silent ferryman, or the night in the hazy, hallucinogenic pipe smoke of the Roma wizard. Jacob looked into the sea, and saw that line going on and on from this point. It was like the lines of Mother's communication criss-crossing the globe in his mantid vision. Perhaps Jacob had ridden a line of power that Mother knew, an axis of the Elders on a map of the world of the Old God.

One of the swamp men shouted from the beach below, snapping Jacob back to the present. Jacob looked and saw the man in the translucent silhouette of his new sight. The swamp dweller was pointing into the surf. Jacob followed his gesture, seeing nothing.

"Look beyond the waves," Theresa said.

Jacob looked to his right and saw her standing there, just behind him. He sighed again, dragging his gaze over the surf, farther out to sea. He wanted to close his eyes, unwilling to see whatever new ancient secret was rolling in the waves, ready to beach itself on Jamesport's rocky shelf and disgorge whatever horror incubated in its rotting womb.

Still nothing, though. He looked farther, to the horizon where the early deep blue of daylight was catching azure and orange from the east, and the glow of his mantid vision had been banished completely.

He saw sails. Six sets of three. Small barques or schooners, black. They shot in a tight line, moving fast and turning toward Jamesport.

"Not much of a watchman, are you?" Theresa asked. "They are an hour or more away, and it will take some time for them to land."

"Who are they?"

He looked at her. She gazed at the ships, and turned to the swamp men on the beach. Tinker now lay in their midst, as the last of them rappelled from the rail of *M'Lass* and the group began to square off around the automaton to lift him.

"Dregs," she said over her shoulder. "Lost sailors, like the men who disappeared from this very ship. They were taken by the horrors of the sea, and they are corrupted in every way. Mother's dregs."

"What do they want?"

"Me." She turned to face him. "And you. And they will kill every man in the swamp village to find us. We must prepare a defense."

Jacob feared that their return through the tunnels would be slow going, but the swamp men carried Tinker deftly through the streams and mud. The collapse that had trapped Jacob, however, stopped them. Tinker would not fit through the gap under which Jacob had become trapped, and efforts to use the automation's feet as a battering ram had no effect on the pile. After several minutes, Theresa shouted and began a frantic conversation with the party. Their voices were quick and full of frustration. Theresa brought them to nods, however, and the swamp men backtracked several yards with Tinker, disappearing in a dark side passageway.

"We go to the swamp," Theresa said to Jacob. "They will take another route and arrive later."

"Why don't we use Tinker in the fight?" he asked. He felt that it was the best idea he could offer.

"Tinker will not fight for us yet. Our witch will work to change that, but it will not be quick. It is enough to have him out of the fight."

Jacob followed her, but was tiring. She was dead, her muscles blissfully empty of fatigue or ache. She could drive her numb body forward forever, no doubt. Jacob, though, was beginning to find his limits. The shotgun in his arms became like a tree trunk. The mantid sight, competing with Theresa's lantern, was causing the back of his head to ache. The mantid's buzzing grew steadily louder, threatening to drown out any thought he might have on his own. But the trial was only beginning. There was a fight ahead of him.

Theresa was speaking, trying to outline the basics of their defense. He could barely pay attention to it, but was able to understand the largest sweeps. The dregs would certainly attack the swamp village. The defense would gather on dry ground, in the abandoned revivalist colony. This was elevated ground, one slope facing the bay and the opposite slope facing the village of the swamp men. They would descend upon the dregs, who would be navigating one of the deepest and thickest parts of the swamp as they left the road.

As much as he could analyze the plan, Jacob found it to make sense. There was nothing that he could offer. She and the swamp men had clearly prepared for such contingencies, choosing the best ground, the best choke points. The abandoned colony would conceal them and provide a defensible position to which they could retreat, It would give them height over their enemy, thus mitigating a chief weakness.

Jacob had no sense, though, of what they faced. He imagined monsters. He imagined villains, kidnappers, and murderers putting to sea and mixing with forces beyond the horizon to become deformed beasts, terrible dark and barnacle-encrusted raiders who fed on the soft skin of land dwellers.

As he pictured them—their scraps of clothing trailing behind in a harsh salt breeze, shreds of nets and seaweed and sailcloth— he felt the prairie wind and the heartbeat of the beast. Monsters pursued him. They crossed vast distances in the hunt for him.

From land, from sea. They built worlds in the stars above. Their corpses lay beneath the water. One curled in the center of the Earth, pressed by stone into a fetal position, and slumbered where it had slumbered forever. Mother was perched in the cliff. She had been their tool, but now she orchestrated them, pulled the strands of her net to direct them like puppets. Beasts and demons from the past, from now, into the future—she arrayed them all against him, to find him.

But it was the singular beast, the beast crossing the plains, that sent a jolt of fear through him at that moment.

He stopped, bracing himself against the earthen wall. Theresa was several yards ahead, crossing from the tunnel into the basement of the old church on the edge of Jamesport. Framed in the light, she looked alive. She was drenched in mud and sewer water, which ran in brown, vein-like trails down her arms and legs. Her hair was wild and stiff. Her robes clung to her here or pulled, heavy and soaked, there. Her feet were caked with dirt. But the muscles in her calf flexed as she pivoted to look back at him. Jacob saw that definition, and thought of the blood running through the fibers of her muscles. Or, did it? Was it blood, or Rutledge's black magic? Or did deathly tar clot and clog in those veins?

His gaze climbed as she bent her knees slightly, perhaps stretching those muscles. The dimples on either side of her left knee, visible beneath the wet robe plastered to her buttocks and back of her leg, deepened and flattened as she worked.

It seemed more than the mantid could handle. The buzz in his mind became a shattering rush of noise, of metal scraping, of great and ancient structures collapsing, filling the deep empty spaces of the Earth with their clattering, cracking debris. His mind flipped between the green fungus glow of the tunnel and the silhouette of Theresa's form in the lantern light. He also saw the beast crossing the rivers and mountains, gripping the dry, glassy tiles of the desert floor with its front claws and throwing them yards, even miles behind it as it coursed closer to him.

"Breathe," she said over her shoulder. "The mantid needs the air."

He was not sure how he heard her. Her voice floated over the noise, even echoed back through it. He took a long draft of air, feeling the mist cling to the insides of his ribs. It ignited in his chest and swelled cool into his head, calming the mantid. Jacob's limbs felt suddenly weak. His knees buckled before strengthening.

"It will not die," she said. "But if it senses enough danger, and it has enough strength, it will leave you. And that will kill you. You must do what you can to keep it calm."

They went into the morning air, and Jacob found even more strength in its clean chill. Clouds gathered overhead. The swamp became almost as dark as night. The mantid glow returned, and he saw every vein of every dead leaf, the pinpoint star at the end of every fir needle. The eddies about the grasses looked like magical smoke, like the smoke of the witch's fire or the steam that billowed from one of Papaya's devilish brews. As they neared the drowned schoolhouse, he thought he could see the corpses of the children. They were curled in the black water, dreaming, some twitching in nightmares. Jacob could not imagine the terror of such nightmares that would upset a child who had already died.

He and Theresa went further, reaching the edge of the slope that rose to the abandoned settlement. Jacob saw the outlines of the squat structures, all once identical boxes that had settled into the hill in different ways, creating multitudes of leaning shapes. Some had not been able to withstand this, and had collapsed in this corner or that, their roofs looking to him like the sheet walls of an army tent. As the two neared, creatures scattered, flashes of light in the brush heading toward the far slope. There was nowhere else for them to go. At first, Jacob thought they were the footsteps of ghosts. But they were a different kind of vermin, a throw-away tinkering of the Elders or slag from the construction of a more substantial creature.

"Stay," Theresa said. "I will rouse the others in the village. Our group will soon arrive with Tinker. They must get through. Shoot any who oppose them. Retreat to this position. We will relieve you."

Jacob nodded, imagining the black barques of the dregs anchoring in the bay. By now, the beasts would be ashore, perhaps penetrating the swamp and marching in sloshing single file between clumps of muddy earth to find the village of the swamp peasants. They would have drawn their nicked, rusting scimitars. Some would be hefting thick warped pikes. The heads of those pikes would be evil barbed spears of salt-rotted metal, a single scratch from which would poison a man.

A gray fog rolled in from the west, from the bay. It was an icy smoke, leaving frost and stiffening grasses and branches, which protested in high-pitched creaking as it washed over them. When it reached the hill, it climbed to the summit. Jacob stood ankle deep in the mist, looking over a flat plain of fog from which rose an occasional clump of trees, the dilapidated shacks of the settlement behind him, and the top of the drowned schoolhouse steeple.

Jacob felt an itch deep behind his throat. The mantid twitched, and the fog disappeared. The phosphorescence shifted. Blue rose sharply, but softened and thinned. He saw no fog, but saw the world beneath in other colors. The water was still black, but his hands were bright oranges and reds like fire. In the distance, toward Jamesport, he saw more colors like that. It was the team of swamp men, and they carried Tinker. A knot of a dozen or more cooler green and blue shapes approached from the bay.

Mother's dregs.

Jacob's heart quickened, which had the effect of startling the mantid, shaking the colors before him for a moment. Gripping the shotgun in his hands, but barely able to comprehend the colors that he saw, he took steps forward, down the slope to the sunken road. The roots of a fallen tree near the base of the hill provided cover. He knelt at this position, waving frantically to the swamp men, unsure if they could see him. His knees squelched in the mud. He pictured himself, fiery reds and yellows, sinking into the cold blue earth. The fallen tree sank with him, the green core of its trunk fading from life, fading into a dead gray.

He wondered how Theresa would appear in this sight.

The swamp men became a tighter, smaller group. Perhaps they had seen him gesturing, and now hunkered to stay out of sight. The group of them began to move to the left, heading toward the back of the hill. They would bypass the dregs, or lead them into ambush. It did not matter to Jacob. The swamp men had seen him, so his first task was complete. Now, he needed to delay the invaders.

He crouched lower, aiming the shotgun through the roots. The dregs were closer, their snorts and heavy, wheezing breaths rising above the rush of the mist. The beasts were huge, deformed men. He could see nothing of their details, nothing of the skin or clothes that he had imagined. He saw only their hulking forms in green and violet, their trunks of legs thrown in wide arcs from their hips as they carved a straight path through the swamp. They would let nothing stand in their way, the dozen of them whose cold forms melded with and separated from the very mist through which they walked. They would cross right over the hill, or right through it. They would trample Jacob.

He waited. The lead of them was now quite close, but not close enough.

Two barrels, side by side, and two triggers. It would take more than a single shot to fell the first of the dregs.

He was the largest, like a bear.

Jacob yanked his finger back through both triggers. The shotgun smashed into his shoulder and sent him back against the slope.

The mist went silent with the report, which repeated across the swamp, echoing from every blade of grass.

The lead of the dregs stood still for one moment, a swirling sun of red and orange burning in his gut. His arms were outstretched.

The others were still as well. They waited.

To the left, the swamp men slipped out of view behind the hill.

The wounded dreg groaned with the deep sound of a sinking ship, air bubbling from every deep pore. He fell back, splashing into the swamp.

The others turned on Jacob, rushing him, tripping over one another and landing all about him. He rolled, smelling their sulfur funk, dodging a pike that sank into the soft slope. He spun and was on his feet, still gripping the shotgun and scrambling up the hill. Jacob could see colors there, shapes amidst the trees and ruined structures. Not ghosts, he knew.

The swamp men had arrived from the village.

Jacob continued up the hill, tripping forward and sprawling to the ground in their midst. The shotgun flew from him, its warm orange barrel cooling in the mist, becoming invisible to him.

The swamp men lined up and fired a volley on the advancing dregs.

It was not enough. The beasts continued.

Jacob turned, watching them crest the hill and swing their great arms, grabbing at the swamp men and smacking them against trees, or ripping their torsos in two. Those bodies stiffened, and the spray of blood was a bright orange stream, liquid light and fire that now painted the top of the hill. The screams of the swamp men died in sudden, gurgling gasps. Their guns went silent.

And the dregs found him. One's fist smashed his left arm, and the pain jolted his sight so that the mantid's vision shattered for one moment. In that moment, he saw the true scene—gray roiling mist, and the black shadows surrounding him, reaching for him.

Jacob shut his eyes and twisted. He pushed himself from their midst with his legs, reaching the edge of the hilltop and rolling. Brush and grasses whipped at him as he rolled. The dregs barreled down after him.

He stopped against a fallen tree and immediately pulled himself to standing. His wounded arm went limp, but his other was still strong. The mantid wounds were alight with pain, but he pushed himself forward.

The dregs were right there with him, reaching to strangle and rip.

Jacob spun, weaving through the water, across the road.

Another shot sounded behind him. A survivor among the swamp men, but not for long. It was long enough, though, for Jacob to break away, to lose them for several seconds.

They found his trail again soon enough. Their hulking green blue forms bounded through the water and over mud, gaining on him.

Jacob found himself at the door of the drowned schoolhouse.

He spun himself through the door and dove for the far end the flooded classroom. He tripped several times, smashing his palms and knees against debris as he fell, splashing in the cold black water. He continued to grope, reaching the collapsed corner and gripping the shaft of the clapper. He took it up, held it like his lost shotgun cradled in his right arm, and made his way back toward the door.

One of the dregs stooped through the schoolhouse door and rose to his full height, waving his arms to grab at Jacob.

Jacob heard a volley of gunshots outside, then gurgling screams. More survivors, and more of them fell.

The beast in the schoolhouse paused at that sound.

Jacob lifted the clapper and swung, its scratched, dented metal ball slapping against the monster's skull. The beast staggered at first, shaking his head clear. Jacob followed through on the swing and set himself up once more. He swung again, going for the same spot. The clapper struck, and that skull gave a sickening crunch as the ball sank deep. The thug stiffened and went lip, dragging the clapper into the knee deep water.

Jacob fished it out as another volley of gunfire, this time sounding from farther up the road, further toward the village, began strong but, as it rolled, fell into disarray.

Jacob could hear the dregs breathing and snorting as they turned their attention from the ripped and broken corpses of the swamp men, the shattered lines of riflemen squirming and twisting beneath hanging mist and the gray smoke of cordite.

He gripped the ladder with his left hand. His wounded left arm went tight with pain. The mantid silenced this. He braced the clapper as he pulled himself up the ladder.

As he reached the top, he shifted his hips and lifted the clapper.

More dregs were in the schoolhouse.

Jacob hooked the clapper into the bell and gave the ball a push. It touched the bell lightly, its ring sending ripples across the swamp water.

"Again!" Theresa yelled.

The dregs turned on her. She was there, in the schoolhouse, standing in the water with her robes flowing around her.

Jacob threw the clapper's ball against the side of the bell.

The glorious deep peal shook the mud and broke the mist. It shattered his vision into a thousand shards that fell with their blues and greens, oranges and reds to the dark water.

The dregs were rushing out of the schoolhouse, the last of them splashing through the doorway as Jacob's vision cleared.

The drowned children rose from the water outside. Regarding the scores of fallen swamp men and the slicks of blood and body matter floating on the surface with confusion, the dead children snarled, their waxy cheeks gray and translucent where they had flesh, glistening where they were bone.

"Attack!" Theresa yelled.

They turned on the dregs.

FOURTEEN

THE DEAD WERE relentless in their attack. They shambled, slow through the water but intelligent in their movement. They maneuvered to surround the dregs and, falling upon them, clawed and bit, gripped with a ferocity that knew no fear. The dregs cried and shouted as their thick black hides curled beneath the gray fingernails of the drowned children.

Jacob watched this for a short moment, ignoring Theresa's pulls and gestures. The mantid sight had dropped and the mist was clearing. Jacob saw the dregs for what they were.

"We must get to the village!"

But he ignored her.

They were every bit what he had imagined. Giants and monsters, they wore bolts of fraying sailcloth tied over their bulk with tangled nets. Where they left their faces uncovered, Jacob saw empty black pupils like those of an octopus, and gray scarred skin, lumpy with barnacle-like growths or strange swirls of sea worms curled beneath the thick, waterlogged layers. Ropey muscles bulged on their arms and calves, twisting in knotted masses that contracted and elongated in rhythms that did not seem to describe any movement, but rather a pulsing heartbeat or other ticking mechanism within their trunks. Seaweed, rotting cloth, ropes and tackle dangled from cuffs and tears of their clothing.

They were transformed or, Jacob thought, born from the unholy coupling of human and an ancient creature slumbering in the silt of deep ocean trenches.

The dead were ripping them to shreds, but were dwindling in their numbers as the dregs tore legs and arms from waterlogged corpses, or lifted the children and smashed their heads against tree trunks.

"Now!" Theresa said.

Jacob, sensing that the dregs were moving to retreat, their numbers severely diminished, obliged.

As he took his first steps, gunshots rolled over the scene. He thought at first it might be an echo from the fight, a delayed sighing of the carnage from the distant hills. It made him think of his shot through Papaya's head, the deed magnified a thousand times and thrown back at him.

The dregs were slinking back to the bay. The dead children, the few who were left, stood maimed or crawled through the muck and water with their faces barely rising into view, like frogs sipping air. But all stopped at those shots.

Theresa stopped as well, her palms facing the bloody water. She listened, staring at Jacob.

The world was silent for one moment. Then, a breeze moved the trees about the schoolhouse before diving through its broken boards and sifting through the tall swamp grasses.

There was another volley of shots.

"The village," Theresa said, and shot across the sunken road, toward the hill.

Jacob followed her, clambering up the slope, gripping fistfuls of mud and dirt. He passed broken corpses of swamp men, slipping in the slime of their bowels and blood. Those empty eyes, those anguished faces watched him go. One, headless, spilling his life into the brush near the edge of the abandoned settlement at the top of the hill, gripped Jacob's shotgun. The barrel was crushed, and Jacob imagined one of the dregs taking it in his giant hand and crunching it shut. Jacob left it to be swallowed by the swamp in the next rain.

Theresa shot through the abandoned settlement, dodging the fallen swamp men. She reached the far side of the hill, the top of a path through the trees and brush, and peered into the distance.

Green swamp grass swayed, spreading far. Thin mist washed the color from the scene beyond, though Jacob could see the witch's hill, the temple of the swamp men from which he had seen the vision of Mother and spotted the tomb of the Elder. The ruined white house looked susceptible to falling against the mere thought of a battle.

The village squatted in gullies and trenches, belching black smoke that gathered about the base of the witch's hill. Sparks appeared from one side of the village, followed by blue white puffs of smoke. A second later, the report of a volley of gunfire shocked the swamp grasses near Theresa and Jacob.

"They are men," Theresa said. Her shoulders deflated and she stumbled back, her hand gripping a stump.

"What do you mean? Not dregs?"

"No. Men. Police or the army."

She was breathing hard.

"I don't understand."

She glared at him, but had no other response.

"Mother," she said between breaths. "The Sisters. They are powerful. They command the kings of industry, and so command the republic."

"The army?" Jacob asked.

Theresa closed her eyes and took a moment to right her breathing.

"After all you have seen," she said. "You cannot be surprised."

Jacob gestured at the scene below the next hill. Another

volley of shots rolled, this time closer to the center of the village, closer to the cold pit of the swamp peasants' bonfire.

"Mother controls the army," he said. It came from his mouth as fact. He was tired of asking. "She orders men, not dregs or insects. Not Tinker. She orders men to slaughter your followers."

"No!" She turned on him with ferocity, with a look in her eyes that reminded Jacob of the cold murder that clotted in the back of the drowned children's skulls, that burned deep in Tinker's moans. "The witches of the college beguile their men to wield their power. The generals order the colonels, the colonels order the captains, and these men march through the swamp to rid Jamesport of gypsies, pickpockets and kidnappers. That is what the newspapers will say tomorrow!"

Jacob sighed, staring into Theresa's eyes until they softened, and her gaze broke into a full welling of tears. She turned to the ground.

"We can do nothing?" he asked.

She launched into him, pounding on his chest and spitting in his face. He backed away, his hands raised.

"Stop!" she yelled. Another round of gunshots sounded. "Stop asking!"

He said nothing. His heart beat faster, and he felt the wind of the plains and the cold of the Appalachian summits. The mantid squirmed, and it paralyzed his thoughts on the vision of that beast coming from the desert, that monster standing atop those mountains and peering down toward the coast, toward Jamesport and Jacob.

"There is nothing we can do," she said.

Jacob swallowed hard.

"The team with Tinker," he said. "They can't have reached the village. They must be hiding. I saw them last heading around this hill."

He spun, getting his bearings against the sun, the hill, the memory of the mantid sight at the moment that the swamp men carried Tinker from the road. He was able to see the road from this vantage, and pointed.

"There," he said. "They left the road there."

"What do you propose?" she asked.

"We find them, and head to the tunnels."

"The church?"

"No. That won't be safe. They must know of that place."

Theresa blinked.

"There is a retreat. If any survive the assault, they will go there."

Jacob waited a moment and gestured her forward.

"You need to lead the way," he said.

Theresa nodded, the last shred of emotion lingering in her eyes before falling away to cold and death.

"You said that something comes for me," Jacob said. "You said it to the witch on the hill."

Theresa stopped. They had not found Tinker or any survivors. They walked the edge of the swamp, their feet cracking thin layers of ice atop puddles in frozen mud. They had travelled far to the eastern side of Jamesport, past the Portuguese quarter. The wall of Fort Madison on Hutchinson's Point loomed not far ahead, its red brick chipped with wars against time and lichen.

"What do you sense?" Theresa asked.

Jacob swallowed. He did not have many answers. The beast came for him. It slaughtered its way across the country. He did not sense whether it would do him harm, but she had said it would destroy him.

"When I was a boy, something happened in the desert, in a cave. It comes from that place." He breathed, watching the heat of his breath swirl in the late afternoon cold. "It feels like it comes from that time, that day. I think it has killed."

She remained still.

"Do you know what it looks like?"

"Somewhat," he replied quickly. "I see it as if...I see through its own eyes. It wants blood. It has claws like a bear. It pounces like...like a lion. It killed a crowd of travelers. I can see the blood in its fur."

Theresa turned to face him, looking him up and down. He shivered at her gaze. He was numb and cold, and his teeth clacked against one another.

"I must apologize," she said. At that moment, she seemed alive and human, innocent. Moments when she seemed alive, those honest moments of guilt or exasperation, only reminded him that she was dead. As warmth softened her face, as her lips appeared somewhat less blue than they had, and her skin seemed to glow with blood and soul, he saw the still, sagging heart in her chest, empty of blood but for the black tar of it that balled in its bottom chambers.

"Apologize?"

"My outburst on the hill. Understand my...my grief."

His own town had died. The plague had taken his family and many others, leaving the survivors as prey to bandits, their corpses food for coyotes with ribs as pronounced as those of the skeletons they dragged into the desert waste.

"I do," he said.

"You will be more valuable to us if you know everything."

"Do you have the answers?"

Theresa paused one moment and looked at the ground.

"Some," she said. "You know much, but not everything that you should know. We are not used to trusting people."

"Is that working?" he asked, then regretted it.

Clouds obscured the sun, and the mantid sight's phosphorescence began to bloom on the edges of the grass and across the icy mud. Anger flickered across Theresa's face, but calmed.

"It did work. It worked for eons. But you bring different times."

She did not continue or add any explanation. Rather, she turned from the swamp and walked onto a wide stretch of sand that ran with deep gullies of water. A thin sleet began to fall. After only several minutes, his pant legs were stiff with ice. A breeze rose, punching from the sea. He held the brim of his hat as he followed Theresa.

Somewhere to the west, Jamesport began and climbed the stone ramp to Executioner's Rock on the opposite end of the island. The legends on this eastern spit were no less severe. Here, locals said, ships beached and the first Portuguese settlers, religious zealots fleeing a sixteenth century Europe that was sending them to the stake, survived by sucking slimy mollusks from dirty shells that they dug with their fingers from the muck. Many died in the winter, but enough remained to pile sand and wood into a makeshift fort, the earthworks of which were still visible just outside of the walls of Fort Madison. Natives descended from the swamps, coming at night and conjuring spirits and dervishes from the stinking black water to sicken those settlers with a vile, erupting pox. It took the children first, filling their mouths and noses with pustules that grew so large as to choke the victims. When the pustules burst, the fluid would drown them.

Jacob wondered if it had been natives. Or, had the swamp peasants cast a curse upon them?

Few had settled here until the army built but soon abandoned Fort Madison. All gave the sandy waste a wide berth as they centered their efforts further west, in a less sensible perch against the poisonous Jamesport Bay.

Theresa now headed for a more recent mansion that stood in sad ruin. Vines with woody stems and spotted dark green leaves shot through its walls and choked its windows, spilling through like tentacles gripping the structure, intent upon pulling it down. They had almost succeeded, for the mansion was but a shell.

The ghost was of a home more modest than the castles on the cliff. The ornaments and accents that still survived in stone and peeling wood were all New England of mid-century, with a pediment and columns that pretended to be Roman, and windows all about the boxy shape of the structure. This was before the New York elite arrived, bringing marble, gold, and Earth-shattering expense to the western cliff.

As they neared, he could see debris littered about the place. The back half of the mansion facing the sea had fallen. A sea squall had perhaps taken two swipes and knocked those sides in flying, splintering planks up the beach and into the ocean.

Theresa was ahead of him, approaching the house on its broken front walk, stepping over running vines that were as thick as saplings. She climbed the stairs of the porch and hopped over a hole in the floorboard, then turned the rusted knob. The door would not budge at first, but she gave it a weak kick and a shove with her shoulder. The hinges popped in a spray of rusty dust, and the door swayed open to reveal a hallway to the open sea behind. Wallpaper curled in sheets between the vines. The second floor was gone. In many places, the first floor gaped open to storage cellars and tunnels below.

Jacob followed her through the doorway, wondering if it would be impossible to simply wander around the side of the house and climb over the low, crumbling foundation.

"Close the door," Theresa said.

Jacob smiled.

"We do not want anyone to know that we are here," she added, seemingly unaware of the preposterousness of the idea. But he did not fight her, and pushed the door closed behind him as he followed her.

She stepped carefully over the soft, rotting flooring. The boards did not creak, but simply sank beneath her weight. Jacob tried as best as he could to step on the joists.

They passed between two rooms, one a parlor or drawing room, and the other a library by the looks of the collapsing shelves and book covers that splayed open on the floor, leaking a custard-looking matter that must have once been pages. Moss had replaced the carpet, and echoed a fine Persian pattern in the same way that a fossil describes the shape of something once alive.

They had stepped from beneath the remnants of the ceiling and, as they walked, the crescent moon started to rise over the end of the hallway where a bulls eye window might have matched one below the apex of the pediment at the front of the house. Thin white trunks of bare trees shot up through the floor. Gray vines wrapped around these, shooting off to cling to the falling walls, working at pulling them down further, inch by inch. Sand piled in corners with debris, and mold gave clear signs of flood.

In the growing darkness, Jacob saw the lines of the house that had been. He imagined men and women moving through these rooms. They were spirits of a finer time when, for a brief moment, this home lorded over the sandy spit to dispel the horrors of the past. But the specter that soaked these sands, that pulsed onto the shore with every wave, would have none of it. And the house would not stand. Perhaps it was a storm, or a gruesome happening that led to the mansion's abandonment. Jacob did not know, but he could sense a furtive nervousness in the lines of the structure and in the movements of those ghosts. This house never intended to stand, despite what its architects and builders had meant for it. In all the days that it stood, it plotted its ruin.

But it still had secrets.

Theresa reached the end of the hall, which did not end so much as disappear into the beach. On either side, however, two doors rose out of nothing. Like standing stones in an ancient monument, they did not serve as portals to actual rooms, but rather gave the sense that they led to other places, other planes.

Smiling, Theresa opened the right-hand door, which moved easily across the sandy, mossy floor at the end of the hall. Stone steps descended into a tunnel of hewn rock slabs. Peering around the side of the door frame, however, Jacob saw only sand and planks. He saw nothing of the tunnel.

"What is this place?" Jacob asked.

Theresa smiled.

"A refuge," she said. "Once a home to artists and writers. A famous sculptor lived here briefly, but wandered into the sea—just walked into the waves to drown himself—after completing a work that the others here destroyed rather than let anyone see. Soon after, several went into the swamp to found the colony there."

"The settlement at the top of the hill, where we fought—"

"Yes, where we fought the dregs. Disease killed those men and women, and their children. The fervor of whatever religion they had found could not save them."

They descended to another door, a braced metal slab like one would find in an armory. Jacob saw a small keyhole. The sounds of the surf and the breeze felt suddenly far away.

Theresa reached into the top of her robes and retrieved a pendant. Indeed, it was like the one that Jacob had taken from Rutledge. Theresa's bore a similar relief, a bat-like creature with wings folded. She gripped its head in one hand, and pulled at its body with the other. The wood separated at the neck and slid, revealing a small studded metal rod dropping like a spine from the bat's neck. Theresa inserted this into the keyhole and turned. A heavy click sounded from deep within the lock. She leaned into the door and it groaned, opening into the dark.

FIFTEEN

ORANGE FIRELIGHT FLICKERED ahead, casting long shadows from the tarred wooden beams that braced the stone ceiling of the tunnel. Jacob's mantid sight began to recede against this light. There was a chamber with tall, thin stone formations, but Jacob could see nothing of the fire or who—or what—might be huddled around it. The mantid amplified his concern, catching and spraying it to all of the edges of his body. His skin rose with goose bumps and his heart quickened.

Theresa, however, did not seem worried. She marched forward with confidence, moving more quickly with each step.

"Wait," he said.

"No," she replied. Simple, insistent and calm.

Anxiety filled him. It settled in the spaces between his bones, and rattled. He could not bear it, and gritted his teeth against it.

"Stop!"

Theresa paused and turned. There was more than just life in her eyes. It was a deep anger that threatened him, putting a sharp point on his nervousness.

"We are safe," she said.

She gestured to the end of the hallway, to the cavern's entrance. One of the swamp men now stood there, his silhouette holding a long rifle against the light. His stance softened as he realized that it was Theresa who approached.

Theresa turned and moved down the tunnel, into a round, seemingly natural cyst in the rock. A tight ring of columns nearly enclosed a small central space, in which swamp dwellers prepared bedding and curtains for her. The columns, like the cavern itself, looked natural rather than hewn, for they curved and leaned as no human architect would imagine. As he looked closer, he saw movement within twisting mineral veins in the columns. Darker material gathered into the shapes of eyes and mouths, and then dispersed as it moved toward the ceiling.

It seemed a trick of light and shadow until the hair on the back of Jacob's neck stiffened, and his spine tingled, carrying a shimmering power that rose from the floor. The mantid curled in his tissue, and he felt its bracing against the vibration as a sharp pain that arced along the bottom of his brain, from the insect's perch to center of his eyes. His vision shifted. It was not the augmented sight that had helped him in the mist against the dregs. Nor was it the view of Mother's vast connections to her demonic kind around the world, and through the universe. Rather, it was a draining, a shutting down. All of that sight and color was falling away, and he was left for that moment with his normal human vision.

And that vision was woefully and tragically flat.

Jacob closed his eyes tight, feeling himself falling through the geyser of power from the center of the Earth. The mantid relaxed at this frantic though oddly calming sensation.

"Jacob."

It was not Theresa's voice. He opened his eyes to her. His vision was still flat, still dull as he regarded her.

"Jacob, come here."

It was the rough voice of the sailor. Jacob turned.

The Historian lay in a battlefield stretcher on the floor. Dark blood spread through a bandage wrapped around his thigh. The left side of his face, already scarred from his temple to his cheek, was now swollen and purple. The bones of his chest rose and fell, one side before the other. He held each breath for a second of wincing pain before releasing it in a long wheeze that rattled in his throat seconds after the air seemed gone. He would pause, perhaps gathering strength, and his chest would rise again.

Theresa sighed and closed her eyes. She pursed her lips against sobbing. Jacob's mind reeled with memories of the countless visits to the abandoned market and the counsel that the Historian had offered.

"I thought that you—"

The deep, breathy voice of the dark interrupted him. It thrust from the Historian unaffected by his injuries, with more strength than the sailor's voice.

"It does not matter," he said. "I go soon, but I am just like all things. Just like you. Created to sacrifice, to discard."

"They say I'm different."

Jacob gestured weakly to Theresa, well after speaking and unsure if he should have said it at all.

"Yes, you are meaningful, but not without her."

"Theresa?" he asked.

He sensed Rutledge's daughter shifting behind him.

"No," the child's voice said. "The other. The one who is alive."

"Isabella," Theresa said.

She gripped his shoulder, pulling him away from the Historian who now coughed and gurgled, blood foaming out of his mouth. The sailor's curses shot at the ceiling.

"The Historian lived among the Elders. He created for them, beasts to kill. With him, the Elders unlocked deep secrets. Everlasting life. Flight. Sight and sound. Endless blood to spill for the Old God. He created your kind. And in your line he placed the keys to all creatures. You carry them all. You alone."

"And that bug in your head," the sailor shouted. "You are ruined. Your secrets cannot fall to Mother. So the beast has been awakened, and it comes to destroy you."

"What—?"

"These are not the answers you sought. But they are answers, and you must have them before he dies. Before I perish."

Jacob stumbled to one side, gripping one of the columns. He turned to the faces flowing in that rock. They were anguished and horrified, fleeing from broken bodies to the sky. Spirits and ghosts.

"The children rebelled," Theresa said. "The Elders slaughtered them. My father found their bones in the cavern of the cliff. You saw them. Some survived to mix their blood with others' in the swamp."

The Historian was now still, his eyes closed. But his deep whisper filled the cavern.

"But there is one woman of nearly pure blood. Generations of breeding, and they have one. Mother has her now, for you and Isabella would revive their race."

Jacob grimaced, clutching the sides of his head. The mantid, this world, dead women speaking strange secrets to him as the ancient Historian died at his feet—Jacob had seen and done much, but the edges of this new world spread so far from him, its enormity growing so quickly in those seconds, that he could not bear it. Mother had promised something much simpler. Kill, and feel icy and glorious numbness fill his veins and blot out the fathomless distances, the black chasms across time and space in which floated these causes, these wars.

Theresa's cause, the Historian's world—these had nothing for him.

He turned, throwing his arms about him in an attempt to ward off all that he had heard.

"Wait," Theresa said softly. "There are things to do. Things that you can do."

"It is too much for him!" the sailor shouted. "I knew it all along! Let him go!"

Jacob barely heard it. He was in the hall and throwing himself against the door. He was in the world, fleeing the ruined mansion, Theresa, and the Historian.

The chapel at the edge of the city had fallen into the swamp. Jacob imagined a hand from the sky pushing it from its muddy shelf, into the black water and dead rushes. Fat blue flies buzzed about the exposed basement, feeding on putrid muck that had been turned up from the cemetery. Jacob wondered, as he wandered the edge of the swamp toward the bay, if the entrance to the mud tunnels had also collapsed. He could not see it.

Jacob shook his head and climbed the earth and gravel ramp. He went southwest, crossing the rail yard. Abandoned cars sat silent and open on the tracks, their dark holds defying the setting sun to reveal their emptiness, their uselessness. They leaned from that weak orange light, their rusted connections to one another holding them from falling completely over into the gray slag and mud.

He darted among the cars, tool sheds, and stacks of termite-ridden ties. He had gotten back to a thought, a cogent mind about his actions. He was done running blindly, but now sought a discreet, dark path into the city.

Money. Theresa's followers could not have found all of it. There were stashes that Jacob had not visited in months, perhaps even years. Any one of them offered hundreds of dollars if they had not been looted.

Over the rail yard, through one of the Portuguese neighborhoods, and to the westbound side of Oceanview Avenue—he emerged into the first darkness of the evening, into polite society, several blocks east of the Mystery Tower. Here, Bristol Street ran north from Jamesport's public beaches and crossed Oceanview. Here, Chang's store sat on a corner, a gilded false pagoda rising at least one story above the building's corner.

The store was shuttered and silent.

Jacob was conspicuous. He was caked with swamp mud. He cradled his swollen left arm and walked with a limp. But the regal men and women who walked the sidewalk in this end of town, the second tier of gentry who had arrived weeks before to stake a claim to a rental property, or to staff a modest home on Hawke Street from the army of Portuguese-speaking porters and cooks who were not fit to work on Millionaire's Row—these lawyers and accountants, their prim wives and children, would not remember Jacob. To them, he was a forgettable truth of life, someone to be avoided in the moment for fear of dirtying a white shirt or dress, or the air about one's breath, but nothing more.

The crowds in the street were surprising on this cold night. Was it a shopping day or holiday? Or perhaps a weekend? Close to Christmas, no doubt. The men, beneath their finery, were flabby cows. They were worthless men, lawyers and accountants. They did not do anything. The women—if they were to slough the layer of powder, a snake's skin, they would be hags, their skin drawn and flaccid for years of soaking in caustic fluids that advertised regeneration. They all must have considered themselves classical gods and goddesses, busts and statues.

Jacob twisted his way through them, gathering his coat around him and bending his hat so as to cast a shadow over his face. He was nauseous. The smell of their perfumes mixed with the vile musk of their dying bodies. When he looked at them, he saw nothing more than yellow twisted teeth, clouds of stinking breath, sweat, and oil.

These city folk were used to ignoring their surroundings. They made haste to wherever they went and, could they afford it, went in carriages to avoid contact with the world altogether.

So, they missed what Jacob saw. They missed the dark, trench-coated agents within the shadows just inside of Chang's door. These agents answered to someone other than the commissioner of police, or even the governor. Their chain of command, Jacob guessed, ran through the vaults of New York banks and halls of power in Washington, to the witches who were wives and mistresses to the men who pretended to rule. Ultimately, to Mother's kind. The ignorant wanderers with their bags of holiday gifts and warm clothes would never see the agents, or venture down Jacob's street to find the bombed-out market. The crowds would never see the federal soldiers stationed in front of his apartment building, chewing tobacco and spitting brown junk into the stinking gutter. The powdered men and women did not question the conventional wisdom about the Mystery Tower or *M'Lass*. If anyone had told them, they would have no capacity to understand, no place even to put the thoughts.

Jacob remembered something that Papaya had said. As he looked across the street, as the crowds passed to and fro between the upscale residential neighborhoods about the corner of Bristol and Oceanview, he heard Papaya's voice.

He was injured. She cared for him. He had just opened his eyes to brilliant light after a long sleep, a sleep of days or even weeks.

He was alive because of her.

"There are things," she said. "There are things that we serve, but that we will never understand. You may get close, closer even than I. But you will never have answers. You may just reach the point where you say, 'Jacob! There aren't answers for you.' And when that's enough for you—well, then, you'll know you're ready to die."

He now blinked and wondered: was he there?

He had answers, to be sure. An ancient race created his kind to carry the seed for all creatures. He was a weapon, a failsafe, created either under order from or in rebellion against the Elders. But the mantids had compromised him, and Mother had come dangerously close to his secrets. Perhaps she read them now. And so a beast came to destroy him, to save his secrets from her, and from her dead masters.

All had and all sought secrets. Answers. Mother wanted the secret to life after death. Rutledge had it, and had taken it with him. Forsythe, perhaps unknowingly, guarded the secret to freeing the spirits that would possess the Sisters. But Theresa was a walking textbook on resurrection. Mother must also have known that Jacob and Isabella were capable of rekindling an ancient race, and its rebellion against her masters.

Secrets and death.

Jacob felt that he knew enough.

Two police in crisp blue uniforms rounded the corner in front of him, parting the crowd as they ran down Oceanview. Women in hats, men in stiff shirts gasped and got out of the way. These pedestrians came from comfortable worlds where the notion of something requiring police was so foreign that the sight of an alert officer provoked horror.

Jacob stared down the police, sure that they were after him. He felt no choice but to stand and fight, but they were looking past him. There was a commotion behind him, a threatening gang of thugs in front of a Chinese laundry. The two officers, running beside one another, had to separate to get past him.

He pushed on, further west. He weaved through the crowds, which swelled as he neared the park of the Mystery Tower. He passed city hall. He walked through the shadow of the Masonic Temple, a structure designed in the flavor of a mosque by a famous architect who had drawn buildings for world's fairs. It promised secrets in the shadows nestled in the crooks of its strange angles, but it was just a facade.

He stood now across the street from the ruined tower, imagining it as the barrel of a cannon, vaulting subterranean power into the sky at the enemies of the Elders. It would have been a beam of power, like the lines that connected Mother to her kind across the globe and perhaps beyond. He remembered lines of power that Chang had once tried to describe. Ley lines, crisscrossing the Earth, their nexi creating immense globes of energy. Jamesport was one such place, Chang insisted. Jacob pictured himself falling into one of those beams and riding it like a bullet through a gun barrel.

Escape continued to promise much. It promised freedom from ancient wars and genealogies. It promised ignorance. Now that he had answers, he wished he had none. And, escape promised safety from the beast that pursued him.

There was nowhere to turn for guidance in this. Sam and Papaya were dead. Theresa seemed to know everything, but spun as many riddles as answers. She had held much from him over the course of the past weeks. The Historian was not much better. Jacob had learned how to deal with him, but the creature was now likely dead. Chang had known something, but was also dead.

Jacob thought of Isabella. At first, he was not sure. Theresa had intended that union. But Isabella had been kind to him. She had cared for him and apologized to him. Her answers, though just as confusing as Theresa's, came from experiences like his. She had gone from knowing nothing to understanding. She had gone that distance in service to powers that she did not fully comprehend. She and Jacob had much in common. He was certain of it, and wanted to know more about her.

The notion of rescuing her filled him with warmth as he stared at the ruined tower through the cold black iron fence. He felt safer when he imagined her at his side.

He turned, walking further down Oceanview, peering into alleys and dark doorways for soldiers and agents, for uniformed police. He was now ignoring the crowd, so many sheep babbling and trotting around him. Ignoring them made him less conspicuous. He relaxed his shoulders and allowed his head to rise. The shadow of his Stetson rose above his mouth. If he were not so dirty, he thought, he would be invisible.

His thoughts were free to turn to more practical matters. Hunger. But first, the money. The Viking Hotel was not far ahead. He knew that there would be vendors there. Across the street, he had a stash of money under a tuft of grass behind one of the Jewish cemetery's oldest tombstones. There, a small box of cheap metal, enameled blue and pink with the design of a samurai, wax pressed into all of the hinges and seams, could hold as much as a hundred dollars. So, his course of action was clear. Retrieve the money. Feed himself.

Rescue Isabella.

The crowd thickened around him as he neared the intersection with his own street.

Pedestrians were not interested in him, he realized, but in a young Portuguese boy hawking newspapers, his left foot upon a stack so high that his knee was jammed into his chin. He was a poor, thin specimen. He had so much ink on him from carting those papers that he was almost as dirty as Jacob.

The boy shouted, "Police sketch Forsythe suspect! Read it here! Millionaire's killer still on the loose! Read all about it!"

A throng now surrounded him. Many purchased papers and that boy, smiling, handed each customer one copy and shouted it all again. Jacob looked over the shoulder of one of these servants to the kings and queens on the cliff, a doctor or lawyer, and saw his own face sketched in artistic detail, Stetson and all. He saw the headline: "Murderer at large!" Beneath it in bold, across several columns, "Man linked to dozens of grisly murders." He saw Chang's name in the print, and Rutledge's.

Jacob looked about. No one saw him yet. They all jockeyed for position about that boy, and all were consumed. It would only be seconds. Without thinking, he reached to his Stetson and pulled it from his head, plunged it into the side of his denim coat and hugged it close with his arm.

He moved back through the crowd, between gatherers who had not yet seen the picture.

There were police on the corner.

A knot of soldiers were climbing his street, coming this way, bayonets fixed to their carbines.

Attention swirled all around him, looking for him, hoping to settle upon him and light him up like a star. Mother would find him. The beast would see him.

He gasped for breath and stumbled down the street. People began to look at him. He was panicked, deranged, a moment's curiosity.

Beside the hotel, a dark alley promised safety for at least a moment. Perhaps a trap, he thought. It might open to the edge of his own neighborhood, or it might end against the old brick wall that marked one of the city's original boundaries. But the promise of cool stone against his cheek was overwhelming.

He fell into the alley, bile rising in his throat and sweat beading on his neck and back. Saliva dripped from his mouth to the garbage that caked on the ground. He stayed there, leaning against his knees and recovering for several seconds as the crowd passed. The thought of their smell stoked his nausea. The funk of the garbage at his feet, the stench of urine and rot, did not bother him. It was the smell of their perfume.

As if it helped, he thought. As if any of that preening helped.

He stood, pushing his back against the brick wall. The cold of it reached through his coat. It felt good.

Horses' hooves clop-clapped on the cobblestone beyond the alley. They were fast. Bells rang. It was police or firefighters bound for the ruckus that rumbled at the laundry, far up the street.

Movement caught his attention from the corner of the alley. There was a deep growl as a shape unfurled, there. Jacob squinted. It was one of the dregs, or something worse. Jacob could see little but the giant shadow, darker than the darkness around it. It spread its arms wide, its claws screeching against the bricks on either side of the alley, and roared with a sound that caused the iron fire escapes to creak and ring. The beast arched, bared long teeth and threw its feet forward, one then the other. It entered a shaft of light from a small window. The creature's ears and snout were snub and scarred, bristling with thick hairs. Blood and mud clotted at the base of those shafts. Its breath filled the alley, clouding it with fog that stank like the fetid muck of the swamp. The beast ducked from the light and shut its black eyes, growling louder and lower, but continued to approach.

Jacob's heart beat faster. Fear flared in his gut. The mantid squirmed and shot something into his blood, something that filled him with a teeth-gnashing, frantic urge to run. His vision went gray, with a tunnel of bright light leading his path out of the alley and into the crowd.

But he knew this would not help. He knew this beast.

Its will and its sight now filled him, as it had in his dreams. The mantid curled, the sharp tips of its barbed legs digging into the top of his spine. The world fell away. The gray went to brown and black. The buildings became ruins. The crowd disappeared, replaced by an army of shambling corpses, their flesh peeling in strips from their dry white bones. The smell of the alley, the stench of the perfume, fled before a howling wind of sulfur.

Howling. It was wind, but also the beast.

The thing was almost upon him. It leaped to attack. Jacob spun and ran into the street, dodging the dead. They did not notice him, but walked east, tripping on chunks of the sidewalk and broken cobblestones in the street. Their eye sockets were empty. Their mouths hung open, but made no sound. The millions of fat blue flies that clotted in their slimy wounds droned as one, hanging upon a vibrating note so low that the grit and grime of the broken city danced.

The growling was behind him, again. He ran, dodging the dead and blocks of fallen facade, finally breaking into the square of the Mystery Tower. Instead of that squat round tower, however, Jacob saw a massive structure of confusing lines, jutting shelves, and spearing buttresses. The design of it seemed intentionally disorienting, a textbook in otherworldly geometry, built to channel his terror and pain into the sky. Squinting, he could make out its pinnacle in the red and gray clouds. It was the tower and it, the cannon he had imagined earlier, shot a pillar of droning energy into the stars. Jacob now heard nothing but the hum of this force. The clumsy footfalls of the dead, the growling of the beast, the wind, the flies—all of these sounds had ceased. The buildings of the square had all collapsed, kneeling to this weapon and the power it channeled from the belly of the planet.

It all shifted. There was a wail as the air was ripped from the Earth. A bright blue and white light framed every shape and flared.

"You all right?"

Jacob turned to the voice.

The stars were bright. The crowd had gone. The beast, which he sensed as still watching from the dark, had receded for now.

An old man with a single tooth looked down at him. Jacob was kneeling, panting.

More wrinkles crisscrossed the man's cheeks than Jacob had ever seen on a single person, more than he had seen on Sam or the shaman in the Chihuahuan Desert. The man's skin was like crumbled parchment. He had a bushy white beard dropping from his chin.

The old man extended his hand. Jacob took it, nearly pulling the man over.

"Do you need something?" the old man asked.

He brought out a piece of bread and a slice of stinking cheese. It smelled like his breath.

Jacob had bought cheese from this man before.

"Go on," the man urged. "They'll arrest you for vagrancy if you stay too much longer."

Jacob stood and bowed his head in thanks. Blood filled his forehead and pounded against the insides of his ears. The mantid twitched, waking from its fright.

Jacob turned, stumbling back up Oceanview.

"Isabella," he said to himself.

SIXTEEN

A NEGLECTED HOUSE IS like a corpse, Jacob thought. As soon as abandonment sets in, rot begins to creep through the structure. The Larchmont estate, untended, was already becoming a ruin. There was a flow of air from within that blew a thin curtain through a hole in the drawing room window. Paint was peeling. Thorny weeds grew among the brown husks of dead autumn plants in the gardens.

This institution, the Eliza Stephens College for Women, had taken fewer students each year. It had made itself inconspicuous. Now, Mother had entered the endgame of her plan and the college was no more. Jacob did not know what it meant. Soon, however, newspaper boys would yell the abandonment up and down Oceanview, perhaps tying it to Jacob's murders.

He had resigned to ignore those things, to concentrate only upon his next steps. These were to enter the abandoned estate and rescue Isabella. Then, as he had been promised so many times, escape.

The door was already open. This did not alarm him at all. The mantid in his skull gave no warning. Indeed, it seemed to be asleep, its energy a steady buzz in the back of his thoughts.

He entered the shadowed foyer, his boots grinding dirt against the tile floor. Open French doors led into the drawing room on his left. A large staircase rose to his right.

Someone had been here. Plaques that had lined the wall were now in a pile on the floor, their inscribed gold plates—names of benefactors and accomplished graduates—stripped away, leaving ghosts of their shapes in the shellac. Here and there, end tables and shelves had empty surfaces that dust revealed had once been set with valuable trinkets.

As he walked further into the house, he discovered that the intrusion must have been opportunistic—a servant or gardener on Oceanview passing this way had taken the chance to enter and steal. Valuable things just out of view of the foyer remained untouched down the hall. But word would spread of the abandonment through neighborhoods like his. It would be a secret among those folk for just several days before someone on that cliff would turn a gaze toward the unfashionable end of Millionaire's Row, toward the darkened earth where Whitebirch had stood, and wonder at the open doors and broken windows of the Larchmont estate. The police would come, and the newspaper boys would shout.

Large double doors opened into the round great room, the room in which the Sisters had interrogated him before burrowing into the ground to join Mother. The chairs were still arrayed in the center of the room, beneath the mural on the domed ceiling.

There were several exits from this room. He turned, went back to the foyer and climbed the stairs. Jacob stopped on the landing and looked over the entrance, imagining a different time. He tried to picture students coming and going, the ceremonies of this college and its sorority. He wondered if the witches had always been here, and if the ceremonies had been arcane services to the Elders. Or, had the witches come later, infesting this place and setting their plans in motion to raise Mother from the sea and resurrect their gods?

He continued, up another flight to the end of the grand staircase and then on to a smaller servant's staircase. This led him to the dormitory hall, where the rooms were silent. He peered into one seeing the bed from which he had risen when he served Mother. The stained glass window at the end of the hall was shattered, now. Colored pellets and shards of glass spread across the floor like handfuls of gems thrown from the dead garden below. With them, curled leaves and bone-like twigs, the lingering debris of early winter, had flown from outside, from across the sea, from other continents and other worlds. It spread far down the hall. He felt the breeze that had carried this stuff. It caused the doors to creak as it shot into the house.

He climbed the stairs to Isabella's nest, walking between the crates to her bed, and found her there. She was so pale and still that he thought she might be dead. But her chest lifted, and her eyelids fluttered with the dreams that played behind them. Her skin was smooth and her hair wild on the pillow. He thought of his sister Ida at that moment. Ida, asleep, clutching a doll.

Isabella's eyes snapped open. Rather than start or scramble back from him, she smiled.

"I cannot leave," she said. "You know that I am trapped here."

"How do I rescue you?" he asked.

She sat up, rubbed her eyes and looked about the room as if her freedom were hidden among the collections, the sacks and crates, all along.

"There is a sigil somewhere in the house," she said. "Break it, and I am free."

Jacob squinted.

"How do I find it?"

"It would be visible to those with a certain kind of sight. If you do not already see it, then I cannot teach you how."

"I won't be able to see it. What if we destroyed the house?"

Isabella sat up, hugging the blanket to her bare chest beneath her armpits. She shook her head.

"Imagine different planes, different times, as separate sheets of fabric." She gestured to the blanket in her lap. "A sigil is like a pin, binding them together. The mark, the symbol itself—it is only half of the thing. The other piece exists in that other plane. To destroy a sigil, you must reach to that other plane."

Jacob closed his eyes.

"Come," she said.

He heard her rise and opened his eyes. The sheet fell from her nude body. Jacob watched her walk from him to clothes draped over the glass organ's bench. She touched the linen of a boy's shirt. Her skin was marble white and smooth. Her hips, her shoulders—the light could find no shadow over those round and graceful lines. The knuckles of her spine, however, were sharper. Their shadows, a trick of the dim lantern light, were like the sail on the back of a lizard or a great fish. He noticed two scars that marred her shoulder blades. As she maneuvered into the brown breeches and the linen shirt, that spine and those shoulder blades moved at odd angles.

"Your scars," he said.

She turned to him, her eyes in shadow. He could sense the sharpness of her pupils.

"You have more sight than you think you do," she said. "They were the first things ever taken from me, hacked away when I was young. They were the first signs that I was close to pure-blooded."

"Mother must have known."

"Of course she knew," Isabella said, almost interrupting him.

"How—?"

"A story for another time." She paused a moment, eyeing him with suspicion. "You still have a mantid in you."

"One," he said. "I don't think it's under her control."

It was the first he said it, even thought it. But it seemed to be true. The mantid had aided in his fight against her dregs.

"It compromises you," Isabella said. "It marks you, and that puts you in danger."

"Something..." he began.

He thought of the beast. It had found him. It had almost killed him in the alley.

Isabella did not let him finish the thought.

"Follow me," she said.

She turned and left the conversation, stepping away from Jacob and into the stairwell. She descended to the hallway, with Jacob in tow, stepping her bare feet carefully over the glass as she went down the hall.

"Before their transformation was complete," she said, gesturing to the dormitory rooms. "They crafted the sigil. Mother pushed the charm into another plane."

"What was it?" he asked.

"Simple. A twig from the garden."

She went to the landing, staying in shadows, looking warily for something to jump at her from the shadows, or for one of the statues to leap from its niche and crush her.

"The house is empty," Jacob said. "Looters have been here, but that's all."

She stopped and turned to him.

"There is no such thing as empty," she said. Her breath clouded in the cold between them as night fell outside. "There are so many things that can cross boundaries and look to you like they appeared from nowhere. Stay on your guard. Always."

She led him to the foyer, and down the hall to the great room. Moving to its center, she leaned against the chair that he had occupied during his interrogation. The group of chairs sat alone in the empty room. Weak gas lamps lit the bottom half of the mural—the canopy of trees above the chair rail, the clouds in the purple black sky, the stars. The zenith disappeared in darkness.

"Do you see the sigil?" she asked.

Jacob looked about, unsure of what it would be and thinking only of the giant Viking rune on the cliff. Theresa had called that a sigil, one that kept the Elder's corpse entombed or blunted another otherworldly power associated with the bay. He also remembered the jar on Forsythe's mantle. It was conspicuous, etched with strange markings. Nothing jumped out at him here.

"I don't even know what I'm looking for," he said.

Isabella closed her eyes and sighed.

"Mother taught us that there was a great temple, here. My kind were wardens. Our fight began here. And, we gathered here for safety. Our last hours. Here, together, in a great chamber beneath a dome, like this dome. The Elders' beasts slaughtered us here."

"I know that place," he said.

"No," she snapped. "You saw the corpse of that time. You saw its fossils. Remember what I said. Fabrics pinched together. That time and place exist now. They exist always alongside of us. Sigils bring them together. Mother, in her cruelty, sent the charm that imprisons me into that chaos and slaughter. The portal to that charm is here. I know it is. I saw them with the charm here."

Jacob looked about once more, seeing nothing but Isabella and the chairs, and darkness lowering over the mural, blending with dark shadows painted between the trees. A mural of a night sky over a forest, and a charm that was a twig. Mother had spun a riddle.

"If you cannot see it," Isabella said. "The mantid in you might."

"I—I don't know how to control that," he said.

"Learn."

Her command echoed through the chamber, spinning with the dome to reach the dark center far above.

He took a long breath and closed his eyes, unsure of what he would see when he opened them. He wished for a vision, for a sign, but saw only her back facing him. The baggy linen shirt made her look so young and frail, like a child.

Jacob reached deep, trying to find the mantid, but it gave no response. He thought back on when he had experienced other visions, back to the battle in the mist about the flooded schoolhouse. He thought of the vision on the hilltop, when he had seen Mother's connections and the graves of Elders. That, he realized, was a moment when saw overlapping fabrics. That was what Isabella was talking about. He had thought it might have been the smoke from the witch's fire that had caused his hallucination. He had also calmed himself and shut his eyes tight. That was all.

And one more thing.

He had remembered Ida.

Memory was the same thing. Remembering Ida, remembering anything—it was the overlap of times and planes, of another time onto now.

He opened his eyes and lurched. He was falling. There was no room, just empty space. He lost trust and put his hands before him. They smacked hard against the marble tile of the floor. He was on all fours.

"There!" she shouted. "What did you see?"

"It was gone. The room was gone."

"Yes! You are almost there!"

He looked at her, seeing the excitement mixed with concern on her face. She did want to see him in this way. She was half-stooped, reaching to him. Something behind her caught his eye. Deep in the dark of the dome, he could see the stars twinkling on the mural. He lifted himself so that he was now kneeling. He looked all around the room. His jaw dropped.

Stars everywhere.

They lit the mural, but it was not the mural. There were actual stars, or a glowing sculpture of a night sky that he did not recognize. Bright blue and yellow stars connected into constellations that he had never seen. Twisting serpentine beasts coiled. Others were shapeless to him—symbols and swirls. Another was like one of the figures on Sam's fortune teller's cards—a man hanging upside down by his feet, but not a man. This being had horns and ridges on its head, and wings spreading down from its back.

As he looked down the mural to the walls, he saw scrawling patterns, writing that made no sense. The mural's trees were covered with these signs. These figures crawled through the doors and went down the hall to the foyer. They, with the stars, lit the house in such a way that the floor itself appeared completely dark. The ballroom's floor was like a new moon in the center of a starlit sky.

"What do you see?" Isabella asked.

"Writing and stars."

She fell into one of the chairs.

"You have the mantid's sight, now."

The mantid was taking what came from his eyes, deciphering it, and feeding it back to him with information from its own senses. He turned his head and all of those glyphs and stars spun into place as the mantid worked.

This was a temple. Or had been. About him, he guessed, countless sigils guarded countless charms. The one that he needed—how could he find it amidst all of these mysterious signs? What, if anything, could that alien sky tell him? The charm was a twig, a simple thing that Mother's servants had enchanted to imprison Isabella. The sigil could be anything.

The signs were mostly geometric, some quite intricate but rough as they ran through the script, painted with a fat bristled brush by a seemingly untrained artist. The script filled him with dread though he had no way of reading it. Perhaps the mantid knew what it said. He imagined descriptions of unspeakable horrors, barbarous and vicious sacrifices.

Jacob stood and walked the walls around the great room.

"Did you find something?" Isabella asked. Her voice echoed among all of those signs, bouncing from star to star and dying in the swirling glyphs.

"It's a book," Jacob said to himself. "This place is a book."

The answers were all here, but he could not decipher them. That was no different from Theresa or Isabella or the Historian telling him their riddles. He was, again, surrounded by answers that he could not read. He closed his eyes at that thought, expecting it to bowl him over. Instead, the fact washed over him with no effect.

He had no thoughts of escape, no dread or panic in the dark behind his eyelids. It was quiet and safe.

When he opened his eyes, he was staring straight at the sigil. It was the same symbol as the college's seal, an eye above an ornate column. A rough circle surrounded the image. In the pupil of the eye, lines like runes or letters piled atop one another. He touched it. The wall felt rough.

He pushed, and it gave beneath his fingertip.

Indeed, the plaster felt damp.

"Do you have it?"

Ignoring her, looking right at that symbol in the pupil of the eye, feeling excitement well up in his body, feeling the mantid twitch with anticipation, Jacob made a fist and, hauling back, sent it through the pupil. The moment his hand broke that thin plaster, the room and the stars, the symbols and Isabella, disappeared.

Jacob was falling fast through darkness, toward a scene of chaos, blood, and panic.

SEVENTEEN

SMOKE FILLED HIS lungs. Heat, fire and blood lifted him into the dark beneath the dome. Cries punched from below. Much of the scene was obscured, but Jacob could see thuggish brutes in armor using the spears and pikes to break wings and legs, smash holes into skulls. Those beasts, ancestors of the dregs, looked up at Jacob. He crested and began falling toward the slaughter. Jacob saw the dregs shoveling the tortured creatures, their wings flapping like broken umbrellas, into a writhing mass. As the smoke parted, Jacob saw the subject of that offering.

A giant gray worm reared from its coiled length. Its entire end opened to a mouth lined with row upon row of dry, jagged teeth that marched into the dark of its gullet. Fleshy antennae surrounded its mouth and probed frantically, wrapping around one another, around the limbs and necks of the victims. This eyeless beast felt its way along the wall and the floor, the rim of its mouth quivering as it sought food. It dove into the pile of victims and reared, catching six or seven in its mouth and gyrating, forcing them to fall into its throat. Screams and cries rose above the growling of the dregs, but ceased as the worm's mouth puckered closed and spasms began to run down the translucent skin of its long body, pushing the victims through it. The slaughter must have been going for a long time, as clean bones had emerged into a pile at the tail end of the worm.

Jacob fell closer to that worm, close enough to see its skin glistening in the fire light.

Suddenly, he was aloft again, rising fast. He was spinning with the stars in the dark dome, seeing flashes of the temple's mural, its night sky and its map of deep heavens from which the Elders had come. There was a whispering voice in his ear, but he could not understand the language. Jacob turned and saw a face in the dim light. She had large, widely-set eyes and a puggish nose, like the swamp men.

Like Isabella.

But she was far more ancient. She was not drawn with the smooth lines of Isabella's body. Rather, ridges ran the crest of her skull and protruded from above her eyes.

He felt now her arms hugging his chest. Bare breasts pressed against his back. Wings beat behind her.

She had lifted him. She had seen him falling and rose from the slaughter, not to break herself against the dome in futile attempts to escape, but to lift him. She knew why he was here. She spoke and held him there, her warm breath a calming thing on the back of his neck.

The worm balled the terror from its whole length into its tail and shot it forward in a horrid bellow. The dome, the sky of all past and future beyond, threatened to explode with that force. Jacob could see his rescuing angel's face wince at the sound.

The sigil. Jacob remembered. The charm was here.

He looked left and right. His shifting was unexpected and his rescuer tilted and twisted, saying something sharp in his ear. He moved with more care after that. She turned as he turned, to help him see.

Jacob focused on the edges of the dome. Ribs of rough stone shot to its apex, which was lost in darkness. A shelf ran the entire circumference, separating the sacrifice that went on below from the map of stars that spun slowly, lazily above it all. Grotesque gargoyles leaned into the space from that shelf, grinning, relishing what their stone eyes beheld. Each beast was unique but he saw in many the wings of the poor victims, in others the eyes of humans, in others bodies of chimps, tails of dogs. The Elders, in this temple, paid homage to their own creations.

One, however, was not a creature at all. A globe, an eye, sat atop a decorated pedestal. Its stone iris stared at him. He pointed. She, leaning, glided forward. She dipped below the statue and beat her wings to rise until Jacob was looking right into that eye.

Below, the dregs exploded in laughter as another group of her kind entered the room. The monsters set upon them, smashing their wings. Many of the dregs had disrobed. As the victims entered, the dregs parted their legs, violating and breaking them. He saw one, a child, lifting above that group. One dreg's thick arm, the sweat and blood on its green leathery skin glistening, shot above the crowd, gripping the boy by the leg and whipping him down, smashing his head against the floor. His body went limp and lifeless. The dreg tossed the corpse like so much garbage to the sacrificial heap.

Jacob shut his eyes and, after a moment, after a whisper from his angel, turned and looked at the statue before him. There was something on the pedestal, in the shadow of the eye. She drifted forward as Jacob reached.

The twig.

It was no longer than his hand, and was thin and curved like a child's rib. As his fingertips touched upon it, his angel lurched.

They bounced on a billow of hot, fetid air. Jacob, looking back, saw panic in her eyes. Below, the gaping mouth of the worm rose to them. It had felt them in the air and it, neglecting all below for the moment, sought them. Its antennae waved all about, whipping their legs. Blowholes riddling the skin behind its antennae quivered and shook. The air reversed as the worm inhaled. The two began to fall, though the angel beat her wings furiously.

Jacob brushed his hand against the stone as he went by the pedestal. The twig went free, floating for a moment in the air between him and the stone as they fell. He clasped his hands together, taking the charm.

She let him go, wrapping her wings about her so that she was a bullet into the worm's mouth. Jacob lost her among those teeth. She, who in the midst of her race's destruction, knew that she could affect a vengeance, was now gone.

He hurtled toward her fate, taking the twig into one hand and clenching his fist around it. He felt it snap into several pieces.

The smoke, the chaos and blood, the death breath of the worm, disappeared.

Jacob fell upon the marble floor of the Larchmont estate's great room, his cheek flat against the cold and bits of that broken twig scattered in front of his face.

Isabella was upon him. She pulled him up by the shoulders and held him across the chest, just as the angel had held him aloft in the temple in this place, eons before. She held him as he looked at his hands. The indentations in his skin from that twig went red for a moment and disappeared. He clenched his fist several times. She held him so hard the he could barely breathe.

"I am free," she whispered into his ear, again and again.

Isabella moved with slow, fluid steps through the foyer. She stopped at the door, perhaps unsure that her escape was possible. She looked to Jacob, who managed a smile before reaching for the knob himself. Together, they turned the knob and pulled open the door.

The night was calm and quiet. Thin scraps of clouds ran in front of the crescent moon, becoming like bolts of exotic gold cloth as they passed before it. The stars were bright markers in the sky, milestones on a trail that Jacob imagined would take him from here, through space to wherever this had all begun. The dead, forgotten home of the Elders. Or, to the heart of their enemy's empire. It would be far from Jamesport, far from the beast that now chased him. Texas and Ida—all of it would be far behind. The Old God would be a secret, a memory.

Lost in this thought, he missed Isabella stepping down the stairs. She was on the walkway, the gaslight lamps shining through her thin shirt. She was unsteady at first, bracing herself with arms outstretched for punishment. But the night remained silent. She took several more steps forward.

All was well.

Jacob joined her, rushing to her side and gripping her arm.

"It is true," she said, laughing.

"How long were you imprisoned?" he asked.

She did not answer. Her faced turned sour and her vision turned to the ground.

"No," she said. "No."

"What is it?"

She looked about. The breeze fell from the shooting clouds, warmer than it should have been. It had dipped into the bay and brought a whiff of that funk across the cliff. She lifted her feet as she might if the ground were hot. Jacob imagined unseen things running between her legs, circling her ankles.

The cliff rumbled. There was a flash over the bay, a moment of silence, and another rumble.

Isabella looked at him, her face knit into frustration and confusion. She sighed and turned, rushing across the lawn and into the street. He went after her, unsure of what was happening.

She was free. Nothing stopped her as she ran into the grass on the other side of Oceanview. She dodged stones and bushes, running at such speed that Jacob worried they would both launch themselves from the edge of the cliff.

Another flash, and the cliff shook once more. Jacob had to stop to steady himself. The ground went still after just seconds. He ran to catch up to her.

Isabella stopped, standing at the furthest edge of the cliff. Jacob saw her in the next flash, and dug his heels into the gravel and dirt. He fell back, landing on his elbows and sliding several yards forward. His feet dangled over the cliff. One more step and he would have fallen.

She looked left and right. Another flash, from the bay. The cliff face to their right exploded.

"What's happening?" Jacob asked.

Isabella dropped to her knees.

"The dregs," she said.

Two more flashes from their cannon answered, revealing the corsairs arrayed in line to send broadsides to the cliff face. A moment passed as those reports reached them, immediately drowned by the cracking explosion in the stone.

"They destroy the runes," Isabella said. "They are freeing something."

Jacob blinked.

"A sigil," he whispered. "They need to destroy the other piece."

"Those are ancient creatures," she said. "They know what they need to do. We have to leave the city."

"I can't leave."

He said it before he had completely realized it. The moment of escape had finally arrived, but this truth jumped like the beast of the plains from the shadow. Perhaps the mantid knew it, or a flash of intuition made him see it.

"What do you mean?" she asked.

"Sam once told me... He said that I belong to him."

She closed her eyes.

"No," she said.

"He said it was written in stone on his wall. He woke and saw it on the wall. I'm bound to him, he said."

Isabella shook her head. Jacob looked into the bay, where another flash of light reached across the bay.

"I'm trapped," he said. "Just like you were."

"You are." Isabella opened her eyes and looked at him. "You freed me. Now, free yourself."

Jacob did not realize that *M'Lass* was gone until after he and Isabella had scrambled atop the stone shelf in front of Sam's cave. They had crossed the city through alleys and thin, maze-like streets as old as the settlement itself. The two waited near the wharf as the tide receded, and then went their way up the beach. They reached the cave just as the sun began to rise over a ridge of clouds.

He had walked by the emptiness of that spot, the place where *M'Lass* had beached. That emptiness nagged at him as he went, though he was not sure what the feeling was. On the shelf in front of Sam's cave, as he lent a hand to Isabella who rose on the slippery stones right behind him, he looked at the pinks and purples of the new day's eastern horizon. His gaze went to Isabella's dark eyes and he realized that the schooner was gone. He nearly let go of Isabella in his shock.

"What is it?" she asked.

He held both of her hands in his right palm and pointed with his left hand. She turned to look as she steadied her stance on the shelf.

"I do not see anything," she said. "The sunrise and the wharf."

"That's it," he said. "There was a ship beached here."

He stared, thinking that he saw the ghostly outline of the schooner. It was just an illusion of memory.

She seemed unsure of what to do with that fact. Indeed, she shrugged and turned to the cave.

"Do you have any sense of where the sigil might be?"

"Don't you understand?" he asked.

She stopped and turned.

"The ship is gone," she said. "A storm took it away."

"She was here just the other night," he said. "I was aboard. Tinker was there."

He expected her to ask questions, and was thankful when she did not. Distrust flooded over him, and he was unsure if he would want to tell her where he and Theresa had gone, how she had led him to a haven, the key to which hid in a wooden charm.

Isabella turned and entered several yards into the cave. She stood at the edge of the rising sun's feeble orange light, her breath clouding in front of her.

"Do you..." she started, but it was much too loud. She lowered her voice. "Do you know where it is?"

Jacob stepped forward, joining her. The sounds of his boots echoed throughout the cave. Each touch of that sound seemed to release a memory from that rock. Sam's laugh. A baby crying. Chopping wood. The pop of wet wood in the fire.

"He said he woke, and it was there."

"But where?" she asked. She let it go loud, perhaps wanting the cave to hear her.

The sun's light became brighter and stronger, reaching almost as far back as the tunnels from the sewers. Jacob squinted into the cave and saw the pale fungal glow of the ramp. He started to notice remnants. He saw scraps of cloth and lumps of coal.

These could have been from any time and, with the tide, perhaps from anywhere.

Isabella stayed, but Jacob began to move deeper into the cave, gripping the tops of the stalagmites as he went. Part of him feared that a wind would rush into the cave and carry him down the ramp to where the bodies had been.

At that thought, a sound rose from below.

"What was that?" Isabella asked.

It was simple and quiet at first. He wondered if it had been there all along. It started to grow in volume and intensity—so many things clicking and rustling. It was like the rush of spirits through the frozen willow fronds behind the Forsythe mansion.

"I don't know," he yelled. His voice bounced from wall to wall and fell down the ramp to lose itself in the rising sound.

Jacob turned, walking deeper into the cave, now hearing scraps of voices in that din rising from the bottom of the ramp. He heard syllables of ancient spells, shrieks of witches on Executioner's Rock, and the banal babbling of children playing in the shadow of the mystery tower. He heard the laughter of crones, the slurred shouts of the drunken men of the bar. He imagined them propositioning the barmaid and they were gone, replaced by a second of Papaya's accent as she stirred gumbo.

He heard Ida's cry falling into the canyon.

Shaking his head clear, Jacob moved further into the cave. He could feel Isabella's apprehension and concern. She was worried about herself in this noise, to be sure. But he also sensed that she was worried about him. He had, after all, rescued her. And now he wandered beyond the sunlight, deeper into the dark of the cave. Her worry for losing him was as palpable to him as the vibration in the air.

Jacob found beds—half a dozen piles of sailcloth and hay. They lined one wall and still showed indentations of those who had slept in them. He looked at the wall behind them and saw nothing.

But there was a hum. It was a droning note that set his teeth vibrating. It filled the spaces within the clicks and rustling from below. He looked about, and saw it. Crystal arms reached from the ceiling and crossed into a familiar arrangement above the foot of the beds. The fungal glow twisted with the orange sunlight to set an image within those girders of glass. Lines and swirls, characters of a forgotten alphabet, joined into the shape of a man hanging by his foot.

It was one of Sam's cards. The Hanged Man.

And the hum came from those crystal beams as they vibrated in the noise, in the light, in Isabella's concern. The tone deepened, setting the grit on the floor to run and scamper like drops of water on a hot skillet. His eyes ached and the animal brain in the base of his skull, the mantid there, were both paralyzed. Worms of light swirled at the edges of his vision. The fluid in his stomach boiled. The air fled his lungs.

This was the sigil. This was his prison.

He stepped forward, wavering like a drunkard. The crystals' drone grew louder until it was all that he heard. He was conscious of nothing else.

Reaching forward, he touched the smooth flat glass. The vibration filled his hand and shot up his arm. It popped through the sinews of his shoulder and set his mind spinning.

For one second, it stopped. In that second, he heard the tunnel erupt below. A cloud spewed from the top of the ramp and Isabella screamed.

With a beautiful note, an angelic chord, the crystals shattered into dust that fell like a shimmering wall in front of him. It filled his mouth and his nostrils. It blasted his eyes.

Jacob fell back to the beds and, opening his eyes, found himself in a different time and place.

EIGHTEEN

THE SOUNDS OF slaughter reached him through stone and
steel. They seemed distant, as if reflected off of the flat face
of the moon from an equally far place. But it happened in the
temple not far from this floor upon which he lay. Jacob knew
that the worm, the armored dregs, the angel who had carried
him into the dome were all close. He felt them through rock.

His fingertips traced the seams between stones. In this way, he
guessed, the mantid imagined the floor through his touch. It saw
the patterns of lines that were so haphazard as to seem without
architecture, like the stones on the shelf in front of Sam's cave.

These were those stones. Under Sam's feet, they had been
chipped and weathered, heaved to different levels by storms and
time. They were so flat and polished now that Jacob stared into
the reflection of his own eye.

Metal implements clinked. Jacob squinted and pushed
himself to his elbows, unable to deny that it was a pleasant
sound. Not far, the giant worm devoured bodies. The panic of
that was in the air, though he heard nothing of it since lifting his
face from the floor. The metal implements sounded again, far
down the hall that ran in front of him. It was not pleasant this
time, but hurried and frustrated.

Jacob stood and immediately began to waver. He could not
walk straight. Indeed, he could not even see far ahead of him.

He pulled his hands into fists and felt sharp pain in his left palm. Something was there, digging into his skin with sharp points. He relaxed his fist and the pain subsided.

Jacob was in a hallway of dark gray stone polished bright like marble. Every few slanting steps through vertigo, he passed doorways into dark cells. There, imprisoned beasts that made noises through open throats and rows of teeth. Their tongues lashed through the air, smacking against invisible fields that separated them from him. He saw different types, different colors and sizes. Some had shoulders wider than twice the width of their torsos. Others had mouths in their necks. They were in various states of consciousness, various stages of construction. The more feral scratched at the barrier. The more thoughtful stared from the darkness of corners. One raised its eyebrows, perhaps wondering if Jacob had escaped from a cell himself.

The hallway was narrow, and slanted in such a way that the dregs would not have been able to pass easily. They simply would not have fit. It widened to reveal cells with larger creatures. Some were formless heaps of jelly with hairs that twitched, sensing his approach. Several appeared like the beast of the plain, the beast that pursued him in his visions.

The noises ahead continued—metal implements. There was bright light around a corner and shadows playing against the wall. Jacob thought of approaching carefully, but his imbalance threw him against that wall. Looking into the room, he saw that the creature there had noticed him.

It was like a man, but stretched to eight or nine feet, its limbs very thin and its chest almost flat. The creature's drawn face had few features. It regarded Jacob through broad eyes set far apart and pursed lips.

It reminded Jacob of the Historian.

The creature worked at a table with shining metal tools upon a mound of coarse hair and muscle, a beast splayed open, its long arms falling so that its knuckles brushed the floor. The beast's chest moved slowly up and down as it breathed in a wheezing, raspy effort. A dog, a bear, and a man—it was the beast of Jacob's visions.

Jacob could see the decisions of its design. Its arms and legs were capable of a far reach. Curled, barbed claws made a snare of that reach. No prey could escape. The powerful, piled muscles of the beast's limbs promised incredible speed. The snout, open, was hinged far back in its skull. Its purple tongue draped over multiple rows of sharp teeth. Its eyes were close in the front. Peripheral vision did not matter. It was a monster of forthright, direct attack. Its speed, its long reach, its wide mouth that, when open, split its entire head—it could outrun and consume anything.

It was coming for him.

The tall creature's arms glistened with the beast's blood. The creature passed curious glances to Jacob as it reached for quivering mounds of flesh in a pan, placing each mound into the open gut of the beast.

Jacob leaned as his vision twisted and tilted. Sweat poured onto his skin to cool his dizziness. He could not move, but simply stared, barely able to concoct the notion of moving. He was able to understand that this creature was building the beast, filling it with power and life, blood and organs. Jacob shuddered and insisted the mantid take him back to Isabella. The beast would wake and it would kill him. The pain sharpened in his left palm as he squeezed tighter and tighter.

The mantid refused to do anything.

Jacob opened his palm and looked.

A medallion. Gold. It was a star. It was the star from his father's holster.

It took several seconds of staring to form the thought, but Jacob knew. This was the charm. This was his imprisonment.

Lost decades ago, it sat now in Jacob's palm, its points drawing blood from his flesh.

The creature lifted its arms and bellowed like a church organ. Tubes snaked from the ground into the beast, then stiffened and darkened with blood and fluid. The beast began to quiver.

Long smooth steps brought the creature to the hallway. It knelt before Jacob, squeezing his arms and poking at his chest. It cocked its head and narrowed its eyes, considering Jacob's construction. Gripping the wall, it pulled itself into the hallway. It was too tall for the space, but its legs bent and it lowered its torso like an insect. It turned to look down the hallway, perhaps looking for an empty cell for Jacob.

Scanning Jacob up and down, it saw the medallion in his bloody palm. The creature moved its gaze between that star and Jacob's eyes. With a long finger and thumb, it pinched the medallion from Jacob's palm. He could not protest.

The creature reentered its room, standing tall. It set the star on the table and, taking a mallet, drove a sharp probe through the center of the thing.

Explosions and screams, calamity sounded outside.

Jacob felt the world opening. He felt weight falling from him.

As the creature looked through the hole in that star and smiled at Jacob, it placed the medallion in the gut of the beast and began to sew the carcass closed.

Jacob slid to the floor. That world fell away.

He was back in Sam's cave. Isabella stood with her hands against her cheeks.

She was screaming.

Jacob sat against the cold stone wall. His vision was cloudy but clearing. He heard everything from a distance, but felt the vibration of the noise below. It was such a force that his teeth chattered and his bones cracked.

He shook his head, trying to wake his own senses and the mantid. It only made things cloudier. He rubbed his eyes and boxed his ears, but nothing helped. His tongue felt fat in his mouth. He tried to swallow, and this simple act set responses in his body in motion that, inch by inch, brought him back to this cave. His ears popped and the sound flooded in. His eyes cleared further with each blink. The mantid stirred.

Isabella screamed from amidst a roar of sound. Her voice was silent. She stood, unable to move on the other side of a low stone formation. Her hands were covering her ears. She struggled to catch her breath between banshee shrieks.

He saw movement to his left, wrapping around the end of the stone that separated him from Isabella. It was like black tar, pouring from the top of the ramp and rolling across the floor to smash against the opposite wall. It had filled the back of the cave from floor to ceiling and spilled now toward the mouth, toward the ocean.

Now, it was upon him. It poured over his legs.

It was not molten or liquid. Indeed, it scratched him. Bits of it rose about his face, humming.

Jacob blinked one more time and swallowed once more.

It was a flood of mantids from the depths, released by the dregs' assault on the sigil.

Isabella fell from view as the tide overcame her. Its chirping and clicking filled the cave, though the cliff had no hope of containing it. That noise threatened to blow the stone to the sky, to every corner of the earth.

The mantid in his brain was silent against it.

Jacob stood. Looking left, he saw the wall of them falling upon itself toward him. The mouth of the cave was still far to his right. The sun had risen above the top lip of the cave's mouth. Though the ground shook—bits of rock and dried seaweed danced and vibrated in that sunlight—it seemed like an unreal other world, still untouched. He knew that they had seconds, if even that, to reach that world, to reach the beach.

This was the beginning of Mother's new world.

Jacob lunged forward. His feet slipped as they crushed the mantids beneath them. His knee smashed against the stone that separated him from Isabella. He gripped that low wall and pulled himself forward, finding solid footing just long enough for him to dive into the current again. He flung his arms through that growing tide. The mantids scratched at him. Their needles plunged into his skin but quickly withdrew. Their kin in his brain convulsed, seizing against their song.

Isabella's hand shot above the tide and grabbed at nothing, gripped by panic. Jacob pulled at her wrist, yanking her free. She gasped as she pulled the mantids from her hair. She bore their scratches across her cheeks and arms. They avoided her once they had tasted her, but her flowing blood continued to tempt them.

"Out!" he shouted.

The noise was too great. She heard nothing as her breath heaved. He pushed her toward the mouth of the cave until they stepped from the teeming edge of the tide. Jacob turned and saw that there was no more cave. The wall of mantids surged forward. The air outside was full of them as they took flight in the sun.

They fell to their knees in their rush forward, covering themselves in the slime of the burst mantids. Isabella emerged first and fell upon the stone shelf. She turned and tried to take Jacob's outstretched arm. Their hands could not lock, sliding apart.

The flood had reached his feet. He felt panic rising. He was flailing. Though they would not consume him, they pulled at him.

Isabella's grip slid down his forearm, locking against his

bunched sleeve at his wrist. She braced her feet against the stone and shouted at the sky that clouded with the insects.

Jacob lurched forward, rising into a clumsy run and grabbing Isabella under her shoulders. He dragged her until her feet found their stride. The two ran from the shelf to the wet sand below, to the edge of the cold ocean.

They waded into the gentle surf, the slime rising into oily slicks around them. The flood exploded from the cave's mouth behind them. It snaked in all directions, took flight, climbed against the cliff face, spread out upon the beach. Millions of the creatures entered this world from their burial, from eons of dark imprisonment in the rock. Their clicking, their celebration of chirping at the end of their hunger, woke the men and women of the mansions, of the wharf, of the Portuguese neighborhoods.

Isabella shrieked with surprise.

Forms surrounded him, grabbing and lifting him into a boat.

He twisted, seeing Isabella beside him and peasants of the swamp all around him. Rising to his knees, he gathered his senses as they rowed him away from the shore.

Not far, *M'Lass* was afloat, listing without mast or sail.

Jacob sat in a splintery chair on the berthing deck of an ironclad. She had an unpronounceable name that rolled in the back of the swamp dwellers' throats.

Six of these vessels surrounded *M'Lass*. A seventh towed her with a heavy chain from which curls and clumps of dark green seaweed waved in the ocean breeze. Jacob recognized these vessels, having seen their type in books. Most of their hulls hung below the water, with the decks rising a single tall step above the surface. A round cheese box of a turret and the top of an armored wheelhouse drew the only profile the boat offered.

The turret spun, bringing the smooth bore barrels of two large cannon to bear upon whatever target the captain determined. Vessels of this type had fought in the war, one rather famously in Virginia.

Jacob stared through twisted short hammocks that hung in waving arcs like cobwebs all about the cabin. The oil lamp on the table in front of him cast their shadows against the lockers.

Twenty or thirty hammocks, he guessed. Swamp men. Their cook shouted at the galley in the cabin behind Jacob. The stove would not light. Above him, a great gear and hissing motor spun the turret wildly as the gunners practiced what seemed to be difficult procedures for aiming the two cannon. Beyond that hiss, those guttural curses and shouts, the clanking hum of the screw spun steady and loud in the aft half of the vessel.

Isabella stepped into the light and approached Jacob, ducking through the swaying hammocks. The orange lamplight sent shadows across her face. For a moment, those shadows made ridges above her eyes, like her ancient kin. As she leaned toward him, however, he saw the smoothness of her skin. No salt air would allow such skin for long. Her brown eyes lost their urgency as they looked at Jacob.

Jacob asked no questions. He picked at the grain of the table, lifted and lowered his gaze. She would tell him. He knew.

"These seven ships come from our brothers. There is an island. It sits well outside of the currents. It is meant to be missed and forgotten. There, our last colony and these ships guard another world from the dregs."

"We're escaping?"

Isabella shook her head. Jacob felt a tinge of disappointment, but escape had been promised and sought so many times without result that the truth largely just passed through him.

"The opposite," she said. "We go to battle. Each of these ships carries thirty men. Two cannon. They mean to attack to dregs in the bay. The captain does not expect to return. He says that this will be the end of us, but he means to take the dregs with him."

She looked to the table, to the light of the lamp that flickered over the soft wood grain.

"Theresa has been captured. The dregs found her. They captured her, and killed everyone."

"The Historian," Jacob said.

"He was probably already dead." She paused. "The secret of resurrection is now in Mother's reach. She will raise the Elder in the bay."

Two shafts of light fell behind her as hatches opened on the deck above. They revealed wooden ladders amidst the swaying hammocks. A round face, the face of a swamp dweller, appeared in the open hatch and shouted into the hold. The flame in the lamp wavered at the sound of that rough voice. Isabella shouted back, a single syllable that Jacob did not believe he could make no matter how hard he tried to swallow his tongue. She moved to the nearest ladder, donned a peacoat and began to climb.

Jacob followed, his back and legs protesting. The mantid shifted and seemed to grumble. His whole body, including the parasite, was content to stay put. Sitting, resting—these were long overdue.

"Hurry!" Isabella called from the deck.

Jacob shook his head hard, hoping to torture the mantid, perhaps to send it flying from one of his ears. Rather, it released noise into his mind, forcing his sight to go brilliant white for a moment before clearing, though leaving scintillating edges to everything for several seconds. He thought of the hanged man sigil, of his imprisonment which was now over, but which still seemed to plague him.

"I'm not free," he said. "I serve one master after another."

"Jacob!"

He closed his eyes for one second and stood, forcing himself forward and up the ladder. On the deck, the wind immediately gripped him. He pulled his soiled denim coat closed with one hand and gripped his Stetson with the other. Choppy waves spilled over the edge of the deck, the wind blowing their foamy tops into a mist that bit into Jacob's face. The deck, though inhospitable, was busy with activity as the crew of swamp men ran to various stations, preparing the vessel for battle. Aft of the turret, they unhooked a temporary smoke stack and sent it below. The engine churned, sending coal smoke in rhythmic shots through the open vent. The smoke rose just inches into the air before the wind caught it, twisting it into nothing.

Ropes secured the lifeboat to the deck of the ironclad. Behind the lifeboat, Tinker stood as a statue, chained to cleats arranged around him. This was not to restrain him. Rather, he was chained much as the lifeboat was tied, so that wind and waves would not carry him away. The swamp men ran about him like he was not even there, with no fear of what he might do.

"Look!"

Isabella pointed. Jacob followed her gesture to the cliff. He did not recognize the land at first. Whirls of fog in dark ribbons obscured the view. He realized, though, that these were not fog at all, but swarms of mantids. Beyond them, veins in the cliff moved.

"The worms are free," Isabella said.

An officer of the vessel offered binoculars to Jacob. He took these, peered through and saw the clouds of mantids. Multitudes of worms, like the great worm he had seen in the ancient cave of slaughter, covered the cliff face. Their antennae probed the rock all about them. Their mouths gripped that stone, taking huge chunks of it into their gullets and forcing the rock through their bodies. Jagged lumps of stone pressed on their shimmering, translucent skin from within.

The officer was speaking as Jacob watched the monsters climb the cliff toward Jamesport's castles. Clouds of mantids already obscured the sky over the town.

"Jamesport is doomed," Isabella said.

Jacob closed his eyes and felt the world rocking. There was a hot wind on his face, and a sulfurous stench burning the hairs in his nostrils. The ironclad was gone. The mantid in his brain quivered. Jacob was in a row boat, sitting on a board. His wrists were shackled beneath his knees. Sweat and grime covered his body. Gangly creatures with oblong heads and loose gray skin rowed in a rhythm that seemed mechanical. They had no mouths, only thin, long nostrils and luminescent eyes. Gnarled hands fused with oars that looked like bones, femurs from a long-extinct striding giant. With each stroke, the rowers snorted and squinted in pain. A cloaked figure stood at the fore, half living and half a statue against the prow. Jamesport burned before them, its fires reflecting in the still black water of the sea. Bright souls shot into the sky and exploded against a low ceiling of clouds. Cracks in the cliff revealed the ancient, reborn city of the Elders, the millions of years since that fall were merely a chrysalis that now fell away, a husk to be discarded and forgotten.

He opened his eyes, and was again peering through the binoculars at the worms on the cliff. Feeling nauseous, he braced himself against Isabella.

"What happened to Theresa?" he asked.

"They took her. It is too late for her. She had done much, well beyond what had been asked of her."

The officer beside them, the captain of this vessel, shouted and pointed. The turret spun with a grating, chilling noise of metal scraping upon metal. The gunports trained on the mouth of the bay. There, two black corsairs emerged from a swirling cloud of mantids. Unholy wind filled their sails. Jacob thought he could hear the rigging creak, the monstrous men of the deck shouting and hooting. They were bearing down on the squadron of ironclads.

The captain beckoned them aft, where sailors led them into the lifeboat. Isabella pulled Jacob after her. Three of the swamp men joined them. All curled into the lifeboat and covered their heads as the ironclad's engine ramped into a fast, deafening roar. The ironclad turned toward the dreg corsairs, joining the others in a headlong attack.

One of the corsairs turned to offer broadsides. Jacob, rising, saw the flashes before hearing the reports. Isabella tried to pull him down into the life boat, but Jacob stiffened. Several of the shots landed near them, sending slicing icy spray into Jacob's face. The ironclad beside them shuddered with a direct hit. The turret exploded, sending a column of fire straight into a cloud of mantids, which swung and dispersed only to recollect closer to shore.

"What are we doing?" Jacob yelled.

"We must make it into the bay," Isabella shouted. "We must—"

The lifeboat jolted to one side, silencing her. Jacob turned to see black wood, marred and scarred with centuries of war, plastered in thick patches with barnacles. A corsair was upon them, aiming to ram them. He saw dregs' eyes on the deck and in the portholes, the red gleaming that burned in the back of that sight. He saw the giants themselves, clothed in scraps and strips, covered in refuse that had clung to them as they rose from the dead silt at the bottom of the deepest ocean trenches. They were nothing but that red sight beneath that refuse. The dregs had once had form. He had seen their ancestors in the slaughter of the temple. But now they were disembodied rage serving

Mother, corrupting the corpses of lost sailors and other beasts, gathering flesh and flotsam to their frames.

The corsair's bow rammed the ironclad, crushing the turret like a tin can. One of the ironclad's cannon managed a wild shot that ran the length of the corsair, flying far wide of the hull.

The life boat tipped, several of its ropes snapping. It slid from the tilting deck into the violent waves. Jacob and several of the sailors lifted over the prow to see the corsair pass over the remains of the ironclad, which bubbled and sank. Tinker was now awake, still chained to the deck. He pulled at those chains, straining their links against one another as he disappeared into the water. His whining went to gurgling and roiling bubbles as he disappeared from view.

The corsair went on, its sails dipping before filling again, sending the ship faster toward *M'Lass*. Two of the ironclads flanked the dregs' ship, putting four shots into her sides. Her belly exploded as her masts shattered into splinters, sending sails to the sea in so much ripped and fluttering cloth. The dregs' shouts shifted from celebration to fury that shattered a cloud of mantids above their doomed corsair.

The rope at the fore of the lifeboat twanged. The sinking ironclad was about to pull them under. The boat jolted sharply toward the water, only inches from dipping under and filling. Jacob leapt to the fore, grabbing at the thick wet knot about the cleat. He watched its fibers tighten as the ironclad went deeper into the channel.

A flash. A blade landed just inches from his hands. One of the sailors had risen behind him. The boat shot back with the snap of the rope that the sailor had just severed. Jacob fell, rolling with the lifeboat, nearly falling into the water.

M'Lass, still chained to an ironclad, slid toward the bay. Five more of the ironclads guarded her passage. The second of the dregs' corsairs, smoking and listing, spun about to level a barrage. Two of the ironclads sent volleys toward her, striking the black beast about its rudder. Her aft section broke away as it turned. Its prow lifted to the sky and the ship went down in a long gurgling slide.

The battle outside of the bay had ended. Shots sounded from beyond the mouth, from beyond the shadow of Executioner's Rock. The engagement within the bay was beginning.

The life boat settled into the calming waters, drifting in the wake of *M'Lass*. Jacob watched the worms tangle upon the cliff. He watched the clouds of mantids. He could see the dull light of Mother in the stone, and the pulsing lines of power reaching from her mass to all corners of the planet, and beyond.

He closed his eyes and saw the ruin of Jamesport. He heard Mother's voice—a low and meaningless hum—as she moved to awaken the Elder in the bay.

NINETEEN

THE SWAMP MEN rowed, trying to give wide berth to the jagged stones in the mouth of the bay, the stones upon which so many had fallen and died. They passed through the choke point to see just the smoke and flashes of battle and to smell the gunpowder. Cannon fire sounded across the bay. Jacob had no sense of the time, but the clouds of mantids were so thick and numerous now as to make it seem night.

"We must put ashore," Isabella said. "We must find Mother and we must destroy her. That is our mission."

"Hopeless," Jacob said.

He was transfixed by the light and the sound of the battle. Again and again, he caught a flash of one of the corsairs or ironclads speeding about the edges of that tumult of smoke and fire.

Isabella maneuvered herself into his line of sight and drilled her dark gaze right into his brain, right into the mantid.

"What do you mean?"

"Theresa is dead. The Historian is dead. I've seen what will happen."

"Change it!" she shouted.

She turned upon the swamp men, urging them to row faster. They shared glances, perhaps feeling as Jacob did, that this was a lost cause. Above, Executioner's Rock jutted from the cliff to remind of eons of death, an endless march of sacrifice to the

Elder in the bay and to the Old God deep below. They knew better than Jacob that the world was not what it seemed. History was not what was known. The Sisters, even if somehow defeated here, were everywhere. They controlled armies, countries, whole centuries of men. If Mother was defeated here, kin of hers would rise elsewhere.

There would be no freedom, no end to this for anyone.

If they failed, Jamesport would die in flames. Mantids would make corpse servants of her men and women, her children. All of this to harness the power of the Old God once more, for how long? How long before that spirit tired of being used once again, and sent the sea to snuff it all out?

Jacob wondered how many times it had already happened. The standing stones, the Mystery Tower, ruins beneath waters around the world—they were layers upon layers of this tale, told again and again. Chang had read it to him from the book. The world had been born many times to this story. The slaughter, the murder, the beast of the plains. They had happened countless times, repeating across the continents as Ida's fall repeated in his mind again and again.

The only end, the only escape, was in defeat.

Ida was free. Rutledge, Forsythe, Sam, Papaya, and all of the others—they were free. Theresa was free. He was sure of it, and could feel her absence.

Isabella grabbed his shoulders, twisting his gaze to lock with hers.

"Break it," she said. "Break it and we make a new world. This can end here."

The swamp men had stopped rowing, and were now watching this exchange.

"It means nothing," Jacob said through gnashed teeth. "We defeat Mother, and there will be another."

"And we will fight that one. And the next."

She narrowed her eyes.

"Why?" he finally asked.

She slumped back, releasing him.

"How many have died?" she asked. "How many have you killed?"

"What does it matter?"

He leaned forward as he shouted this. She lowered her eyes, then lifted her gaze once more.

"How many saved you?"

He remembered the angel in the temple. Papaya. Theresa.

"I saved you," she continued.

Jacob could not look her in the eye. He turned to the water, sighing. She had saved him for nothing. Papaya and the rest—they had all saved him for nothing. Chance had brought him to that cave, had killed Ida. It could easily have been him. Perhaps it should have been.

He felt pressure in his head. A dull ache quickly grew to an intense and squirming pain, as if the mantid were trying to push itself through his forehead. He blinked several times and squeezed his eyes shut. The vision of the fiery world, the world of Mother, returned. The empty sockets of the tortured rowers stared at nothing. Their moans were like ribbons of black cloth through the sulfur fog. Jacob saw a dark form in the center of the bay. It was vaguely human, but the height of ten men at least. He could not focus upon it. It was a black void in the air, warding away light. It brought pain to the back of his head to look directly at it. The rowers delivered him to this blackness.

It was the Elder. He would serve the Elder.

Jacob opened his eyes. The swamp men and Isabella were upon him, pulling at his coat. Vertigo sent the world spinning as scraps of the vision flew across real sight, mixing the two. The pressure in his head intensified. He righted himself, dropping his forehead into his hands.

"What is it?" Isabella asked.

"Something..."

"What?"

"Something is happening."

The smoke in the bay was clearing. He could see the ships maneuvering, the ironclads engaging the dregs' corsairs, and *M'Lass* drifting on the far shore. The mantids were coursing above. Streams of them moved to the center of the bay. Rocks fell from the cliff as the worms followed, twisting and tangling into the black, poison water, slithering through its muck.

Jacob turned to the water and saw movement. Ivory forms sailed beneath the surface, turning gracefully. They were broken bodies trailing slimy scraps of flesh. Some were just bones. They rose like divers, turning their empty skulls to the sky before twisting and spinning toward the bay. Some came from the ocean, wearing all manner of clothes or nothing at all. Some were sailors, others children, others women. Some were wrapped in cloth and marked with symbols. Sacrifices.

The inlet was now churning with these corpses. Where they backed against stones, they piled above the surface and folded upon one another, squeezing putrid fluids and evil gasses from their cavities. Some were so old as to disintegrate in the force of the current. Their matter became a cloud of specks and an oily slick on the surface. Others were freshly dead, wounds in their skin trailing brightly colored organs that had not yet gone gray. They still had expressions of frozen horror and shock on their faces.

They were carrying the lifeboat in their stream. The sailors could find no space for their oars in the water. Not far, a spit of gravelly sand reached into the inlet and widened as it disappeared behind the cliff. Jacob thought that it might be the beach below the broken runes, the beach of the standing stones. He rummaged in the belly of the life boat, retrieving a hook and rope. He swung the hook over his head and launched it toward the beach, where it caught on a pillar of stone, wrapping itself several times and holding fast. The life boat was moving quickly, threatening to rip the rope out of his hands.

"Pull!" he yelled.

The swamp men grabbed at the rope and drew the life boat closer to the stone. Jacob knelt and wrapped the slack tightly around the cleat. The three swamp men continued to pull, but the boat ground against stone and sand below the surface.

"Jump!" Isabella shouted.

Jacob ushered them out, the sailors and then Isabella lined up to launch to the beach. The current of dead was pulling hard. The cleat made a snapping noise and the life boat lurched. Jacob, about to jump, stumbled out of the boat and landed flat in the water. The current immediately began to pull him. He flailed for the rope, finding it with two fingers and throwing his other arm to it, wrapping it around his elbow. The cleat snapped from the life boat. The rope shuddered, then groaned as the current gripped Jacob. On the beach, the swamp men moved to the edge of the water, trying to reach the rope looped around the stone some yards into the bay.

Jacob pulled, able to make some progress toward the beach as he moved sideways to the current. His knees hit a shelf of sand and he scrambled up, falling forward into the much shallower water. Turning immediately, he looked for the boat but could not see it. The mantids were gathering into a single writhing mass above the center of the bay, which roiled as corpses flailed and piled. The last of the ironclads and corsairs battled around this, but seemed insignificant against it. He looked to the beach and saw the three swamp men and Theresa, all frozen in mid action, relief playing on their face.

The party gathered on the beach. Jacob moved to the stone and unwound the rope, bringing it in with him. They counted various blades as their only weapons. One of the sailors presented the hilt of a fascine knife over his forearm. It was practically a sword to that man. Jacob took it. He had seen the type. Indeed, he and Ida had once found the skeleton of a soldier in the West Texas desert. The man had perhaps abandoned his unit, or they had left him to a cruel fate of exposure in the waste. His bright white bones were dry and cracked. The bony puzzle of his hand gripped a rusted fascine knife. Jacob remembered kicking the faded blue cap from the man's head and seeing yellow strands of hair, like his own. Flakes of skin floated in the air but barely moved. There was no breeze. The soldier's buttons, his belt buckle, his knife—they were all badly rusted.

"Mother is there," he said.

He pointed up to the cliff face, to the gaping cave where the Viking runes had been. He could see her dull light.

The thin warmth of the sun entered the channel and threw the shadow of Executioner's Rock across the bay, like a finger pointing at the tomb of the Elder where the mantids and worms now gathered. With that heat, a light breeze like a puff of breath upon a candle sent the smoke of the battle into the swamp.

Jacob took a deep breath. The smell of gunpowder clung to the rubble around him. He stood in the cave where the Viking sigil had been the night before. The sulfur burned at the back of his throat. He imagined gunpowder there, a small pile lit and fizzing, melting the thin skin and threatening to burn the mantid from his skull.

The battle in the bay seemed over. *M'Lass* had beached against the mud on the north shore. Jacob squinted and thought there was activity on her deck, but he was not sure. The ironclad that had towed her was gone, the chain trailing down the schooner's length. Jacob could see the burning wreckage of ironclads smoking in the bay. The water was not deep enough to cover them entirely, or to extinguish the fires that consumed their turrets. Likewise, the corsairs of the dregs were shattered wrecks that rose above the water line. The wrecks sank as Jacob watched, the silt below the water swallowing them into its velvety depths.

One corsair remained afloat. Its masts had fallen to either side and dragged with its slow drift like two giant oars. Scraps of sail covered her deck, billowing violently as the dregs moved underneath them.

Water roiled and bubbled in a muddy churn at the center of the bay. Worms writhed with corpses there, below a swirling black cloud of mantids.

Behind him, hewn tunnels went beyond this broken wall, but he could not see far into the darkness. Wooden beams braced the walls and ceiling. He squinted, thinking that the mantid would come to life to give him sight in the dark. It did not. He was not sure in this moment, in this anxiety, how to make that happen.

He heard skittering, like a handful of pebbles thrown across the floor. The sailors bolted forward, shouting and wielding their blades. They had seen something. Isabella braced herself and brought her knife forward. She pointed into the dark and shouted at him, but he did not hear her voice. In fact, where her mouth moved, another voice spoke to him.

"It does not matter," Mother said. "The battle has ended. It does not matter what you do. I will always be able to find you. The mantid will always betray you."

Jacob clenched his jaw and looked back at the bay. The water was now leaping and gurgling, no longer black but gray and white and pink from the worms and the sea's corpses.

"I control the mantid," he said.

"Do you?"

At that moment, his vision changed. The bay went dry like a desert with cracked plates of mud. A giant sarcophagus opened in the center of a crater. The memory of the Elder's corpse clotted like ice in its black emptiness. Beyond, it was not day and there were no clouds, no mists over the swamp. Indeed, there was no swamp, just ash and rock that marched to the horizon. There, unfamiliar constellations were terribly close.

"Behold your world," Mother said.

A flash and a wind, and he had moved. He was afloat in the sea. The sea was calm and silent. There were no waves, no tides or currents. The harsh smell of sulfur and rot clung to the surface of the water. The spires of the new world rose from the ruins of Jamesport, splitting the old brick buildings apart. But not all—the Mystery Tower reached above it all and shot a pillar or swirling fire from its barrel into the heavens.

Next, he lay on a gravel beach.

"Go," Mother said. "See for yourself."

The mantid compelled him to rise. As he stepped stiffly from that beach, the sky shot with lightning that arced from the beam of the tower. The thunder from these discharges was a wailing groan.

Jacob walked across the gray stones, his feet sinking into them. Flakes of ice floated in the air as snow, but never reached the ground. It was like ash, but it melted on Jacob's skin. He was exhausted, but the mantid pushed him on. It seemed detached, its consciousness given over to Mother. It was almost still but for a twitching around its edges that sent signals through his body to move at her command.

Structures rose in front of him. Inside, Mother's insect servants tended to formless beasts in stables. The insects threw them offal, and those beasts took it in toothless maws.

He walked an aisle between the stables, to a chamber in which the formless beasts birthed larvae. These spawn splashed to the ground, knocking chitin against the floor and one another as they flailed oblong heads and thin, long limbs. They opened wide eyes that moved independently, sending frantic gazes in all directions. The insect servants fed some of these into crematory niches. The whole chamber was full of the rush of those flames and the roaring drone of the mother beasts as they pushed the larvae from their wombs. And the cries of those infants—they were harsh in those new throats.

"You see," Mother said. "The human is the most malleable form. It can be anything we imagine. It is the pinnacle of our design. These larvae, some are fit for sacrifice, while others join the Sisters."

Jacob saw the remaining larvae transforming before his eyes, becoming insects with vaguely human forms but with sharp horns, razor mandibles and arms ending in lethal barbs. These marched and separated, some climbing ramps into giant shapeless craft, boundless shadows in the smoke and clouds. Others developed lighter frames and moved to chambers where their barbs were removed and their mandibles blunted, so that they might serve the Elders, tending the needs of those great and silent creatures whose ancient and evil dreams fueled the war against the stars.

"Behold your children," Mother said. "For it is your seed that conceives them all."

He had no capacity to be stunned at that, no permission.

He was in the cliff again, looking over the empty bay and hearing the fire from the Mystery Tower above and beyond him. The whole cliff shook, and the sky lit with that demonic fire.

"The Old God wants only what the Elders want—to sleep and to dream. As long as we understand that, as long as we ration its power, the Elders can live in worshipful slumber forever. And the power will hold their enemies at bay forever. Your kind is bred for this. Birth. Death for sacrifice. Transformation for service. The perfect form."

He stepped deeper into the cave. He could see Mother's glow through the mantid's sight, as he had once before. He entered the chamber in which he had first seen her, the chamber where she had ordered him to kill Chang. As he went, he noticed brittle and ancient skulls about him. He knew these to be the party that had climbed the cliff with him. One was larger.

Isabella.

She was unimportant to Mother except as bait, as a lure.

"We control what will happen," Mother said. "We control the mantid."

"No," he said.

Jacob clenched his jaw. This lit pain at the back of his skull that spread forward to his eyes in pulsing heartbeats.

"I control the mantid," he said through his teeth.

Mother was silent, but the mantid began to screech. He was not sure if it was a real sound, or something that the mantid injected into his senses. As it waned he could do nothing but look at the skulls at his feet, at Isabella's skull.

He saw himself from above, as he had on the mountaintop when first awakened to the mantid's sight. He saw Mother and the web of her connections spreading from her mass. She was much more powerful. Those lines pulsed back and forth as her kind were now awake and strong. The lines of power across the Earth bent toward the cannon that rose from the ruins of Jamesport. All the energy rising from the slumber of the Old God led into that weapon and shot into the sky.

The Elder was sleeping deep in the cliff. Jacob saw flashes of its dreams as it tortured figments of its own mind. It had built the world that Jacob now saw, enslaved the Old God, all to protect those fantasies.

He looked back to Isabella's skull, into those dark sockets. He imagined her body, white skin, sleeping. She slept without breath, like Ida.

Ida. Once again, thoughts of her broke the mantid's link to Mother. It felt like the popping of a joint, then blood flooding into a waking part of him. It prickled in the roof of his mouth and lit his mind.

Now, simply by willing it, he moved from sight to sight. The sight of the swamp, the sight of the world and the connections between things, the sight of things in the darkness. There were many more types of sight laid over the real world that he did not understand. Fabulous colors. Swirling currents. Layers of time dropped upon one another like a deck of fortune tellers cards, falling with a speed that made him dizzy.

"Stop," he said.

And he was not in the future. He was back in the cave of the present.

TWENTY

THE SAILORS WERE dead on the floor around Isabella. Their bodies were broken and split, their blood splattered across the wall and glistening on the talons of two standing insects, the Sisters transformed. Jacob could see the scene of the future, the arrangement of the swamp dwellers' bones untouched in all of the millennia that would march from this moment until then. Isabella was trapped against the wall, covered in the sailors' blood and ready to take her final position on the floor. Three smaller creatures, transformed children, nipped with their bloodied claws and mandibles and waited for the end of the kill, the beginning of their feast.

Jacob flexed his right hand, finding the hilt of the fascine dagger within his palm. He hefted the blade and launched forward, sweeping the weapon wide against the smaller monsters. The blade only banged against their chitin. On a second swing, the blade dented and cracked one carapace. Piercing cries shot through the stone as the creature flailed out of control, spinning and rolling, trying to grip its open, oozing wound. Jacob gave the creature several kicks, sending it over the edge of the cliff. The two remaining children fled into the darkness of the cave. The two Sisters turned on him, deep growls bubbling through the blood that covered their alien mouths.

They flanked Jacob, pummeling him and forcing him back toward the cliff. Jacob stumbled under their blows, landing flat. He rolled from beneath their feet nearly to the edge of the cave and threw down his arm to stop himself. Gravel fell to the beach below.

Ida.

He squinted, clenched his teeth again to force back the thought, and rose to his knees.

One of the Sisters gripped his left arm, her claws sinking into his skin. Jacob yelled and willed the mantid to calm the pain. It took just a moment, but the numbing toxin flowed from the base of his brain, through his veins, throughout his body. The pain in his arm went dead.

The beast's weight shifted as it launched an attack from the lower legs on its other side. Jacob caught the barbed, hairy limb at a knuckle just above its talon and pulled. The Sister spun and lost balance, but grabbed Jacob's coat and pulled him as she fell toward the cliff.

Jacob twisted, trying to free himself. Her weight brought him to the floor, heading face long toward the cliff. She tumbled over the edge, just as Jacob planted his elbows against a dip in the rock. The denim of his cost ripped loudly as he broke free of her. She reached back, trying to grab him again, but missed by inches. His Stetson had flown off, and was hanging in the air above her, spinning like he had thrown it by the brim. The hat arced to the left out of view. The insect plummeted, her piercing cry ending with a sickening crunch as she struck the stones below.

Jacob looked back into the cave. The mantid offered the dark sight. The edges of the cave and tunnels drew themselves brightly. Isabella had collapsed against the wall, her own blood mixing with the carnage of the sailors. Beyond her, deeper in the cave, Jacob could see the edge of Mother's chamber. The two children ran quickly toward her, out of view.

He felt them, and Mother. But there were other presences. Theresa, and something else.

Closer, the second of the Sisters stood between him and Isabella, backing toward her.

Jacob stood. The insect circled as he approached. She leaned into him, and had a longer reach than he. She shot forward, her claws clipping his thigh. Blood streamed from that wound, though he did not feel it. She struck again, but he was able to step aside. He noticed a membrane sliding over her eyes in the brief second before her lunge.

The membrane slid again, and Jacob sidestepped her attack.

He watched her. She stood still but for her clicking mandibles and the twitching ends of her talons. Her empty eyes, many eyes, reflected him in the light from the cave opening. Jacob waited, pain starting to rise in his leg and arm as the mantid reached its limits. Tingling faintness crept up the back of his head. He was losing blood from the wounds on his leg and arm. He took a deep breath and held it, hoping to fuel his blood for just one more second.

Her eyelids closed and one of her lower limbs shot forward. Jacob had enough time to lean, swinging the fascine blade as he went. The blade rang as it severed the insect's limb. She stepped back, shrieking. Strands of yellow slime dragged from the wound to the floor. As she opened her eyes and looked at the broken stalk of her limb, Jacob rushed forward, sinking the blade straight into her belly, and then pushed down. It did not cut through her chitin so much as break it. Her whole body shuddered from the wound to her mouth, the screams shooting through her splayed mandibles, sending cracks through the stone and ripples across the bay.

She sank forward, her two top limbs draped over his shoulders. Her claws clacked in spasms of shock and death, or in a last effort to strike at him. He withdrew his dagger, its blade glistening with her matter. Jacob twisted from beneath her as she fell, her legs and jaws still twitching.

Isabella moaned. He turned to her, ran to her side, and cut scraps of clothing from the sailors to bind her wounds. Her bleeding slowed, and he turned to his own wounds.

"Go," she said. "Kill her."

He tested his grip on his blade once more and strode into the dark.

There was Mother, eyes and ropy flesh hanging in a web of cords. She was like the egg sac of a giant and vile spidery thing dwelling in the stone. The two insect children cowered beneath her, gripping one another in a shifting mass of glistening chitin.

"Do you think you matter anymore?" Mother asked. "We have already harvested your seed. We have stolen your secret. We can create anything, now."

Jacob stopped.

"Look," she said. "We have also taken the secret of resurrection."

Jacob looked past her and the children squirming beneath her. He saw a form bound to the wall, arms and legs spread far.

It was Theresa.

Her chest and stomach were pinned open. Inside, her bones and flesh—long dead and dry—had all been broken, pulled from her and laid upon a shelf of stone beside her.

Theresa's head lolled. Her eyes were open, but she saw nothing. Her dry lips parted, but there was no voice left in her.

"You are too late," Mother said again. "Even I do not matter. My mission is done. The Elder rises now. Even if we fail here, another will rise."

Rage rose in him. The mantid moved to govern that, then withdrew. It knew to let him go. He stepped forward, readying himself to strike, when a hiss shattered his focus. The children beneath Mother chirped as the hot air hit his back. He ducked and turned, just as a barbed limb swung from behind. It missed him and withdrew into darkness. Jacob raised the dagger as another limb shot at him, swinging across him and knocking the blade from his hand. It twisted, revealing a sharp edge, and returned. Jacob saw the blur but felt nothing. He felt the mantid releasing something that flooded him with numbness.

His right hand was gone.

The blood at that severed edge welled but slowed as the mantid's toxin clotted. He opened his throat to scream but nothing came. As he slumped, eyes and mouth wide, silent breath emptying his lungs, he saw his assailant emerge from the dark. This insect was hunched beneath the ceiling of the cavern, taller than the two Sisters though with an only slightly larger head that looked almost comically small on bulky shoulders. Small wings fluttered, useless but for buzzing an evil determination through the fabric of the air. It stood on two thick legs, but had an array of hairy, spidery limbs sprouting from the back of its head. These were identical, with barbs and edges. Each was a weapon, and ran and weaved in wild paths in front of Jacob.

"There is no escape," Mother said.

This queen, this most horrid of the Sisters, stepped forward and lifted Jacob to the wall, pinning him beside Theresa. He kicked wildly, but his feet glanced off of her thick chitin.

He knew her. He had seen her. A shock of red hair still clung to her carapace. A scrap of black cloth was tangled in the root joint of her spidery arms. She was the one on *M'Lass*. She had wooed the captain and raised Mother. She was the first.

She sensed his realization and stared into his eyes. The mantid went still. Her countless eyes blinked, membranes closing and opening in a wave across those shining black beads. Her intent was in him, and the mantid began to squirm. The pain and pressure shot through Jacob's body. He gnashed his teeth and groaned as the mantid moved to leave him, to burrow from his head and crawl out his throat. Jacob was done. It knew it. It was now abandoning him.

He closed his eyes and turned his head, resigned. He was holding his breath but opened his lungs and let it flow.

"Go," he thought.

Mother had said there was no escape, but here it was.

Jacob opened his eyes, meeting Theresa's dead gaze. Her life after death, her ultimate destruction, the risks she and everyone had taken to empower him, to save him—it was all in vain. The frustration of that more than anything else was left in her dull, dead eyes.

And all he had killed, his life and mysterious call to Jamesport—for nothing. Ida's death had started it all, and it was now meaningless. It was not Theresa's gaze in this dark cavern now, but Ida's from a bruised and broken face. She stared past him to the high, hot sun.

The mantid stopped at that thought. Jacob turned back to the beast holding him against the wall. She pushed him harder. Her mandibles fluttered, but the mantid still paused.

"No," he said. "Give me strength."

A small release, but his limbs stiffened and numbed. He began to kick, but the blows were ineffective. His frantic movements brought his feet back to the shelf below him, where they knocked the metal implements of Theresa's dissection to the floor with clanging and ringing. His foot hooked onto a larger implement, and he flung this upwards, gripping it in his left hand. It was a clamp of some kind, a large metal thing that he began to smash against the carapace. The beast ignored him at first, but shuddered with each successive blow, twisting her head to avoid his attacks.

She finally stepped back, shaking her head in a daze. Jacob fell to the floor, smacking his back against the stone shelf. He writhed in pain, gnashing his teeth and struggling to keep his thoughts on the mantid.

"Stay," he said again and again. "Stay."

And the mantid gave him sight. White lines, fleeing darkness— there was Isabella at the mouth of the cave, surrounded by corpses of insects and sailors. He saw the beast, still somewhat stunned but moving to him. And, near his left hand, his dagger.

He took it and, weakly and awkwardly, plunged it into beast's leg. The shock jolted through her countless arms but she made no sound. Her breath merely stiffened, hitting so hard against the ceiling that it threatened to gouge a hole in the rock. Jacob pulled the blade free and rose to his knees. Turning the blade in his hand, bracing his left arm with the stump of his right, he thrust the weapon up, into the insect's lower abdomen. Slime and matter rained from that split.

Jacob stood as the beast stumbled forward. Her head lowered. Perhaps she did not mean to, but she presented herself for destruction. He turned the blade once more, pointing it down and driving it into the base of her head. The whole body shivered. Her spider limbs shot straight.

She fell in a heap as the mantid's numbing elixir left his blood, replaced by a liquid rage that was all his own. Jacob launched upon Mother, swinging at her cords so that they snapped with twangs and shot to the floor and the ceiling. He plunged the dagger into her, again and again. Putrid, viscous fluid shot from those wounds, from her punctured eyes. The ropes that coiled to make her being withdrew like worms from where he struck. Gasses bubbled from her.

He stepped back, watching her deflate, watching her drip to the floor.

The children screamed in the shower of Mother's matter, their mandibles clicking. One turned on him, angry, rushing him. It was nothing to impale that beast on the fascine knife and throw it to the wall below Theresa. The other cowered. Jacob approached and brought his foot down upon its head, sending spurts of yellow slime across the floor.

He turned again on Mother. As he hacked at her, as he made her a shapeless pile on the floor, he heard her laughing.

It drifted away into nothing, and she was gone.

Jacob knelt beside Isabella, joyed that color was returning to her cheeks.

A moan rose from the bay, sending shivers up his spine. He stood and moved to the edge of the cave's mouth. A geyser now shot from the center of the bay. Streams of black fell from a rising, bubbling core. It grew more and more violent, so that the surface of the rest of the bay became a choppy scape. *M'Lass* and the last corsair, both grounded, barely moved against those waves.

It was him and Isabella—no one else standing in the way of the Elder that awakened in the bay. That was surely what was happening. Mother had promised it. She had worked for eons. It did not even matter if she still lived. Indeed, herself, her consciousness might have vaulted across the Earth to another vessel. If not, if she was truly gone, there were others like her. There were Sisters spread across the globe, ready to sow terror and wrath to bring the world to its end. They did not need her, but they needed the Elder to rise.

Poor Theresa had given her second life to this. She was now the corpse she had always wanted to be, but she would not have wanted to serve this evil. He had hoped at one point that he could join her, but he was left with Isabella, tasked with bringing an end to this horror.

Impossible, he thought.

There was no one to answer him. The Historian would have rebuked him. Papaya would have told a riddle. Sam might have laughed. Theresa would have been frustrated.

The mantid was silent. It never answered. Though he commanded it, though he could will his way through its various sights and fill his body with its toxins to create different effects, it was silent. He heard just the wailing across the bay.

Something broke the surface. It seemed like a pile of stones at first. He recognized more detail—faces and limbs, scraps of clothing. Waterlogged flesh, gray and rotten. He saw those shapes twist together into form. The corpses that had flowed from the sea had risen into a mound that now moved. It undulated, lifting one end and the other—shoulders. There was a back, and the back of a head. All of that flesh and bone formed into the body of a demon that had no body of its own any longer, the body of a witch king whose flesh had, millions of years before, rotted into silt and made the water black and poisonous.

Now it had a body again. The corpses that the sea had claimed, the crew of *M'Lass* and so many others over the years, gathered with the worms to clothe that ghost as it lifted from the sulfurous mud of the bay. Its moan rose, barreling through the channels and organs formed by those bodies gripping one another.

The thing was now on hands and knees. Standing, it would be twenty or thirty yards high. It stayed in that bent position, a bridge over the center of the bay. The corpses writhed and tightened, squeezing fluids and vile, infected seawater from between their tissues to slick upon the choppy surface. That mess and bits of flesh fell like rain. The sickening smell reached the mouth of the cave. Isabella woke, startled, and immediately covered her mouth and nose. The smell went into Jacob's mind, past the mantid.

It was a humanoid form with barbs on its shoulders and down its arms, fins down its back like a reptilian creature. Its head had giant fluting ears, horns made from bones of those poor souls, and tentacles flowing from beneath a single eye. From the midst of those tentacles, the screeching continued, shattering the clouds and sending the water away in ripples all about it.

The Elder rose to its knees. As it moved its arms before its great eye, an eye made of ten thousand swollen and rotting eyes, it regarded its claws. Each of the mouths that made up its matter, each of the skulls peered and moaned against its great moan. In this body of corpses and worms, inside of its shell, the soul of the waking demon stretched against the sun. The mantids gathered above it and swirled about its head like wild hair blowing in the wind.

It turned to face the cave, to face Jacob and Isabella. Its eye narrowed. It knew who it faced. It knew what Jacob had been and what he was now with that mantid in him, servant to no one now but himself. Its arms swept before it as it tested its sinew.

The Elder would rise to its feet. Once it did, it would level Jamesport. It would dig the weapon and the ruins of its ancient city from the cliff. Its era would begin anew, spreading from this place to destroy everything.

Isabella gasped as she watched, pushing herself back into the dark as if the cave would protect them. The sigil was gone. The Elder was free.

But *M'Lass* moved.

The chain from her bow tightened. She spun. The Elder, staring at its hands and flexing its fingers, did not see the ship approaching from behind. She slid, listing over the chop, between the Elder's legs and banged against the inside of its thigh.

The beast looked down and reached to the ship. As it laid its palm across the deck and gripped the hull, as it flexed, the corpses of its hand screamed. The sound of this echoed against the cliff and over the swamp. Fluids gushed from its hand like water from a twisted wet cloth. A moment passed, just one moment in which Jacob saw the end once again—not like he had seen the future that Mother had presented, or the future he had experienced in his dreams. No, it was the actual point, the moment at which the world would look back and say the Elder had risen. It was the moment at which the Old God's second imprisonment would begin. None of the thoughts and deeds of humanity, or of the angels from which Isabella descended, mattered now. It was all utterly empty, amounting to nothing but rotting flesh clothing the soul of a demon.

Jacob saw the flash before he heard it, like cannon fire but much greater. The scene slowed.

The mantid wanted him to savor it.

Fire burst from the schooner's hull. It was a giant explosion, the size of the sun fallen into the bay. It began by tearing the Elder's arm to shreds. Those scraps of dead flesh, each a small black shape against the blooming fire, shot in all directions. As the explosion grew, it slammed into the Elder's chest, collapsing it into the beast's soul. It slammed against the bottom of the Elder's jaw, sending the tentacles like spears into the sky. They separated into their bodies, then into limbs and glistening parts. The Elder's head jerked back and disintegrated, like seeds flying from the head of a dandelion.

The explosion split the beast down its middle. All of the flesh, all of the dead who had drifted at the bottom of the sea, who had gathered under whatever power Mother had summoned into this form, unraveled like ropes. The worms burst, expelling their fluids in thick splashing walls. Flesh sailed across the bay, into the swamp, dropping into the muck.

Isabella lowered her hands and stood, shuffling to Jacob's side just as the sound of the explosion filled the cavern and sent air swirling about them.

As quickly as the Elder's reign had begun, it ended. *M'Lass*, packed full of explosives, had been ignited in the Elder's hands. The beast's spirit, still hanging in the center of the bay, began to drift into the swamp. It would wander those reeds and trees to raise odd lights through gas into the night, to bring a chill to those who passed by train or carriage, to do no more than that.

Before Jacob could wonder who had ignited the explosion, a trail of bubbles appeared in a straight line from the center of the bay. Tinker's head broke the waterline. He walked, dropping the broken chain behind him onto the beach of stones below the cave. He looked at Jacob and Isabella. His shout, his gurgling cry through the tube that snaked into his young, dead throat, filled the bay with his victory.

TWENTY-ONE

THE WIND BLEW from the southeast, carrying the exhaust of rattling generators. It bounded over the stone walls between the mansions and whistled through the charred debris that had been Whitebirch. The wind did not know anything of the landscape that might have been. It did not know that it might have discovered the Elder here, that it might have found a cliff torn away, and the ruins of an ancient city revived. It went unaware, cutting through a thin rain and skidding over the inch of ice and snow that had settled since the battle in the bay.

The mantids were gone from the sky. Many perished in the explosion, bits of their husks now drifting through the grasses at the north shore of the bay. Some had survived, disappearing into the swamp. The worms were all gone, large sections of their hides floating in the black water or draped over short trees at the edge of the swamp, curling in the cold wind.

Large snowflakes still fell, buffeted by the wind.

Jamesport was in ruin. The Mystery Tower stood, as it had for millions of years of both tumult and quiet. The wharf was also untouched, and so the army was landing in force. Soldiers gathered the dead and tended to the survivors. The small units that had patrolled in the days prior, under orders from unknown commanders, had either withdrawn or melted into the larger mustering. The official story would be of a freak hurricane, far too north and far too late in the season, followed by a string of disasters so improbable as to be impossible to disbelieve. A fire. An earthquake that no one could explain. Tornadoes. When all was rebuilt, those who remained or who scattered throughout New England would tell stories of ravenous insects swarming into deafening and droning clouds, and giant slug-like beasts gouging ruts in streets and holes through brick buildings. A demon rose in the bay. They would speak of soldiers securing the city for days prior and then, untouched by the events around them, looking for someone or something in the rubble. Some would speak of the insects burrowing into the dead, and the corpses rising to become insect beasts themselves. Academics and officials would disregard these stories, describing them as mass hysteria, in the vein of folklore of witchcraft and headless horsemen. They would point to the sources, immigrants and simple folk, as a rude peasantry that was not ready, perhaps even unfit to enter the twentieth century. The barons on the cliff would deny everything, either through fear or conspiracy. All would forget the gun and cannon fire in the days prior, the explosions against the cliff that brought the Viking symbol to the beach as so much rubble, the operations to eradicate the swamp dwellers, the fire at Whitebirch and the murders of Forsythe and the kindly man who ran the import shop.

There would be thousands of dead. A disaster, and a number. That is what the world would remember, if even that. The Sisters would make sure that there was nothing else. Jacob wondered why they would even make the effort to hide their work. The insignificance of humans—it did not matter if people knew the truth about what happened here.

Unless, of course, if it did matter. If there were measures to take, or others like Jacob to act against the Sisters, then there would be reason to cultivate a lie.

"We do not have much time before the patrol returns," Isabella said.

Jacob nodded.

Tinker carried Theresa. She, wrapped in sailcloth emblazoned with symbols, would be a sacrifice like her father. Tinker carried her past the standing stones and on to Executioner's Rock.

This was her end. Her death was complete. It had lingered for years.

More of Isabella's folk had arrived in Jamesport. They had commandeered the surviving corsair and dispatched of the last dregs aboard. Lashing that wounded ship to an ironclad, they prepared to set out to sea. Tinker, Isabella, and Jacob would go with them.

That would be his escape.

Let Jamesport rot, Jacob thought. But let it die its own death, not hastened, not resurrected. Let it be what it would be.

Countless cities across the world—there would be other Jamesports. Other servants like Mother. Other Elders for her kind to resurrect.

For now, rest. There was much to learn about Isabella and her kin. From what Jacob understood, there was an island with a secret that would not only keep him safe, but would open doorways into even more understanding, even more answers.

Tinker howled. It was a much more human sound than any Jacob had heard him make. It was a cry, fury at a death that both he and his sister had already experienced, but which he now at last had a chance to lament. Jacob had no idea what the swamp dwellers had done to Tinker, but the automaton had been freed from Mother's control. He was something of a living, feeling thing.

The boy stood long in the wind. Jacob feared the gusts would blow Tinker from Executioner's Rock. There was a weight of history about him, anchoring him to that stone. It was not just

his own history or his sister's, not just their lives and deaths, but
' the history of thousands who had leapt from that stone or who
had fallen in sacrifice, who had gathered into the Elder's body
that morning. There was the history of the slaughter in the cave
below them, the history that Jacob had seen when he destroyed
the sigil that imprisoned Isabella. Death was all around them.

Now, Tinker held one more death in his arms. He offered
one more corpse to the sea. Isabella and Jacob watched him,
silent as Tinker shouted and moaned at the stars that spread
across the cold sky as the snow ceased and the clouds fled.
Distant stars, homes of the Elders and their enemies—no one
knew what ruins or thriving cities might stand upon the rocks
spinning about those lights. There was the root of all of Tinker's
turmoil, the wellspring of all of their lives and so the source of
their deaths.

Tinker let his forearms fall. Theresa rolled from him and
disappeared into the dark.

Jacob heard the wind rushing into the bay, and the surf far below.

Tinker stood for a moment longer. Jacob thought that he
heard weeping. Tinker turned, his whirring rising above all
other noise. Jacob imagined Tinker dropping others to the sea.
Might he have sent Jacob to that sacrifice at some point?

At what point, Jacob wondered, did Mother know what he
was? She might have collected his seed before sending him to
the rock. Jacob might have been useless to her all along.

The three turned and began toward the road, where
one of Isabella's kin drove a carriage. This driver huddled
in a thick wool coat, warm and sleeping, his snores almost
indistinguishable from the rising and falling of the waves.
The carriage would take them to the eastern spit of the island,
to the ruined mansion and a boat that would secret them to
an ironclad that hid in the night. They would have to move

quickly to beat the sunrise, and the naval squadrons that were certainly bearing down from Providence.

Jacob felt a presence.

He had forgotten. He stopped and looked, taking on the sight of the heat of things. Tinker and Isabella continued to the road. Jacob scanned the horizon, the cold dark emptiness beyond the cliff, the ruins of Whitebirch that still glowed with yellow heat, like the memory of the fire.

A hole in his sight, colder than anything, leapt from the stone.

He reached with his left hand, too late for the fascine dagger at his belt.

Its claws were still hot with blood from the slaughter at the train. That was all that Jacob saw as the mantid sight focused after his fall to the ground under the beast—the heat of its claws. The sun had once warmed the bristling hair of its back, but now there was nothing. Jacob imagined a fire in the beast's gaze, hot breath from its dust-choked throat.

There was nothing but hot orange claws emerging from black.

Jacob willed his normal sight and saw two red pupils staring from a dark bulk that blotted out the stars. He heard the growling of thousands of eons as it stood over him, pinning his shoulders to the snowy ground.

He kicked to no effect.

The beast of the plains was his. It had his father's medallion in its gut. It had come to rid the world of the danger that Jacob had become. The rebellious architects had planned for this in the last days of the Elders' reign. Mother had compromised his mind and extracted what she had needed. The beast came too late, but it would carry out its mission. It would sate the hunger that had been in its gut forever.

Isabella pummeled the beast with her fists, hoping to distract it for she certainly had no chance of harming it. But she would sacrifice herself, the last of her kind, as the angel in the cave of slaughter had sacrificed herself for Jacob. Isabella would give herself, her life.

The beast did not even have the patience to kill her. With a kick of its rear leg, it sent her across the field to slam into one of the standing stones. Isabella slumped, unconscious. But the beast shifted its weight as it kicked, freeing Jacob's left arm to reach for the hilt of the blade. He whirled this from its loop and swung weakly with his wrist. The end of the blade, though razor sharp, glanced off of the beast's thick hide. The red pupils shot to meet his, bore into his head and found the mantid. The growling became a fury. The claws lifted and opened, catching starlight to become the hot orange things Jacob had seen through his other sight. The mantid shot fear and panic into Jacob's veins. He flailed in its grip.

The beast seemed to smile, but the expression died quickly.

Tinker's footsteps crunched through the snow, and the automaton crashed into the beast. He smashed with his metal ball and plunged his blades into the beast's haunches. It reared, releasing Jacob to roll through the snow, leaving his fascine knife out of reach.

It was a jackal in the face, a lion in its legs. Its torso was that of a gorilla. Fans and razor fins marked its joints. It was all of these things beneath hair as thick as quills and sharp-edged muscles that were of such power to define themselves against its inch-thick leather. Like the statues in the temple above the cave of slaughter, the statues that peered upon Jacob and the rescuing angel as he destroyed that sigil, it was a thousand familiar and terrifying things stitched together into the invention of the predator. The architects had created it to pursue and kill.

Tinker and the beast grappled with one another, two immovable forms clasping their hands and settling their weight into their heels, pushing to break one another. They passed Isabella, who lay with her head lolling, sitting bent against the standing stone. Her skin was dead white in the reflection of weak moonlight from the snow.

Tinker's high-pitched whirring and hard clicking sounded across the cliff. It roused memories of blood and heat from deep in the stone. It went through the tunnels, to the quivering mass that had been Mother, filling empty dark spaces. The beast answered with yelps that shot from deep history. It swung its paws against the automaton's body. Its claws, the claws that had scratched the earth of eons, the claws that had scored blood and water and night from the dry plains, sent long screeching marks down Tinker's torso.

Jacob watched, still stunned as the pair wrestled in circles, swinging one another against the stones. Blood steamed upon the beast's back. It limped, its muscles punctured by Tinker's blades. But the automaton fared no better. One arm, the arm of the iron ball, fell limp. His torso was thin to the beast's attacks. The beast punched dents into Tinker, punctured the automaton's chest with its claws and ripped through the metal.

Jacob stood and ran low to Isabella. He reached for the fascine knife with the stump of his right arm, stopped, and reached across with his left hand to pluck the cold, wet hilt from the snow.

Tinker hooked the beast's right arm and spun, sending the monster into a dizzy whirl. Tinker turned and slammed his back against the beast's, throwing his bladed arm up around the thick neck. He dropped to his knees, and the beast's impossibly heavy frame lifted from the ground, standing straight into the air one point before pivoting down and landing face-first into the snow.

Tinker, still kneeling, did not rise.

Faint warmth leaked from Isabella's nostrils as her chest rose and fell. Jacob straightened her head as if straightening the head of a sleeping, sitting child.

The monster rose, shaking away dizziness with violent throws of its head.

One of Tinker's feet shot forward and he tried to rise. Jacob heard the whirring and a metallic snap.

Jacob was running to the fight, now. He was not sure what he would do. The mantid filled him with numbness, making thick leather—thicker than the beast's—of his skin.

Tinker went stiff, rolling to the side. A dying moan followed him.

The beast reared. Jacob saw the scar of its construction down its chest like the seam of a garment. He lifted the fascine knife as he ran, pointing it forward with the strength of his arm, buttressed by the force of his run. The mantid filled him with speed and abandon.

The beast rose above Tinker, its claws lifted to the night, to the stars and the moon. The monster's roar sent the snow into a cloud and froze the surf far below.

Isabella stood, shaky, leaning against the stone.

Jacob's blade found the seam. The beast shuddered and Jacob drove forward, his body slamming into the beast. The blade sunk to the hilt, beyond. Jacob's hand slipped into the monster's warm gut. Blood gushed to the frozen ground—the blood of the beast, the blood of its victims, the blood pumped into its frame before history began, the blood that gelled in those vessels as it slept in the deserts, waiting for Ida and Jacob.

Whirring and clicking, a wailing moan. Jacob paused one half step, the sound of Tinker's rise coaxing an instinctive fear. But the automaton was standing beside him, pushing the beast away from him. Jacob stepped back as the two went through the standing stones, to the spit of rock that had seen so many falls, so many sacrifices.

Jacob dropped the blade in the snow. It steamed with the monster's blood.

Tinker pushed, one sure step after another until his knees began to buckle. The beast's pupils, however, were fixed on Jacob. They were sharper and brighter than any star.

The two fell from Executioner's Rock, silent and slow, like one giant thing tipping over that edge.

Jacob stood still, the heat of the beast's blood cloaking his left arm in a cloud of stinking vapor. That blood mixed with his own blood, which seeped from cuts in his palm and drew thin rivers through the valleys between his knuckles.

Isabella approached.

Tinker and the beast fell, spinning in the automaton's frozen grip, to Theresa and Ida and all of the rest.

Jacob opened his palm to find his father's bent star, its points sunk into his flesh.

TWENTY-TWO

HE STOOD ATOP the cheese box turret, leaning against the railing. The mist had condensed on the metal. Drops crawled along the metal toward the rear of the ironclad and fell into the wind. The boat's churning propellers sent a wake into the calm sea, the white froth disappearing into mist behind them. There were no close landmarks, only water and fog.

The rising sun set fire to the mist. It was a strange scene. Fore and aft and both sides, swirling mist was orange and red like the heart of an explosion. The dissolving fog soon revealed an endless scape of gray sea.

Jamesport was a memory behind him, at least a day's journey. Now, they headed into that rising sun to an island of Isabella's kind, and a secret beyond.

That sun painted orange clouds upon the blue and purple sky. Behind were night and stars, and a quarter moon that sank into the ocean.

He was between.

He was between questions and answers, between pieces of land, between night and day. He was not sure of the date, but remembered something of December, of Christmas and New Year's approaching. Perhaps. Maybe he was between two years.

Jacob closed his eyes. Awakening the mantid, he brought forth different sights. He saw lines in the oceans, communication between Mother's kind—quiet and cold, but there nonetheless. One dark line led straight behind to Jamesport. That was Mother, dead. Looking to the horizon he thought he saw the resting places of Elders along the edges of the Earth. He could head straight toward any one of them, destroy them one at a time.

He sighed, and with his exhale layer upon layer of history rose from the dark depths of the ocean. Jacob saw whalers and merchants, warships like fat-bellied fish. He saw Vikings and explorers. Before them, impossibly small boats rocking in the chop. Irish monks. Celtic gods in magical chariots. Groaning, cracking ice fell across the sea. As the mantid sight moved backwards, fire raged and melted rock into molten glass. The ironclad bobbed in that hell for just one moment before returning to the cool, misty Atlantic. But all of the layers, all of the history of this lane of the sea, remained visible to him, each transparent and offering sight through to the one below. In that chaos, he saw glimpses of all of the answers he had ever wanted. But he could not study them. They defied his gaze, darting away faster than the muscles that moved his eyes. They dodged behind ships, slipped beneath the water, or shot into the smoke of the fiery, prehistoric sky. But he did not need them any longer. He knew all that he needed to know.

Now, he went with Isabella to the island of her kind. Beyond, he would go wherever she led him to rebuild her race. He knew that the war was not over. The beast that pursued him was dead, and he hoped there were no others. But Mother's kin lived in rocks and gullies, beneath seas that flowed into dark and deep crevices of the Earth's crust. She had uncovered secrets, and so the dead Elders might rise. The Old God had communicated through shamen, through wizards like Sam and witches like Papaya. It had communicated through books and visions. He thought of alerting it. There must, he thought, be a way.

Perhaps the Old God did not care.

Isabella was behind him. She was close, her warm sighs stroking the back of his neck. He continued to look to the gray sea. Under the water—under snow and ice, dirt and rock—caverns still smelled of air that was eons old. Whispers echoed, breathy and cold, as fragile as the thin ice that creeps across still puddles. Witches and ghosts haunted cold stone worlds that he could never know, no matter what sight he possessed.

Isabella, perhaps reading his thoughts, said: "You will never have all of the answers you want. You will never know everything."

"I wanted to know nothing," he said. He imagined himself in the desert. His sister, his father, his mother—all ignorant. "I wanted to escape."

"That is not true," she said. "Everyone has said it. Theresa. The Historian. You are in the center of all of this. You have no choice but to know things. There is no escape. You might not like it, but you have no choice. You know that."

He looked into the water and nodded.

"Where are we going?" he asked.

"We go to an island of my people."

"Then?"

"Come below," she said, turning. "Eat."

Jacob followed her, descending through the turret to the galley. There, an old cook who looked every bit like the witch on the hilltop handed two bowls of stew. The meat was stringy and white, of a creature hauled from the bottom of the sea. The gravy was like snot. The cook offered the bowls with her head bowed, a thin smile on her lips. She was proud, or playing a joke. Jacob could not tell. Isabella took the bowls and moved toward the fore of the boat, to the berthing deck.

"Hab'muk," she said over her shoulder. "The Elder we destroyed was Hab'muk, weakest among his kind. He was Lord of Spirits, ethereal and shapeshifting. He presided over the sacrifice."

They sat and ate and said nothing for some time.

He smiled. When others had delivered puzzles and riddles, she had always given him answers.

It was not an island so much as the summit of a sunken mountain. Buildings, walkways, rope bridges all clung to its crags as if the seas had risen, forcing these structures to float to the top.

He and Isabella occupied one of those homes. It had been days on this rock, in these quarters which became warm and comfortable, familiar. A dome of mist surrounded this sanctuary. Time sped or slowed under strange rules. Ironclads came and went, one towing the salvaged corsair of the dregs to a dock where Isabella's kind, the swamp men who had built the perches on this rock, crowded aboard and began to work at its barnacles and the mud caked to its planks. She was a prize. They would make her seaworthy to a higher standard than that which concerned the dregs, and scrub the disease from the grain of her wood.

It was going to take him somewhere. That is all that he knew. It was going to take him somewhere hidden and safe, somewhere that Isabella knew. He did not care to know more. He cared only that she would be with him.

Jacob tried to count the days on that rock, like he had counted questions and answers, phases of the moon, bullets in his revolver, and his victims. He tried to take something from each day, to keep each. One day, it was the smell of Isabella's breath as she slept, naked in the bed beside him. Another, it was the howl of the cold wind that wrapped about the rocks as it came from the sea and spiraled up, billowing the rope bridges and sending a salty musk to the sky. The cries of sea birds. The sound of the bell that pealed hundreds of times each day, a guide to the ironclads, their engines chugging and arriving at the rock through the mist that seemed to distort all sound of the outside world. Seven or eight days.

He healed, the pain at the end of his right wrist settling into a fiery itch that Isabella said was a good sign. He also ate well. The rock dwellers made stew of fish and crab with bright green kale or seaweed. It reminded him of Portuguese dishes in the poorest quarter of Jamesport. They also grilled sea birds that they trapped with complicated arrangements of nets that led the bird into cages.

Isabella's kin were stoic. They enjoyed their food but did not laugh or talk. They averted their eyes from him, tending to him with deference. There was no leader among them. They fulfilled their roles, did their work. Their lights flickered out early in the night.

They dressed his wounds again and again, those fresh like his severed right hand and those from the beginning of this trial, which reopened and neared necrosis. The dirt and blood, Mother's slime—it was all gone from him. His clothes were clean and mended, even his denim coat. His hat was gone, but he found his father's badge in the coat pocket.

Jacob looked at himself in the mirror each morning. He looked older and thinner. The blue of his eyes was a little less sharp. He imagined the mantid nestled in the matter of his brain. As the water gathered into a drop in the cleft of his chin and his hair fell forward in thick wet strands, he thought again of a crazed ex-Confederate. He dismissed the ghost at once.

He had been an assassin, a criminal. He had lived outside of the world. Now, the distances to which he had gone made him a whole different thing. And he was a different thing, perhaps not human. He was, as Isabella said, a being at the center of things. He had been and would still be hunted.

Jacob woke her. She was wrapped in warm quilts, naked beneath. He had counted the times they made love. Coupling with her was a promise, each time a promise to protect and care, to carry on together, to fight, to escape by one another's side, to create, to recreate. Each time.

He woke her and, looking into her brown eyes, simply said: "It's time to go."

Jacob turned to the door of their room and stood there, watching his profile in the mirror from the corner of his eye. Jacob waited for her to rise and dress, plunging his left hand into his pocket, wrapping his fingers around his father's star. He pushed its bent arms flatter with his thumb. It was cold at first, but warmed as he worked it. He imagined the smell of its metal on his hand and his fingerprints across its back, smooth but where the Historian's kind had punctured it. He was not sure if he should keep it or not. It seemed a dangerous thing as a sigil's charm, but it was now done.

He put it back into his pocket, with the smell of her as she slept beside him, the sounds of the wind, the birds, the ironclads' engines.

He woke to a roar. He had been asleep just one night on the corsair, or perhaps a hundred years' worth of nights. He woke groggy and unsure, rolling himself from the hammock and peering across the deck. Gray, dim light fell from the hatches above. It had followed them everywhere.

Isabella and her kind were gone. There were thumps on the deck above. He stood and shook his head. Gathering his coat, he moved to the bottom of the ladder. He saw blue sky above, and could not remember the last time he had seen empty blue sky. All of his memories, brief efforts that he made then and there at the bottom of the ladder, evoked his childhood in the desert.

He climbed the ladder to the deck. There was still a smell about the ship, a smell that he could sense when he was close to the wood. He could still see black in the grain of the planks. The deck was splintery and rough. This was still a ship of the dregs, still poisoned and foul. The smell was like mold and death, how he imagined the muck at the bottom of the sea would smell, the muck from which *M'Lass* had pulled Mother.

Most of the dozen sailors aboard were standing along the port rail. He moved toward them, toward the roaring, pausing beside the pilot at the wheel. The pilot held fast, though the wheel seemed intent on spinning out of control. But he held the ship steady, straining and groaning. Noticing that Jacob was watching, he threw a glance to the compass. Jacob saw the needle moving slowly counter-clockwise. The ship was in a gentle turn, though there was nothing gentle about the pilot's effort at the wheel.

Jacob went to the side of the ship, standing beside Isabella. They were all calm, looking over the ocean. Clouds roiled all around them. The ship was in the eye of something. The sails were unfurled but limp, rippling slightly in light breezes that punched from all directions. In the distance, the clouds rolled and twisted with almost violent abandon. Here, there was none of that.

But there was the roar.

The sun sat in the zenith so that the whole blue sky framed in clouds with that sun was like a giant eye. As Jacob's eyes became accustomed to that light, he saw a hole in the ocean. The ship rounded a whirlpool, edging closer and closer.

Panic began. The mantid shuddered, offering him all manner of responses and different kinds of sight. Chemicals pumped into his veins to make him faster and stronger. He gritted his teeth and held it all down.

"What's happening?" he asked.

Isabella turned to him, a blank look on her face, and back to the whirlpool.

"There," she said. "We go there."

Whether it was fear or thoughts of betrayal, Jacob let his composure slip. He nearly collapsed on the rail. A great sigh escaped him and he closed his eyes.

"Why?"

She leaned over him, putting her hands on his shoulders.

"Do not worry," she whispered in his ear. "We are going to a safe place."

He watched as the horizon of the pit drew closer and heard the groans of the pilot who led the ship around and around the hole. The corsair went faster and faster. All about them, vague and unreal, the clouds fought. Worlds appeared within their shapes and then, in catastrophe, dissolved. Figures smashed into one another, dancing and warring like the statuettes in Rutledge's collection. The sun above remained still rather than crawl across the sky, though it felt like hours of movement toward their end in the whirlpool.

Jacob had wished for it. He had wished to be taken from the world, to be relieved of what he knew and what he had done. A large part of him did not care that they circled to catastrophe. Even the mantid seemed resigned to the fate. A cool and calming ice moved through Jacob's veins, and he felt sleepy. It was a different slumber, like the sleep he had known when Papaya nursed him back to health. Empty and blank, dropping him from the world.

The ship slipped gently over the edge of the hole. He felt for a moment as if he would fly forward and off the boat, but everything righted like a cork plunged into water. The world turned sideways and proceeded as if it had not dealt anything strange at all. Jacob looked behind and saw the sun in the opening of the tunnel behind them. The barest, slimmest circlet of blue shimmered around the sun's fiery edge. Sunlight poured through the tunnel, shining through the limp sails. As the entrance to the tunnel shrank behind them, Jacob realized how fast they were moving, or perhaps falling.

Soon, there was nothing to see of that world above and behind but a star in an otherwise empty field of black. He felt the mist against his face and heard the water moving like a fast stream all above him and on either side of the boat. It was dark and cold. Time disappeared once again.

They moved about the ship as it went almost on its own. The pilot, at one point, tied the wheel to the deck so that it could not turn at all.

After just one or two days, Jacob realized he would have to count meals to know how much time was passing. But meals became unimportant. The crew grew weary of the emptiness and the dark. Tempers flared in games, or when their captain ordered lamps to be shuttered so as to conserve oil. Soon, in the dark, they all felt alone. Jacob felt separate from Isabella, and lost her for long stretches in the dark. He knew the ship and the crew through the sight of the mantid, but gave up searching for her.

A week, or more—he could not tell. He withdrew to his hammock and passed the time in sleep, or begging the mantid to flood him with something that would shut him down through this. It answered by calming the itching of his right wrist, which eventually subsided on his own, leaving nothing but a dull ache and the occasional sensation of still having a hand, holding the grip of his revolver or turning Papaya's rosary in his pocket.

He imagined sights and remembered things. He saw Tinker and Hab'muk in the bay. He saw Mother's eyes looking at him, surrounding him like he was inside of her. Unblinking, pale, moonlike eyes. He began to fear the deck. When lamps were stowed, the mantid's sight was dizzy and vague enough to leave a real chance of his stepping from the side of the ship, into the black. He imagined one of the great worms spearing silent and sudden from the side of the tunnel and snatching him from the deck, pulling him into the water.

One day, a star appeared in front of them.

Isabella was at his side.

"We are almost there."

It became a singular thing to watch, that star in front of them. It was not a star, but an exit. It seemed a strange and forced realization, though logic told him it could be nothing more. When he dropped the mantid sight, letting the darkness surround him, he imagined flying through space. He even let himself believe that it was so. From one star to the other, from one epiphany to the next, from knowing nothing to knowing all that he needed to know. Through the darkness, in between.

Then, over the course of one fragment of time—a day, a week, or more—the star behind disappeared and the star ahead began to grow. Jacob could see yellow sunlight, but no sky or clouds. Just yellow so bright that it was impossible for him to see it directly. He could only view it through the corners of his vision. He saw a shimmering aura around its edges, flowing into it. He realized that this was the water flowing out of the tunnel.

The sails filled, and the portal grew larger and larger.

Their exit was as quiet and calm as their fall into the tunnel had been. The ship crested the edge of the portal and settled into a sea that spread away in bright blue ripples. The sails fluttered and the mast creaked like it had from its first wind from the island of Isabella's kin, like it had embarked upon a simple voyage rather than falling into a whirlpool and coursing through the Earth's crust.

Above, seemingly close enough to touch, a raging sun blinded and burnt him. He squinted. The world curved up all around him. Isabella gripped his hand and pulled him to the front of the ship. She pointed to a green land, a wild and ancient land. Spires of a ruined city—tall, thin, and crawling with vines to their sharp peaks—defied explanation even of the most modern construction. Ancient trees dropped seeds and twigs to silent walkways through abandoned plazas.

The city was empty and forgotten, but it was there for them.

The crew looked upon that approaching shore.

The smell was of time, of long and undisturbed emptiness. It was musty and sharp, tickling the back of Jacob's throat. It was somewhat short of filling his lungs. He took long and desperate breaths.

"You will adjust," Isabella said.

Her words were enough to beat down the panic in him.

The ship ran aground in the soft sand of a bar some distance from shore. They dropped the anchor and lowered the life boat. In groups of four, the swamp men went ashore. Jacob watched them go until the boat became a small thing, and the men were mere specks on the brilliant white sand of the beach.

"We will be safe here," Isabella said. "We are protected here. This place is delivered to us, for us to rebuild."

She gripped his fingers in hers and lifted her eyes to the sun at the center of the world. She moaned against its heat.

"Go ahead," she said. "Look."

The light blinded him.

"No," she said. "Let the mantid show you."

He looked at her for a moment, feeling warmth and hope. He turned to the sun and willed the mantid to see through the light. There, suspended with wings folded about its body, the bat, the Old God slept. Its power radiated and its dreams showed him all, answering questions he did not yet even know to pose. It showed him his history and hers. It showed him the future, the world that they would build, the dangers and trials ahead. Beyond that creature, Jacob saw vistas and ruins, valleys and forests and lakes of the world inside. And the Old God's light bathed it all, never ceasing.

"Who made this?" It was all the he could manage to mutter. He was not sure if he meant the city, or Earth, or the Old God itself.

Isabella did not answer for several seconds.

"I do not know," she finally said. "It is a question for us to answer together."

– THE END –

www.ingramcontent.com/pod-product-compliance
Lightning Source LLC
Chambersburg PA
CBHW031114030726
47496CB00002BA/543

* 9 7 8 1 8 9 7 4 9 2 8 8 8 *